Light Sleeper

The two assailants inched toward the fire, closer to Colt's sleeping form. Lon watched closely for signs of movement, waving Brownie on as they stalked their intended victim.

When they were about fifteen feet away, Lon suddenly split the stillness of the night, yelling, "Git up from there, sleepyhead!" and pumping two shots from his pistol into their victim. Without giving time for a response, both men dived upon the body, only to find they had attacked a blanket wrapped around a saddle.

"What the hell?" Lon uttered. The next sound he heard was that of a Winchester cranking a cartridge into the chamber.

Whirling around at once, Lon tried to get a shot off. But he wasn't fast enough to counter Colt's .44 slug, which shattered his sternum and sent him over on his back.

RANGE WAR IN WHISKEY HILL

Charles G. West

BERKLEY
New York

BERKLEY
An imprint of Penguin Random House LLC
penguinrandomhouse.com

Copyright © 2008 by Charles G. West
Penguin Random House supports copyright. Copyright fuels creativity, encourages
diverse voices, promotes free speech, and creates a vibrant culture. Thank you for buying
an authorized edition of this book and for complying with copyright laws by not
reproducing, scanning, or distributing any part of it in any form without permission.
You are supporting writers and allowing Penguin Random House to continue to
publish books for every reader.

BERKLEY and the BERKLEY & B colophon
are registered trademarks of Penguin Random House LLC.

ISBN: 9780593441459

Signet mass-market edition / July 2008
Berkley mass-market edition / July 2022

Printed in the United States of America
1 3 5 7 9 10 8 6 4 2

For Ronda

Chapter 1

Like two old bulls, they stood eyeing each other. Two big men, determined and defiant, the gray-streaked manes of each bearing testament to a life of tests and survival. In Frank Drummond's mind, this confrontation was to be the final one. It was the third time he had made an offer to buy out Sam McCrae's Bar-M Ranch, a section of range that he needed and intended to have. Peaceful buyout or otherwise, his patience was exhausted. He figured he had gone as far as he intended with the stubborn old son of a bitch, and it was time for a showdown. "Well?" he demanded.

"How many different ways do you have to hear the word *no* before you get it through that thick skull that you ain't gettin' the Bar-M?" Sam McCrae replied defiantly. "You and that gang of outlaws that work for you have scared most of the smaller ranchers out of the territory. You even got to Sessions last year, but by God, you ain't gettin' the Bar-M or the Broken-M. Me and my brother were here before you ever saw this valley, and we, by God, plan to be here after you're gone. You've had your say now, so you can climb back in that buckboard and get the hell off my land."

Frank Drummond stood fuming, his heavy eyebrows glowering like dark storm clouds as he glared at Sam McCrae. Barely able to control his rage, he nevertheless spoke quietly but clearly. "You've gotten my final offer, McCrae. Now we'll see who stays in this valley and who doesn't." He turned away and climbed back in his buckboard.

Sam stood on the top step of his porch, a deep scowl etched across his weathered face, watching until the buckboard disappeared behind the cottonwoods at the bend of the creek. *I hope to hell he finally believes he ain't running me off my land,* he thought. Drummond already owned all the land from the north bank of Lodgepole Creek to the stream that formed the boundary at the beginning of McCrae range. That wasn't enough for Drummond. He wanted to control all the land between Lodgepole Creek and Whiskey Hill, more than fifteen miles of open range.

The price Drummond had offered was a fraction of the value of the land between his spread and the free-flowing water of Crooked Creek. Even if the offered price had been reasonable, Sam had no intention of selling. He and his brother, Burt, who owned a spread adjacent to his, had first come to settle here when the town of Cheyenne was known as Crow Creek Crossing. There was plenty of land north of Crow Creek Crossing for everyone then. Sam and Burt weren't the only settlers who claimed portions of the vast prairie convenient to the proposed Union Pacific Railroad line. There were a good many more, enough to establish a small town called Whiskey Hill, a half-day's ride from Crow Creek Crossing. Drummond moved in a couple of years later with a crew of men more at home on wanted posters than tending cattle. His intentions were soon apparent; he was building a cattle empire, and he went about acquiring all the land one way or another. The smaller ranchers fell one by one; some sold out to Drummond at desperation prices and some had unfortunate accidents, and before long only the McCrae brothers and Walter Sessions had remained to stand between Drummond and Crooked Creek. Now Sessions had also knuckled under after too many cattle had gone missing or been found shot.

With the completion of the railroad in November 1867, Crow Creek Crossing was renamed Cheyenne, and had already earned a reputation as one of the wildest towns in Wyoming Territory. The little town of Whiskey Hill naturally inherited some of Cheyenne's undesirables. When the Union Pacific moved on to Laramie City, the construction workers and many of the riffraff that had contributed to Cheyenne's sinful ways followed along. "I wish to hell Frank Drummond and his crowd had moved on with them," Sam mumbled as he stepped down from the porch and turned to go to the barn.

Vance should be back from the south ridge before supper-time, Sam thought as he saddled the sorrel mare. *I'd best ride up as far as the north fork to make sure we ain't losing any more strays.* It bothered him that he had to tell Vance to check the south ridge. His oldest son should have learned by now to think of it himself. Sam shook his head, perplexed by the thought. Vance showed no evidence of ever being able to take over the management of the ranch. "He needs a little more of his brother's grit in him."

His muttered comment brought a familiar moment of regret to the gray-haired patriarch of the Bar-M spread. Vance's younger brother, Colt, the fiery young mustang, was as different from Vance as night is from day, and Sam blamed himself for the distance between father and son. In looking back to find a reason, he regretfully admitted that it was probably because Colt was clearly his mother's favorite. When Martha was taken by pneumonia, it seemed to change the thirteen-year-old boy. He missed his mother, and Sam knew he should have been more patient in his expectations for the boy to become a man. Colt seemed to be mad at the world for the senseless death of his mother, and consequently exhibited a show of resistance to any form of authority.

Sam often thought about Colt while the boy was away these long years. He was convinced that if Colt had been allowed to sew his wild oats, he would eventually have settled down to run the ranch. "If *if* was a tater, we'd have somethin' to eat," Sam said, and sighed sadly. For Sam's young firebrand son had been shipped off to prison at the age of eighteen, for a crime Sam faithfully believed the boy did not commit. Colt said he didn't have anything to do with it, and reckless and wild as he had been, Colt had never been a liar. "Damn, I miss that boy," Sam whispered as he guided the mare toward a path that led up to the ridge.

His thoughts returned once more to Drummond. *I'd*

better go over and tell Burt that Drummond was here again, he thought. "We'll probably start missin' some stock again." He had barely gotten the words out when the stillness of the late afternoon was suddenly shattered by the sharp crack of a single rifle shot. Sam McCrae stiffened, then, without so much as a grunt, slid to the ground, a .44 slug embedded between his shoulder blades.

"McCrae, you've got a letter."

Colt McCrae looked up, surprised. The last letter he had received was two years before, when his father had taken the time to write. "Who's it from?" he asked.

"Burt McCrae, it says on the envelope," Bob Witcher replied, handing the letter through the bars. "Is that your daddy?"

"Nope," Colt answered. "That's my uncle Burt." His curiosity aroused by the unexpected letter, he hurriedly tore it open, fearing it must hold bad news. Uncle Burt was not one to write letters unless it was a dire necessity.

Bob Witcher watched with interest. Of all the guards in the prison, Bob was the only one who had taken a personal interest in the solemn young man from Wyoming Territory. He had watched the hostile, wild eyed kid develop from a skinny, tough-talking hothead into a soft-spoken man of few words. Bob had seen a strain of decency in the young prisoner, and after knowing him for a few years became convinced that Colt really was innocent of the crimes with which he had been charged. He liked to think that he had been influential in Colt's maturing into a man. Aware of the bitterness festering in Colt's soul, Witcher had spent quite a few hours talking to Colt about the evil erosion of a man's mind when consumed with thoughts of vengeance. Over the years, as Colt grew in maturity, Witcher witnessed the silent strength of that maturity. There was little doubt, however, that the penitentiary's prisoner work program had to be given credit for Colt's physical development, turning the skinny boy into a prison-hardened man.

Colt read his uncle's letter; then, without comment or even a change of expression, he placed the letter on his cot. Witcher sensed a feeling of trouble. "Bad news?" he asked.

His face void of emotion, Colt looked up and replied, "They killed my pa. Shot him in the back."

"Damn, son," Bob responded, "that is bad news. Do they know who shot him?"

"Yeah, they know," Colt replied, his words soft and measured. "Uncle Burt says nobody saw it happen, but there ain't any doubt who was behind it. Maybe they don't know who pulled the trigger, but they damn sure know who ordered it done."

Witcher shook his head solemnly. "That is sorrowful news, but don't you go gettin' all riled up and have the warden order you into solitary for a few days. You don't wanna add no time on your sentence when you're this close to gettin' out." Witcher had seen it happen before when a prisoner received bad news from home that prompted an attempt to escape. It was the warden's policy to impose a cool-down period until he was convinced the inmate was no longer inclined to attempt some fool scheme to run. It would be a shame in Colt's case since the young man had only six months to go. Witcher cocked his head to one side, giving Colt a hard glance. "It's against the rules, but I won't report this to the warden if you'll promise me you ain't gonna do somethin' stupid."

Still with no show of emotion, Colt said, "I ain't gonna cause no trouble, Bob. I aim to do my time and leave this place in six months." He picked up the letter again and gave it a brief glance. "Uncle Burt wants me to come back to Whiskey Hill when my time's up. Says he and Vance need my help. There's a ticket in here from Omaha to Cheyenne, but I'd have to make it to Omaha on my own." He paused again. "Maybe I'll think on it."

Bob nodded. He knew that Colt had not intended to return to Whiskey Hill when he was released, having had his fill of the community that had stripped him of almost ten years of his life. Although he thought he had a limited window into the man's mind, Witcher could not know the depth of sadness the report of Colt's father's murder caused. Colt had never been especially close to his father. He was closer to his uncle Burt. Maybe it was because Burt McCrae's nature was closer to that of the wild young boy who felt more at home in the foothills and mountains than on a cattle ranch. A sad smile formed on Colt's face as he pictured his uncle—husky and rugged, bigger than life. Like Colt, Burt had been the black sheep of the family, a stark contrast to Colt's father, who was a man of few words and steady as a rock. Colt wondered how the years had changed his uncle. Then he reminded himself that nothing outside an act of God could change

Burt McCrae—he with his prized possession, a derby hat bought in Omaha, cocked jauntily to one side as he rode herd on his ranch hands.

The coolness between Colt and his father was cause now for regret on the son's part, for he felt it was his fault, and now the opportunity to atone for it was lost. It would have been better if he had been more like his brother. Then the gulf between him and his father might not have been so wide. Like his father and his uncle, Colt and Vance were miles apart as young boys. That, too, was a shame. Maybe now it could be fixed. As he had said, he would think on returning and bide his time.

Six months after receiving his uncle's letter, Colt McCrae stood outside Kansas State Penitentiary's eighty-foot walls, a free man after having first entered the prison nine years, two months, and thirteen days before. He took a few cautious steps away from the wall and turned to look back at the harsh masonry that had sealed him off from the world. Gazing beyond the guard tower at the sky above, he saw dark, gunmetal gray clouds hanging over the walls, threatening rain, and could not help but remember that it had looked the same on that sorrowful day in his young life. He looked at Bob Witcher and permitted a nervous smile to form on his rugged face. The prison guard, who had become a friend, answered with a broad grin.

"You take care of yourself," Witcher said, extending his hand.

"I will," Colt answered, and turned to leave. He paused, turned back, and said, "Thanks, Bob." Witcher

nodded, then watched as the solemn young man from
Wyoming walked toward town.

It was August 1868 when he had been brought in
chains to the godforsaken prison in Leavenworth
County, along with two of his accused accomplices,
Billy Watts and Roy Barnes. The third, Joe Tucker, who
had actually shot the bank guard, had been hanged in
Whiskey Hill.

A skinny eighteen-year-old at the time, Colt was
guilty of nothing more than having the wrong circle of
friends. Joe, Billy, and Roy were all older than Colt, but
they tolerated him and another boy his age, Ronnie
Skinner. Fascinated by the three hoodlums' big talk,
Colt and Ronnie would while away countless hours
hanging around the Plainsman Saloon, listening to
their talk of cattle rustling and bank robberies that
never came to pass. There were many times during the
past nine years when Colt had wished he had taken
his father's advice and sought his formal education
elsewhere.

Although a wild and reckless boy, Colt was not dis-
honest, and for that reason he carried a nagging sense
of guilt for not warning the sheriff about a planned
robbery of the Bank of Whiskey Hill. In his defense, he
had not been certain that it was not just more of Joe
Tucker's big talk. Ronnie was not so skeptical, and
asked to go along on the robbery. It was Ronnie that
Eunice Fletcher got a glimpse of on that fateful day as
he held the horses behind the bank. But it was Colt
who she pointed out in the courtroom. They looked
enough alike to be mistaken for each other at a dis-

tance. Colt never expected Ronnie to step forward and confess, but he felt that when he got his day in court Mrs. Fletcher's identification might not stand up to a good lawyer's questioning. Actually she had seen Ronnie holding the horses from the back door of her husband's dry goods store, over a hundred yards from the bank.

Unfortunately for Colt, times were not favorable for fair trials back then. It was a time of wild and lawless behavior with the influx of the railroad construction crews and the riffraff that followed them—the gamblers, the outlaws, the saloons. It was too much to handle for the sheriff and his deputy. As a result, a vigilance committee was formed that was swift on punishment and not prone to lengthy trials. The bank guard named Joe Tucker as his killer before he died, and the Gunnysack Gang, as the vigilance committee was called, swept down on the three robbers while they were still counting the money at Tucker's shack that evening. The fourth member of the gang, who held the horses out back, was not at the shack when the posse struck, but it didn't matter. They had an eyewitness. Colt McCrae was arrested the next morning.

Now, over nine years later, Colt thought about that morning as he peered out the window of the train when it gently rocked around the long curve before the straight shot into Cheyenne. There had been no trial to speak of and no lawyer for the defense. The four prisoners were marched before Judge Blake, who listened to the sheriff's account of the crime, then promptly passed sentence. Joe Tucker was hanged on the spot. The crowd who had gathered to witness the trial wanted the other three to hang as well, but Judge Blake did not submit to their lust for punishment. Billy and Roy were sentenced to twenty years while Colt got ten.

Thinking about that day now, Colt could not suppress a bitter smile as the train slowed down, passing the stockyards on the east side of town. He had no desire to return to Cheyenne, but his curiosity prompted him to peer with interest at the houses and stores that were not there nine years ago. If he had a choice, he might have remained on the train and continued on west to the foothills of the Laramie Mountains, where he had often gone as a boy to escape the monotony of ranch work. With no horse and no money other than the few dollars in his pocket, however, he felt forced to respond to his uncle's request for help. In return, his uncle could provide the horse and rifle he would need to find his father's killer. During the long lonely nights in prison he had held on to the image of the hills and mountains only a good day's ride from Whiskey Hill. It was a land of gently rolling hills with low grassy meadows and steep granite formations that led to the mountains farther west.

Screeching in protest, the train wheels came to a stop, and he stared out at the town he had last seen when he was shipped away to prison. There were two other passengers bound for Cheyenne, and he waited until they had made their way to the exit. In no hurry, he got to his feet and followed them down the aisle, carrying his earthly possessions in a tiny bundle tied with string. It was a long walk from Cheyenne to Whiskey Hill, a half day's ride on a horse. Walking would take considerably longer, but he had no other means of transportation. Fortunately for him, a teamster driving a wagonload of supplies for Fletcher's Dry Goods gave him a lift before he had walked a mile. It wasn't much faster than walking, but it was easier on the feet.

The time was only a little past noon when he hopped off the wagon at Fletcher's store. It would take his uncle most of the morning to ride in from his ranch, so he had time to kill. Standing before the store, he looked up and down the street. A lot had changed since he had been away, but the Whiskey Hill Kitchen was still there next to the hotel, so he decided to spend most of the little bit of money he had on a meal.

Chapter 2

Mayor Roy Whitworth slid his coffee cup over to the edge of the table for Mary Simmons to refill. He paused to give the young half-Cheyenne waitress an approving smile before resuming his conversation with Raymond Fletcher. He was about to expound on his plans for his reelection campaign when he was interrupted by the sudden appearance of Barney Samuels.

Bursting through the door, Barney made straight for the little table in the back room where the town's leading citizens routinely met for lunch. Seeing the mayor and Fletcher already seated at the table, he announced, "You ain't gonna believe who I just saw get off a freighter's wagon . . . at least who I *think* I saw."

"Who?" Roy Whitworth asked, not really that interested.

Barney grinned, anticipating the reaction to his announcement. "Colt McCrae," he said. "He looks a helluva lot different, but I swear it's him."

As Barney expected, his statement caused both men at the table to suddenly sit upright. Whitworth hesitated to comment for a moment while he thought about it. "Hell, Barney," he said, "you musta started drinking a little early today. Colt McCrae's still in prison—won't get out for some years yet."

"I ain't had a drop today," Barney replied, his grin expanding, pleased by the mayor's reaction. "He's been gone longer than you think, I reckon. I swear, if it ain't him, it's sure as hell his double, only this one's a helluva lot bigger."

"What in hell would he want to come back here for?" the mayor asked. He was about to dismiss Barney's claim as mistaken identity when the sheriff walked back, accompanied by the owner of the diner, Oscar Anderson. Whitworth turned his attention to the sheriff. "Say, J.D., Barney here thinks he saw Colt McCrae get off a wagon that just pulled into town. You hear anything about him coming back to Whiskey Hill?"

J. D. Townsend grimaced and shook his head, not bothering to answer the mayor until he had seated himself at the table. "I expect he mighta seen McCrae. I got paper on him a week ago."

"A week ago?" Whitworth exploded. "And you didn't say nothing about it?"

"What the hell was I supposed to say?" the sheriff responded, obviously irritated by the grilling from His Honor, the mayor. "All it said was that he was released from prison. It didn't say he was comin' back here. Tell you the truth, I didn't think he'd ever show his face here or in Cheyenne again. Ex-convicts generally go somewhere they ain't known."

"Well, I expect it would be best if you told him to

keep right on moving," the mayor said. "We don't need his kind in Whiskey Hill. We cleaned up this town eight years ago, and we sure as hell don't need any jailbirds in our community."

Obviously perturbed, Townsend responded, "Well, Roy, I can't lawfully tell him he can't stay."

"But you can let him know he ain't welcome," Oscar Anderson interjected.

"Well, of course I'll have a talk with him," J.D. said, still perturbed. "I expect he ain't plannin' to stay for long, anyway." He paused while Oscar's waitress placed a cup of coffee on the table before him. "Thanks, Mary," he said, then continued. "Hell, it mighta not even been McCrae that Barney saw, anyway. It's been nine years, and he wasn't much more than a boy at the time."

"It was him," Barney insisted, "and he sure as hell ain't a boy now."

The topic of the back table's discussion was at that moment standing before the door of the Whiskey Hill Kitchen, thinking of a time over ten years before when Oscar Anderson had thrown him out of the diner with instructions never to come back. The thought of it brought a thin smile to Colt's face. He had probably earned Oscar's wrath, although all he had tried to do at the time was buy some breakfast. He was promptly hustled out the door by the burly Anderson simply because Oscar didn't want "his kind" in his establishment. He took a moment to count the money in his pocket to be sure he had enough left to buy a meal, then opened the door and entered.

The place hadn't changed much since the last time he had seen it, with the exception of a row of wooden booths along the far wall where a long table had been. He glanced around the open diner for a few seconds before walking over and seating himself in one of the new booths. He sat there for a minute or two before the waitress, a young girl, walked over to take his order.

"What can I get you?" Mary Simmons asked. "You want the lunch special?"

"Is it too late to order some breakfast?" Colt asked. "I just got in town, and what I'd really like is some scrambled eggs and bacon." He didn't express it, but he also thought that it would be fitting to be served the breakfast he had tried to buy when Oscar threw him out.

"I didn't think I'd seen you in here before," Mary said. "Sure, you can get some eggs. Pearl will fix you breakfast any time of day." She flashed a warm smile for his benefit. "You new in town, or just passin' through?"

Colt returned her smile as he took a moment to study her face. Dark hair and eyes, pretty in a wild way that suggested a strain of savage blood. If he had to guess, he would say that there was Indian blood somewhere along her family line. "I may stay for a while. I'm not sure yet. I used to live near here, but I've been away for a while."

"Well, welcome back," Mary said. "I'll get you some coffee." She turned and went to the kitchen where Pearl Murray was busy filling up plates of meat loaf and potatoes for the table in the back room. "I need an order of scrambled eggs and bacon," Mary called out as she walked through the door.

"The hell you do," Pearl replied gruffly. "Who the hell for?"

"Customer in the first booth," Mary replied cheerfully, anticipating Pearl's reaction to someone ordering something different than the lunch offering.

"Why can't he eat meat loaf like ever'body else?"

"He said he just got in town, and I guess he missed breakfast," Mary replied. "I told him sweet ol' Pearl would be more than thrilled to fix him whatever he wants." She graced the peevish cook with a wide grin. "Besides, he's not bad looking."

"I shoulda known," Pearl retorted. "It ain't enough I got the town big shots in the back room. Now I've got to stop and fix some drifter breakfast."

Colt glanced up when Mary approached with a steaming mug of coffee. Placing it down before him, she slid into the booth across from him. "So, you've been away for a while," she said. "What brings you back to Whiskey Hill?"

"Came to see my uncle," Colt replied, thinking that the girl was prone to ask a lot of questions.

"Your uncle? Who would that be?"

"Burt McCrac," Colt answered, still wondering how far the girl's curiosity was going to take her.

"Oh, Burt," she said. "I know him. He comes in once in a while when he's in town. Vance, too. You know Vance?"

"He's my brother."

"Oh," she replied, stopped for a moment by something in the back of her mind. She was relatively new in town, but she seemed to have heard something about Vance McCrae's brother. At this moment, she was unable to recall just what it was.

Since she seemed to have run out of questions, Colt asked one of his own. "Does Oscar Anderson still own this place?"

"Yes. Do you wanna talk to him?"

He laughed. "No, I just wondered. That's all."

She remained there for an awkward moment while he sipped his coffee. He seemed nice enough—soft-spoken—but there was something guarded about his demeanor that made her wonder if she should be so friendly. "Well," she suddenly stated, "I'll go see about your breakfast."

"I was about to holler for you," Pearl said when Mary returned to the kitchen. "You can take these dinners back to the big shots." Just as she said it, Oscar joined them. "It's comin' now," Pearl said to Oscar, anticipating his query.

"I was wonderin'," Oscar commented. He picked up a couple of the plates to help Mary.

"What about my breakfast order?" Mary asked as she picked up the other two plates.

"In a minute," Pearl replied. She glanced at Oscar, grinning. "Mary's got a new customer she's shining up to."

"Who?" Oscar asked, ready to tease his waitress.

"Some stranger," Pearl replied.

"He's Vance McCrae's brother," Mary offered, then stopped abruptly to keep from bumping into Oscar, who had come to a sudden halt.

"Where?" Oscar demanded. When told the stranger

was in the first booth, he put the plates down and went to the pass-through window behind the counter. After staring at the man calmly drinking coffee for a long moment, he uttered a whispered "Jesus! It's him, all right." Remembering the wild, skinny boy, he found it a little unnerving to see the filled-out, solid version that was the man.

"Oscar, what is it?" Mary asked, concerned by her employer's obvious alarm. She and Pearl crowded in beside Oscar to stare at the man as well.

Oscar turned to face them. "That man is Colt McCrae. He's been in prison for the last nine years." He directed his next remark at Mary. "Don't go gettin' friendly with the likes of him."

"He seemed nice enough," Mary uttered in her defense, shaken by Oscar's remark.

"Them dinners is gettin' cold," Pearl reminded them, unconcerned with any threat from the stranger in the booth.

"You mind yourself," Oscar instructed Mary. "Feed him and get him outta here." The thought of refusing him service was but a brief vesper across Oscar's mind. He had no urge to confront the man he saw in the booth. He might still be harboring bad feelings about the last time he was in the diner. Reluctant to even glance in Colt's direction, he hurried toward the back room just as Turk Coolidge, who owned the Plainsman Saloon, came in. He paused to let Mary precede him with the other two plates of food. Mary, however, could not resist sneaking another peek at the mysterious stranger in the first booth.

As soon as he was inside the door, Oscar made his

announcement. "Well, boys, Barney was right. Colt McCrae is settin' in my front booth right now, pretty as you please." As soon as he said it, all heads turned toward the door, although it was impossible to see the booths without actually stepping to the door.

Mayor Whitworth was the first to speak out. "He's got some brass, coming back here. Maybe you oughta go in there and arrest him, J.D."

"For what?" the sheriff responded.

"I don't know," Whitworth shot back. "I don't care. Make up something. Let him know he ain't welcome around here."

Immediately defensive, the sheriff replied, "I told you I aim to talk to him. I can tell him it's best to move on, but unless he breaks a law, I can't do much more than that."

"Maybe it's time to call up the old vigilance committee again if you can't keep criminals out of town," the mayor said.

"There ain't no cause for talk like that, Roy," J.D. responded indignantly. "I do a damn good job of keeping the peace around here. I'll have my eye on this jailbird, and the first time he steps outta line I'll nail his hide to the wall."

Turk Coolidge, an interested bystander to the conversation to that point, made a suggestion. "It's your establishment, Oscar. Why don't you throw him out?"

"Like J.D. said," Oscar was quick to reply, "he ain't done nothin' to break the law, so it wouldn't be right to throw him out without no reason. Now, if he was upsettin' the customers or something, I'd throw his ass right out in the street."

"Yeah, I reckon," Barney said with a chuckle.

While the town's leading citizens were debating the possible actions available to them to rid the town of this latest threat, the object of their conversation was contemplating a plate of scrambled eggs just set before him. He could not help but notice a change in the waitress' expression as she refilled his coffee cup. Glancing beyond her toward the bar, he also noticed a woman's face in the pass-through window. "These eggs really look good," he commented, guessing that she must have discovered his past. "Tell the cook—what was her name, Pearl?—that I really appreciate it."

"I guess they didn't care how they cooked 'em in prison, did they?" She couldn't help herself. She just blurted it out. Embarrassed then, she immediately apologized. "I'm sorry. I shouldn't have said that."

He smiled. "Why not? It's a fact. They looked like leather and tasted worse."

She couldn't help but laugh. She started to turn away, then hesitated. She sensed no threat of harm to come her way from this man. "What are you going to do, now that you're back?" she suddenly asked.

He glanced up to study her eyes for a moment before replying. "Rob banks, hold up trains, murder innocent people, I reckon. You know, the things that ex-convicts do."

She gave him a look a mother might cast upon a petulant child. "Well, the way they're talking about you in the back room, I think that's what they expect. You need anything else?"

"One more cup of coffee," he said. Then glancing up when the front door opened and a big man wear-

ing a derby hat walked in, he added, "And maybe one
for my uncle."

She stepped back as Colt untangled his long legs
from the booth and stood to greet his uncle. Burt
McCrae said a brief hello to Mary before stopping to
scrutinize the man standing next to the booth. Struck
speechless by the transformation of boy to man, he just
stood there for a long moment shaking his head in disbelief. When words finally returned, he said, "Damn,
boy, I wouldn'ta known you if you didn't look so
much like your daddy in the face."

"How you doin', Uncle Burt?" Colt replied, taking
his uncle's outstretched hand. He didn't voice it, but
his father's brother had aged a great deal since he last
saw him. The dark hair had turned almost completely
gray, and the cheerful face he remembered as a boy
was now lined with wrinkles, but he still wore the
determined expression of a bulldog. The derby was
weathered and faded from the Wyoming sun, but still
cocked at a jaunty angle. The exterior was frayed and
worn, but Colt suspected there was no change inside.
"I'm glad to see you got my letter."

"Yeah, got it last week," Burt replied. "Sorry the
only letter I wrote you was one tellin' you about your
pa."

Colt smiled. "Hell, I was surprised to get that one. I
didn't think you could write."

Burt continued to look his nephew over from head
to toe, astounded by the change. When Mary broke into
his fixation to ask if he wanted coffee, he nodded, then
slid into the booth opposite Colt. "Damn if it don't look
like prison life was good for you," he said, his face

breaking into a wide grin, much like the picture of his uncle that Colt remembered. "I swear, it's good to see you. I'm just sorry you couldn't have got out before your daddy was murdered. Those bastards . . ." he added, his words trailing off.

"What bastards?" Colt prodded quietly.

Burt shook his head in frustration. "Drummond's men," he answered. "Who did the shootin'? It's hard to say, but there ain't no doubt in my mind that it was by Drummond's order. Course J. D. Townsend ain't been able to find out who the shooter was, since he don't as much as take a shit without askin' Drummond where to put it. You know how your daddy was—he wasn't about to roll over for Drummond like some of the other small ranchers did. And I ain't, neither. I reckon I'll be the next one on Drummond's list of killin's, 'cause I'm just as stubborn as your pa was. He's gonna have to kill me to get my land. It's Vance I'm worried about." He paused briefly when Mary brought his coffee. "I've been losing a few head of cattle here and there, but Vance has lost more than I have. Not only cattle, he's lost three of his regular cowhands. They just up and quit for no good reason, but I've got a pretty good idea some of Drummond's scum has been puttin' the fear of God in 'em. I'm afraid Vance is gonna knuckle under and sell out to Drummond, and if he does, that's gonna cut me off from water."

"Did Pa leave the ranch to Vance?" Colt asked.

"He left it to both of you," Burt replied, "and that's one of the reasons I sent for you. Your daddy wrote his will, leaving the ranch to you and Vance, and the house to Vance and Susan about a year ago. I wrote one, too, when the cattle rustlin' started. We put both wills in the bank for safekeepin'."

Colt didn't reply right away while he thought that over. *Landowner*—one thought he had not considered over these past years. He had no desire to be a rancher. The one driving thought that had dominated his mind since being incarcerated was to be free, free of all things restricting, free to wander wherever he chose. "What does Vance think about that?" he finally asked. "He probably expected to get everything, and maybe he should have. He's got a wife and child, and I don't give a damn about workin' a ranch."

A look of disappointment immediately flashed across Burt's face. He had obviously hoped that Colt would return to help manage both the Bar-M and his spread, the Broken-M. "That ranch is rightfully half yours," he insisted, "and if somebody don't stop Drummond, you and your brother are gonna lose it."

"Don't misunderstand me," Colt said. "I aim to put a stop to the cattle rustlin', and I aim to find the man that shot my pa. All I want from you and Vance is a horse and saddle, a good rifle, and supplies and ammunition, and I'll help you keep the land."

Burt smiled. "I knew I could count on you." He was about to say more, but was interrupted by the sight of J. D. Townsend approaching the booth. "Here comes the sheriff to welcome you back," he said facetiously.

"Burt," J.D. acknowledged briefly before directing his attention toward Colt. "I heard you was gettin' out, McCrae. I was surprised you'd show up in Whiskey Hill again. You just passin' through?"

Colt didn't answer at once, taking his time to study

the heavyset lawman. He remembered J.D., but only as the young bully he had been as a deputy. "So you stuck around long enough to be sheriff. I expected you to be gone by now."

Bristling just a bit, J.D. responded, "Yeah, I'm the sheriff here, and it's my job to keep the peace. This town has got rid of most of your kind, and I wanna make sure you understand that I don't stand for any jailbirds makin' trouble in Whiskey Hill."

"There ain't no call for that kind of talk, J.D.," Burt said. "Colt's served his time."

"Yeah, well, there ain't no welcome here for him. The best thing for him is to get on outta town while he's got a chance."

Colt's gaze held steady on the sheriff's face during his exchange with Burt. When J.D. returned his attention to Colt, he asked, "What have you done about findin' the man that shot my father?"

"That's over and done," J.D. replied. "His killer is long gone. Figure it was a drifter—no way I coulda caught him."

"What are you doin' about cattle rustlin' off of Bar-M and Broken-M spreads?" Colt asked, his words soft and even.

Showing his irritation at being questioned, J.D. blurted, "I ain't but one man with one deputy. I'm more worried about the likes of you comin' back to cause trouble in town."

"How many cattle has Frank Drummond lost?" Colt asked, his words still calm and measured.

J.D. took an angry step backward. "I don't think I like your attitude."

"Is that the next charge you and the fine citizens of Whiskey Hill are figurin' to send me to prison for?"

The sheriff pointed his finger directly at Colt. "You've been warned. You'd better watch your ass around here, jailbird, or I'll be on you like a chicken on a June bug." He promptly spun on his heel and returned to the back room.

"Well, I reckon you've been officially welcomed home," Burt said after the sheriff had gone. "You'd best watch yourself around J.D. Everybody knows Frank Drummond owns him." He paused to make sure Colt was paying attention. "I expect we'd best get started if we're gonna get back to the ranch before dark. I drove the wagon in since I figured I might as well pick up a few things at the dry goods store."

"You go along," Colt said. "I'll catch up with you at the store. I just want to pay for my food."

"You need some money?" Burt asked, but Colt shook his head.

Burt hurried out to his wagon while Colt walked over to the kitchen door. The two women turned to look at him when he stuck his head inside. "I need to settle up," he said. Then, nodding to the plump little woman standing by the stove, he added, "Thanks for the eggs, Pearl. I hope it wasn't too much trouble."

Quite surprised by his polite comment, she couldn't think of a reply at once. After a moment, she remarked, "If it'd been any trouble, I wouldn'ta done it."

Mary walked him to the front counter and took his money. "Will we be seeing you again?" she inquired as casually as she could affect, for she had overheard the confrontation between him and the sheriff.

"Most likely," he replied.

"Can I help you, sir?" Eunice Fletcher asked when Colt walked into the store. "No, ma'am," Colt replied. "I'm with him." He walked over to stand beside his uncle. Burt made no introduction, both men aware of the irony of the moment. The eyewitness who identified Colt from more than one hundred yards away failed to recognize him when ten feet from him. "Here, let me get that for you," Colt said and stepped forward to lift the heavy flour sack that Mrs. Fletcher was dragging from behind the counter. "I'll throw this in the wagon, Uncle Burt," he said.

Burt nodded as Colt hefted the fifty-pound sack up on his shoulder. Eunice Fletcher smiled at him as he turned and left the store. Burt paid her, gathered up the other few articles he had bought, and followed Colt out the door. "Well, there's the judge's eyewitness," Burt remarked as he climbed up in the wagon seat.

An hour later, Raymond Fletcher returned to his store and was greeted by his wife. "Burt McCrae was just in, had a nice-looking young man with him."

"Eunice!" Raymond replied in alarm. "That was Colt McCrae."

"My stars!" Eunice gasped, clutching her throat. "He coulda killed me!"

Chapter 3

Vance McCrae stood on the lip of a deep gully, staring down in frustration at the rotting carcasses of two cows. At ten or twelve feet below him, he couldn't see the brands clearly. This point on the east range was close to his uncle's property, so the carcasses could be either Broken-M or Bar-M. They looked to be three- or four-year-olds, and should have been part of the herd driven over to the railroad holding pens a few weeks past. There was no need to climb down to the bottom of the gully to verify the cause of death to be from bullet wounds. This was not an unusual discovery during the past year. It had gotten to the point where circling buzzards were a daily occurrence on his grazing land. There was also little doubt who was responsible, but he felt helpless to do anything about it. He had no way of proving Frank Drummond responsible, and he could not ignore the fact that his father had been shot in the back after making accusations against the town's wealthiest landowner.

Vance had faced Frank Drummond with the problem back in the early fall during roundup. He didn't know what to expect when he rode over to the Rocking-D to confront Drummond, but he knew he had to do it. As he had expected, his complaints were met with smug indifference on Drummond's part and the suggestion that maybe the McCraes were just an unlucky family. He offered to take Vance's problems off his hands with a ridiculously low offer for his ranch. With no evidence to support it, Vance could not openly accuse Drummond as the source of the trouble, so he had no choice but to shamefully retreat, much to the amusement of two of Drummond's henchmen, Lon Branch and Brownie Brooks. The thought now of the two sneering miscreants made his blood boil as he stared down at the carcasses.

Turning to go back to his horse, he hesitated when he heard the sound of another horse approaching. Standing by his mount, his hand on the butt of his rifle, he peered over the saddle at a rider approaching from his uncle's spread. Thinking it to be one of his uncle's hands, he relaxed his grip on the rifle, and waited. As the rider drew near, however, something very familiar about the way he sat the saddle struck Vance. It had been a while since he had seen anyone move with a horse quite like that, as if a part of the horse instead of merely aboard it. "Well, I'll be damned . . ." he finally muttered.

He stood there staring at the man approaching. As Colt drew near, Vance made note of the obvious physical changes in his brother. Remembering the chasm between the two before Colt was sent to prison, he could only wonder what damage the years of incarceration had wrought.

"I heard you were back," Vance offered in greeting. He made no move to step forward and extend a hand as Colt pulled up and dismounted.

"Hello, Vance," Colt said. "How've you been?"

"All right, I guess," Vance answered guardedly, not knowing what to expect from his brother after so much had happened. "You've changed a helluva lot."

"Yeah, I reckon," Colt replied. Then the hint of a smile tugged at the corners of his mouth. "You look like you picked up a few gray hairs—married life, I reckon."

Vance grinned. "Maybe so."

"How long has it been now? Seven years?"

"Six," Vance said, correcting him.

"Six," Colt repeated, "and you've got a young'un, a boy, I heard."

"That's right. Sammy's five this month."

Colt nodded, then remarked, "Damn, you didn't waste much time, did you?" There followed an awkward moment of silence while both brothers searched for conversation. Finally, Colt broke the casual impasse. "Susan Sessions, I heard. Always figured you two would tie the knot."

"Yeah," Vance said, changing the subject. He nodded toward the big buckskin Colt had selected. "I see you picked out a good horse. Uncle Burt always liked Buck. Looks a lot like that horse you used to ride before. I reckon that's why Uncle Burt named this one Buck, too . . ." His words trailed off. Changing the subject again, he nodded toward the saddle sling. "You got Pa's Winchester?"

"Yeah. Uncle Burt said it was all right with you. Is it?"

"Sure. I've got my own rifle. I don't need two."

With both brothers feeling the strain of making casual conversation, Colt finally got down to business. After Vance showed him the carcasses at the bottom of the gully, Colt told him of the arrangement he had made with their uncle. "I guess that's going to be my job, to try to cut out some of this business. I'm going to be ranging over both spreads, yours and Uncle Burt's, so you need to tell your men they might be seein' me when they're ridin' winter range. How many have you got?"

"There aren't but two that's stayin' this winter," Vance answered. "You know them—Bill Wilkes and Tom Mosley. They worked for Pa." Colt nodded, and then Vance asked, "You stayin' with Uncle Burt?"

"Well, yes and no. I don't plan to stay at the house. I'll be campin' most of the time, so I can cover more ground. I'll just be checkin' in with Uncle Burt every now and then."

"The weather's kinda cold to be livin' outdoors all the time. Course, I remember you never minded the cold much. Looks like you haven't changed in that way."

Colt laughed. "I suppose. Anyway, when you've been locked up as long as I have, the open spaces feel kinda good."

Vance smiled in response. "I reckon you're right. You know, Pa left the ranch to both of us. You've got as much right as I have to live there."

"Yeah," Colt said. "Uncle Burt told me, but I'm not

figurin' on workin' this ranch. It's yours as far as I'm concerned. You're the one who's been takin' care of it. I've got a few things to take care of. Then I'll most likely be movin' on."

The somewhat cautious reunion between brothers over, they climbed back in the saddle and started in opposite directions. As an afterthought, Vance called back over his shoulder, "You're welcome to come by the house and meet my family." Even as he said it, he knew Susan would raise hell with him for extending the invitation.

"Thanks, maybe I will sometime," Colt answered.

He reined the buckskin to a halt on a ridge overlooking the wide shallow valley that served as the Rocking-D headquarters. The last time he had ridden through this part of the hills, the valley was an endless sea of grass. Now he gazed at the huge white house with its expansive porches and the barns and out-buildings beyond. It was an empire, all right, with three separate corrals. "You'd think this would be enough for one man," he remarked to his horse. "No explainin' some folks, I reckon." He nudged Buck with his heels, and proceeded down the gentle slope.

Although he saw only one or two hands over near the barn, he drew his Winchester from the saddle sling. Holding it with one hand, the butt resting on his thigh with the barrel straight up, he approached the house at a slow walk. No one seemed to notice him, except one man repairing a fence around the garden, who paused to stare at the stranger for a moment before resuming his work.

Colt walked his horse up to the front porch. Remaining seated in the saddle, he called out, "Drummond! Frank Drummond!" There was no answer, so he called out again, still with no response from anyone inside. He considered the fact that no one was home, but decided that they simply could not hear within the massive house. So he raised his rifle and fired it in the air. He got a response within a few seconds.

Frank Drummond, along with two of his men, both armed, came storming out on the porch, only to be stopped short by the sight of the stolid horseman calmly awaiting them. Colt, his rifle resting upon his thigh again, registered no emotion, except for a slight shifting of his eyes as he considered the men on either side of the commanding presence of Drummond.

"Who the hell are you?" Drummond demanded.

"Colt McCrae."

Drummond paused a moment, scowling. "Oh, the jailbird," he said with a sneer. "I heard you were out of prison." He walked over to the edge of the porch and pointed a finger at Colt. "Let me tell you something, jailbird, it ain't healthy to come into my home shooting off a rifle." His rage was building, accelerated by the obvious cool disregard shown for his threats by his visitor. "Something like that could get a man killed. If I want you to set foot on my land, by God, I'll send for you. Now turn that horse around and get the hell off my range."

Colt shifted his gaze momentarily to the man standing to the right of Drummond. "Are you nervous?" The man did not reply, but moved his hand away from the pistol he wore. Looking back at Drummond again, Colt said his piece, speaking in a calm, unemotional voice. "I came to tell you somethin'. Bar-M and Broken-M cattle are no longer gonna be used for target practice. Any more cows I find with bullet holes in them, I will automatically figure were shot by your men, and they will be dealt with. Any missing Bar-M or Broken-M cattle found on Rocking-D land will be assumed stolen—"

Furious, Drummond interrupted. "Why, you insolent son of a bitch! You come riding into my home, talking to me like that. You don't know who you're messing with. I own this country! I'll have you sent back to prison." He paused for emphasis. "That is, if you get off my land without getting shot for trespassing."

Already having considered that risk, Colt lowered the rifle barrel slightly in the irate man's direction. "That could happen, I guess, but you can be sure of one thing. It better be a damn good shot because the next one is gonna get you." He leveled the rifle, aiming it directly at Drummond's gut. "Now you've been warned." Pulling the reins with his free hand, he backed his horse slowly away from the porch. Drummond's two men watched nervously, undecided on what to do until Drummond told them to let him go. Though still enraged, he was not brazen enough to kill a man right in his front yard. Colt backed up until clear of the garden fence before turning his horse and galloping away.

"He's had his little show," Drummond said, "and all it did was dig his grave."

• • •

Lon Branch rode up to the wide porch that wrapped around three sides of Frank Drummond's white frame house and dismounted. After looping the reins over the hitching post, he stepped over to the porch and knocked on the plank flooring, then stood respectfully waiting for Alice, Drummond's housekeeper, to come to the door. Lon, like the other ranch hands on the Rocking-D, would not walk up on the porch and knock on the front door. He had never been told not to. It just seemed to be disrespectful to do so.

After he'd knocked three more times, Alice finally heard him and came to the door, properly gracing him with the scornful look she reserved for all Drummond's hired hands. Lon respectfully told her that Drummond had sent for him, so she told him to wait. After approximately ten minutes, Drummond appeared in the doorway. He stepped out on the porch. "I got a little business I want you to take care of, Lon," he said.

"Yessir," Lon replied.

"I had a little visit today from another one of those McCraes, the ex-convict. And I don't like brass-balled jailbirds ridin' right up to my house and threatening me." Drummond was trying to hold his temper as he spoke, but Lon could see that his boss was clearly irritated. "A man like that could very well have an accident, maybe his horse might throw him, or he might wind up gettin' shot like his old man."

Lon didn't reply at once, slow to get the meaning of his boss' pointed remarks. After a moment, it hit him. "Oh, yes, sir," he then quickly replied. "Ain't no doubt about it, a man like that is damn sure ridin' for a fall.

Me and Brownie was thinkin' that same thing yesterday. We took a little ride over towards McCrae's range, thought we'd thin out his herd a little more." He paused to give his boss a wink. When Drummond failed to respond, he quickly continued. "Anyway, we found a bunch of strays near the creek, but before we crossed over, we spotted Colt McCrae settin' on his horse on the ridge above the creek. He saw us, too, so we didn't do nothin'. A couple of the boys heard some shootin' over that way yesterday mornin'. When they rode over to take a look, they saw him takin' target practice with a rifle."

Confident that his wishes were known and would be carried out to his satisfaction, Drummond considered the problem solved. It was no more than a minor irritation, but an irritation nonetheless. He had felt certain that when he had eliminated Sam McCrae, the son, Vance, would crumple soon after. This latest development with the other son might serve to inspire Vance to stiffen his resistance just when Drummond figured he was close to breaking him.

"All right, then," Drummond said, ending the meeting. "Just be sure you take care of business so that it's neat and tidy." He stood on the porch for a few moments more, watching his hired hand ride off to do his bidding. Lon was a good man—had just enough rattlesnake in him to take care of jobs like this, and enough sense to keep his mouth shut. That's why he and his partner, Brownie, were well paid.

In Frank Drummond's mind, there was no right or wrong when it came to his methods in building his cattle empire. It was simply business, and sometimes stringent methods were called for to eliminate problems that stood in the way of progress. He planned to own Whiskey Hill, and stubborn people like the McCraes were minor delays that, from a business viewpoint, had to be handled. Satisfied that this latest problem was as good as taken care of, he turned and went back inside.

"Lookee comin' yonder," Tom Mosley said, tugging Bill Wilkes' shirtsleeve.

"Well, I'll be . . ." Bill responded, grinning broadly. "It's the ol' wildcat hisself. I wondered when he was gonna come around."

The two old cowhands walked out of the barn to meet the rider on the buckskin horse, both men sporting grins on their faces. When he saw them, Colt couldn't help but grin himself. He guided the horse up to them and climbed down. "I thought you two old coots would have dried up and blown away by now," he teased.

Bill Wilkes stepped back, pretending to be shocked, turned to Tom Mosley, and exclaimed, "Damn, Tom, I thought this young whippersnapper mighta learnt some manners in prison. We might oughta turn him over a knee and dust his britches."

Taking visual inventory of the rawhide-tough adult version of the skinny lad they had last seen, Tom replied, "Maybe you oughta do it. I ain't sure I could get the job done."

Joking aside, they both descended upon Colt, shaking hands and back-slapping, all three grinning broadly. These two, Tom and Bill, had worked for

Colt's father since before his mother passed away. They had remained close to the boy even when he had shown his wild streak and got on the bad side of his father.

"I figured I'd better come by in case Vance hadn't told you I'm gonna be ridin' Bar-M range," Colt said. "I don't want you takin' a shot at me if you see me pokin' around after dark."

"Yeah," Bill said, "Vance told us he saw you yesterday, said you was plannin' to do some scoutin'.'"

"I reckon it's a good thing you came by," Tom commented, "'cause I ain't sure I woulda recognized you at a distance."

On a more serious note, Colt said, "Vance told me you and him were running the ranch by yourselves. I guess it's been pretty tough over the past year."

"It has," Tom said. "Drummond's boys has scared everybody off but me and Bill. I reckon if we had any sense, we'da left, too, but, hell, we're too damn old to go anywhere else."

"Maybe I can help," Colt said. "At least, that's my intention."

"We can sure as hell use the help," Bill said. "We're losin' cattle every day to lead poisoning, if you know what I mean." He shrugged. "Vance is doin' the best he can, it's just that he ain't Sam McCrae."

Vance pulled the curtain aside and peered out the kitchen window. "That's Colt out there talking to Tom and Bill. I oughta go out there." He turned to look at his wife, who was stirring a pot on the stove. "Oughta invite him to eat supper with us," he added.

"You should not!" Susan hastily informed her husband as she moved closer to the window to stare out. "I don't plan on feeding that ex-convict. I don't want him around here, and I don't want him around Sammy. I don't know why they let him out of prison."

"He's served his time," Vance said in defense of his brother. "I talked to him yesterday, and I really believe he's changed."

"Well, I doubt that. You can put a wolf in a pen for as long as you want, but when you let him out, he's still a wolf."

"Well, I'm at least gonna go out and talk to him," Vance said. "He's willing to help, and we damn sure need him."

"I'm warning you, Vance, I'm not cooking for the likes of Colt McCrae."

It was a mystery to Vance why his wife seemed to have developed such a strong dislike for his brother. As far as he knew, Susan had never really had much exposure to Colt before he went to prison. And although there was never a close bond between the two brothers, Vance had never overly criticized Colt. To the contrary, he had seldom even spoken of him during the nine years he was away. He decided it was just simply a mother's natural tendency to protect her son from what she considered a dangerous individual. He shrugged his shoulders and turned away from the window. "I guess if he needs to see me, he'll come to the house," he said, preferring to keep peace with his wife.

Over at the barn, Tom Mosley asked Colt if he was going to the house to see Vance. Colt glanced in that direction and hesitated for a moment. "I reckon not," he said. "I talked to Vance yesterday. I just came by to make sure you two old men didn't accidentally take a shot at me."

"Huh," Bill joked, "might take a shot, but it won't be accidental."

Colt laughed. "I've got to get goin', anyway. I figure to camp over on the north ridge tonight. Uncle Burt said he found a couple more dead cows over that way, and I wanna stop by the house to pick up a few things."

"You be careful, boy," Tom said as Colt stepped up in the saddle. "That's close to the Rocking-D."

"I aim to," Colt replied and turned Buck's head back toward the Broken-M.

The two old cowhands stood watching the younger of the two McCrae sons as he rode away at a gentle lope. Still marveling over the transformation from boy to man, Bill Wilkes felt inspired to proclaim, "I got a feelin' things is about to change in this valley."

"I know what you mean," Tom said. "I've got the same feelin'." He pushed his hat back and scratched his head thoughtfully. "Damn! Don't he remind you a lot of his daddy when he was about that age?"

"Come to think of it," Bill agreed. The thought brought back memories of long ago when the four of them, Tom, Bill, and Sam and Burt McCrae, had first brought a small herd of cattle to the valley. And now everything they had helped Sam build was in jeopardy of being consumed by Frank Drummond. Bill and Tom were too old to be involved in a range war, but they both felt it was their place to try to help Sam McCrae's sons hold on to the land. "Yessir, things is liable to get hot around here."

Letting his horse set its own pace, Colt rocked along easily in the saddle, thinking about the two old ranch hands he had just left. Tom Mosley's question—if he was going to the house to see Vance—stuck in his mind for a moment, for it brought back troublesome thoughts of a time when he and his brother were not so different. His mind drifted back to a summer day nine years before.

Barely a week past his eighteenth birthday, he had gotten into an argument with his father because he had slipped off the day before to go hunting for antelope, leaving his chores unfinished. The argument was pretty heated, and being a hardheaded young rebel, he took off again in protest, instead of mucking out the barn as he was told to do. Since it was a rather warm day, he decided nothing could be better than a dip in the creek that ran along the north ridge and, at that time, divided his father's range from that of Walter Sessions. The picture of that day came back to him clearly, for it was a day that would influence the rest of his life.

The water was cool and deep, and he wasted no time shucking his clothes and plunging in, thoughts of stables and chores far from his mind as he splashed around in the dark water. He had not been in for a quarter of an hour when he was suddenly startled by a voice from the bank behind him. He turned to find Susan Sessions leaning against a cottonwood tree, watching him, a mischievous smile displayed across her face. She was holding his clothes in her hand.

"Whoa!" he blurted. "What are you gonna do with my clothes?"

"I've not decided yet," she teased and made a motion as if to throw them in the creek. "Maybe I'll just hold them and let you come get them." She held them out toward him. "You want them? Come on out and get them."

"I've got a better idea," he replied. "Just drop 'em by the tree there where you found them. Drop yours on top of 'em and come on in. We'll both go swimmin'."

"Why, Colt McCrae, you've got a sassy nerve to think I'd be found in the same creek with the likes of you." She reared her head back, pretending to be shocked. "I've got a good mind to tell your father about your sassy mouth."

Colt laughed. "If you had a good mind, you'd shuck those clothes and jump in. It's nice and cool."

She favored him with an impish smile. "If I did, you'd probably tell everybody in Whiskey Hill."

"Wouldn't say a word—wouldn't be nobody's business but yours and mine."

"It is awfully warm," she said, her eyes locked on his.

Colt shook his head slowly, the cruel irony of that day so long ago having returned to his thoughts many times while he had languished in his prison cell in Kansas. They had made love on the grassy bank of the creek. Susan soon abandoned her veil of innocence and aggressively offered her body, demanding his most virile response to her hunger. When it was over, she climbed back in her clothes and assured him that if he breathed a word of what had just happened, she would denounce him as a liar. The cruelest stroke of irony, however, was the fact that while this illicit encounter was taking place, twelve miles away in Whiskey Hill a bank robbery was in progress, resulting in the death of a bank guard.

"I was wonderin' if you were gonna show up for supper," Burt McCrae said when he walked out on the porch to watch Colt loop his reins around the post.

"Tell you the truth, I hadn't thought about it," Colt replied. "I was just gonna pick up a few things I needed, but if you're offerin', I might take you up on it."

Burt looked surprised. "You ain't plannin' on stayin' at the house?"

"Nope. I don't figure on bein' much help to you and Vance if I'm stayin' around here at night. If I'm gonna help you at all, it's gonna be out scoutin' the ridges where I can maybe see what's goin' on." When Burt started to protest, Colt stopped him. "Let me do it my way. All I need from you is some grub from time to time, and cartridges for my rifle. Fair enough?"

"Why, yeah," Burt stammered, "fair enough. Now come on in the house. Rena's got supper on the table." Colt followed his uncle inside where Rena, his Indian cook, had loaded the table with food. While Colt filled his plate, Burt sat back and grinned. "It's damn good eatin', ain't it?"

Colt did not reply, instead looking up at the silent

Cheyenne woman, and nodding in agreement. Pleased, she smiled in response. Rena had been his uncle's cook for as long as Colt could remember. His aunt Vera had been dead since Colt was no more than a baby, and as far as he ever knew, there had never been any other woman in the house but the somber Rena.

Thoughts of a wild young Colt McCrae returned to Burt's mind as he watched the imposing figure of a man seated at his supper table. When he gave it a second thought, he was not surprised that Colt chose to sleep under the stars, rejecting a bed in the front room. The boy had always been more at home in the hills and the open prairie. Rena had always been partial to his nephew. She used to say that Colt may have been born to a white woman, but his heart was Cheyenne. It struck Burt then how cruel a penalty it was to lock this free soul away in a prison cell. Burt continued to study his nephew intensely, so intensely that Colt wondered if something else was on his uncle's mind. "What is it, Uncle Burt?" he asked.

Burt didn't answer at once, still wrestling with the decision to broach the subject or not. Maybe it was best to let old wounds alone. It had been almost ten years. Maybe Colt preferred to let past sins and grievances lie in the past, but Burt thought he should at least let him know. Finally, he said what was on his mind. "I don't know if you still care or not, but I was over to Cheyenne last week and I saw an old friend of yours." Seeing Colt's interest, he went on. "Ronnie Skinner—I saw him comin' out of Bailey's Saloon on the edge of town. I'da recognized him anywhere—still the sneaky little rat he was ten years ago, only a little older."

Colt didn't say anything for a minute or two, his mind obviously going back to darker times. Finally, he asked, "Did you talk to him?"

"Nah," Burt replied. "He didn't look like he even knew me. I didn't have nothin' to say to him, anyway." Colt just nodded thoughtfully. Burt continued. "The bartender said Ronnie hangs around the saloon most of the time—when he ain't in jail. Seems like he's stayed in some kind of trouble around Cheyenne for the last several years. I don't think he's been back to Whiskey Hill since you and them other fellers were sent off to prison."

He continued to study Colt's face closely, but his nephew gave no indication of his reaction to news of his boyhood friend. Behind the expressionless face, however, Colt's mind brought back the image of the man guilty of the crime for which he had served time. "Well, I'll be goin' along," was all Colt said. Then he got up from the table, nodding a thank-you to Rena as he went out the door.

Chapter 4

He followed the north ridge for a mile and a half, on the lookout for strays before reaching the little stream that marked the corner of his uncle's ranch. He had always called it Crooked Branch when he was a boy because of the many turns it made at the bottom of the ridge, and it eventually flowed into Crooked Creek. He didn't know the real name, if there was one. Maybe the Cheyenne Indians had a name for it. Beyond the stream was most likely Drummond land now, since there was very little range on this side of the railroad that didn't belong to Drummond. He decided that Crooked Branch was as good a place as any to camp for the night.

He pulled the saddle off his horse and hobbled the buckskin to graze while he looked for firewood among the cottonwood trees. Soon he had a fire going and coffee working up a boil. His uncle had supplied him with everything he would require, including .44 cartridges for the Winchester his father had left him. Thinking of the rifle, he propped the coffeepot on two smoldering sticks in the edge of the fire, and drew the weapon from the saddle sling to inspect it. It was a fine rifle, a Winchester '73, and his uncle had told him how much his father admired it. *I can see why*, Colt thought as he turned the rifle over in his hands as if examining it for the first time. He ran his fingers over the wooden stock, remembering how smoothly the lever action had operated when he had taken target practice to become familiar with the weapon. Satisfied that he and the Winchester would work well together, he laid it across his saddle and returned his attention to the coffeepot in the embers.

Finished with his coffee, supplemented by some cold biscuits Rena had given him, he washed the pot in the stream and packed it away. Alone, under a clear night sky, he felt at peace with himself, forgetting for the moment the bitterness that was never far beneath the surface of his mind. But those moments were few and short-lived for Colt McCrae, and soon replaced by memories of the years of silent angry brooding of the soul-killing confinement of prison life when the frustration of his wrongful incarceration would drive him to the point where he would hammer his fists against the wall of his cell. It had been hard, but he had learned to deal with the harsh and unfair realities of his life. Looking back, he felt that he owed a lot to Bob Witcher's interest in him for the patience he eventually acquired. When black thoughts of revenge had finally faded with time, they were replaced by dreams of leaving Kansas and Wyoming behind him. It would have been easy to climb in the saddle in the morning and ride away from a town that didn't want him, but things had changed with the murder of his father.

There were some things that needed fixing. *So I reckon I'll hang around until I get 'em fixed*, he thought. Before long, it was fully dark and time to turn in.

"I told you we'd find him near the corner of Rocking-D land," Lon Branch said smugly, his voice barely above a whisper. "Look at him, all cozied up to the fire. It's a damn shame to ruin his sleepin', ain't it?"

Brownie Brooks snickered softly. "I reckon so. He'll be wishin' he was back in prison pretty soon." Drummond's two henchmen continued to lie there at the brow of the ridge for a few moments longer, both men savoring the fun about to begin. "We could just shoot the bastard from here. How far did Mr. Drummond say we was supposed to go with this jasper?"

"He didn't say," Lon replied, his eyes never leaving the motionless form close by the fire. "He just said to take care of him." He considered Brownie's suggestion for a few moments before deciding. "Hell, shootin' him wouldn't be that much fun. Whaddaya say we tie his ass up, hook a rope behind his saddle, and let that big horse drag him all the way back to the Broken-M?"

"That suits me," Brownie quickly agreed, "but it might not hurt to shoot him first to take some of the fight outta him. From what he looked like taking target practice, he might just be a handful."

Eager for the fun to begin, they left their horses on the ridge and made their way as quietly as possible down the slope toward the unsuspecting camp. Lon took the lead, his pistol drawn, and Brownie followed close behind holding a coil of rope. "You be quick with that rope when I jump him," Lon whispered.

"I'm right behind you," Brownie replied.

Moving with great caution, the two assailants inched closer to the sleeping figure by the fire. Lon stopped and held up his hand when Colt's horse snorted and blew. He watched closely for signs of movement, but there was no indication that the horse had awakened the sleeping figure. After a moment, he waved Brownie on and continued his silent stalk of their intended victim.

Reaching a point about fifteen feet away, Lon nodded to Brownie. When Brownie returned the signal, Lon suddenly split the stillness of the night, yelling at the top of his voice. "Git up from there, sleepyhead!" and pumping two shots from his pistol into their victim. Without giving time for the prone figure to respond, both assailants dived upon the body, only to find they had attacked a blanket wrapped around a saddle.

Stunned by their discovery, they were both rendered motionless for a long moment. "What the hell?" Lon uttered. The next sound he heard was that of a Winchester cranking a cartridge into the chamber.

Whirling around at once, Lon tried to get a shot off, but he was not fast enough to counter the .44 slug that shattered his sternum and sent him over on his back. Screaming in pain, he dropped his pistol and rolled over on his elbows and knees. With no threat from him for the next few seconds, Colt turned his rifle on Brownie, who had dropped the rope and was fumbling with his revolver in an attempt to draw it from his belt. The front sight of the pistol had snarled in his shirt, holding it fast. Colt waited, his rifle aimed squarely at Brownie's chest, watching with bemused patience while Brownie struggled to free his weapon from his shirt. Noticing that Lon was now up on his hands and knees, and struggling to get to the pistol he had dropped in the sand, Colt, with one quick motion, sent the fatal bullet into Lon's body. Lon collapsed heavily. Back to Brownie again, Colt cranked another cartridge into the Winchester's chamber. Still struggling unsuccessfully to free the front sight of his pistol, Brownie saw the futility of his efforts, and promptly decided to run for his life. Colt unhurriedly raised his rifle and stopped the terrified man with a bullet in his leg. Brownie tumbled in the sand on the stream bank, holding his leg and wailing in pain.

Colt casually walked over to the fallen man and stood over him for a long moment before speaking. "Shut up your crying. I ain't gonna finish you off just yet." Fearing for his life, and uncertain what the stoic rifleman had in store for him, Brownie could do nothing but cower at the tall man's feet. "Get on your feet," Colt ordered.

"I can't," Brownie groaned. "You done put a hole in my leg."

"If you don't get up from there, I'm gonna put a hole in your other leg."

"All right, all right," Brownie protested painfully, "I'm gittin' up!" He dragged himself over to a willow tree and pulled himself up on his feet.

Colt reached down and picked up the rope

Brownie had dropped. Following the wounded man to the tree, he ordered him to put his hands behind his back. In response, Brownie made one more desperate attempt to jerk the pistol from his belt. Colt casually cracked him on the side of his head with the barrel of the Winchester. Yelping with the pain, Brownie meekly obeyed Colt's orders. Once Brownie's hands were securely tied around the tree at his back, Colt took the rest of the rope and bound him head and foot to the tree. Then he grabbed the stubborn pistol by the handle and yanked it from Brownie's belt, ripping the shirt in the process. Satisfied that Brownie would be there waiting for him, he then climbed the slope to fetch the horses they had left there.

After a few minutes, he was back. He released Brownie from the tree and untied his hands. Prodding him in the back with his rifle barrel, he shoved him toward Lon's body. "Drag him over here," he ordered. Limping heavily, Brownie took a few steps toward his late partner, then suddenly made a move to get to his horse. Before he could take two steps, Colt was right behind him and tripped him with a kick of his foot. Brownie fell on the ground. He tried to break his fall, but landed face-first in the sand.

"You don't learn very fast, do you?" Colt said, as he grabbed him by the back of his collar and jerked him to his feet. "Now drag him over here," he said. When Brownie balked, and stood sullenly staring at the rifle leveled at his midsection, Colt said, "The only reason you ain't dead is because I want you to tell your boss that I mean business. Now, if you don't drag him over, like I told you, I'm gonna shoot you and be done with it."

Realizing only then that Colt was not planning to finish him off, Brownie became eager to obey. He grabbed his late partner by the ankles and dragged him over to his horse. At Colt's order, he lifted Lon's body up to lay across the saddle. Once the body was resting across the saddle, Colt instructed Brownie to mount up and take Lon back to the Rocking-D. After pulling both rifles from their saddles, Colt said, "When you get across the creek on Rocking-D land, you might wanna tie his hands and feet together to keep him from sliding off of that saddle. You tell your boss this is the price he'll pay for slaughtered McCrae cattle. Next time I catch you on Bar-M or Broken-M, I ain't likely to be in such a generous mood." He stepped back then and watched as the would-be assassin splashed across the stream leading Lon Branch's horse behind him.

Standing now in the cold darkness of the November night, Colt felt a chilling sensation run the length of his spine, a feeling that had nothing to do with the temperature. He had just killed a man. It had all happened so fast that there had been no time for conscious thought, but now as the sound of Brownie's hoofbeats faded in the gloom, the sober realization struck him. He had taken a man's life. The fact that it was a life that needed taking did little to minimize the impact it would forever have on his life. *What choice did I have?* he asked himself. *They came to kill me.*

He had to admit that he had prepared himself to kill. Leaving prison, he had promised his dead father that his death would be avenged. He wondered now if Lon Branch had been the man who shot his father. Would he ever know who murdered his father? *Well, there's no turning back now*, he thought as he returned to his camp to pack up. *There's gonna be a war.* His thoughts went to Vance and his uncle. How could he confine the war to himself and Drummond, and not endanger their families? He decided, by letting Brownie go, Drummond might see that the war was with him, not his uncle, and not Vance. *I've started it, so be it. Let the devil get ready for visitors.*

It was almost daylight by the time Brownie urged a tired horse into a gallop to cover the final fifty yards from the gate to Drummond's front porch. He jumped down from the saddle, wincing as he landed on his wounded leg, and staggered up the steps, forgetting the customary respect usually shown his boss' front door. After repeatedly banging on the door, he suddenly found himself facing an irate Alice Flynn, who had been stoking the kitchen stove in preparation for cooking breakfast.

"What is the matter with you?" Alice shrieked at Brownie. "Have you lost what little sense you had?"

"Lon!" Brownie blurted. "He killed Lon!" He pointed at the corpse draped across the horse. "And he shot me," he added, pointing to his blood-soaked trousers.

Only slightly more concerned than if he had reported he had killed a snake, Alice cast a disgusted glance at the body. "Mr. Drummond ain't up yet—" she started.

"I'm up," a gruff voice came from behind her in the hallway. "What the hell is going on?" He stepped past Alice to confront Brownie.

"He shot Lon," Brownie repeated excitedly. "Killed him, and shot me in the leg."

"Who did?" Drummond demanded.

"Colt McCrae," Brownie blurted.

Drummond didn't say more for a moment. He glanced down at Brownie's bloody leg, then shifted his gaze to the body lying across the saddle, his anger growing rapidly. Turning to his housekeeper, he said, "Alice, go on back to the kitchen and fix breakfast." When she had left them, grousing to herself about the riffraff her employer hired, he turned back to Brownie. "What in the hell happened? I sent you two over there to take care of that convict, and you come back here like a dog with your tail between your legs?"

"Nothin' we could do, Mr. Drummond. He was waitin' for us. We never had a chance." Brownie groaned to draw attention to his wound. "Poor ol' Lon—that bastard cut him down before he could get off a shot." He remembered then the message he was told to deliver. "He said to tell you that anybody else ridin' on McCrae range would get the same."

"Oh, he did, did he?" Drummond responded, his face twisted in an obvious display of his growing anger. This was not the way Frank Drummond wanted to start his day, by hearing of the incompetence of the two he sent to do what he considered to be a simple job. At the moment, his anger was more a product of Lon and Brownie's failure than the threat of one ex-convict. Feeling no sympathy for the wounded man standing chastised before him, he glowered at Brownie while he considered the next course of action. "Get on back to the bunkhouse before you get blood all over my front porch," he finally said. "Take Lon with you. Pete will have to have somebody dig a hole for him, I guess. Tell Pete to patch you up if he can." Then he paused, thinking of a better plan. "No, tell him to take you in to see the doctor." It wouldn't hurt to let the sheriff know that this ex-convict was on a shooting rampage. Drummond could build on his justification for killing Colt McCrae, and maybe his brother and uncle, too, if they got in the way. From the talk he had heard, the whole town of Whiskey Hill would like to be rid of Colt McCrae. "Tell Pete to come see me before he goes," he said, dismissing the wounded man.

When Pete Tyler, the foreman of the Rocking-D, pulled a buckboard up before the house, Drummond came out to meet him. Ignoring the silent suffering man on the seat beside him, he gave Tyler instructions. "When you take Brownie into town, make sure everybody sees him. As soon as I get my breakfast, I'm going into town to see the sheriff. But here's what I want you to do first. Pick a couple of the men you trust, and send them on out to find that damn McCrae jailbird, and take care of him. Understand?"

Pete nodded. He understood. "I'll take care of it," he said. Lon and Brownie had always been the boss' choice for doing any dirty little jobs that needed doing. But Pete had a crew of eight more men, and in his opinion, any one of them would have been a better choice than those two saddle tramps. He climbed up on the buckboard, turned the horse around, and headed back to the barn where two of his men were loading wire on a wagon.

Not having been privilege to Pete and Drummond's conversation, Brownie complained when Pete turned back toward the barn. "I thought we was headed for the doctor's. My leg is painin' me somethin' awful."

"Hell, you ain't gonna die," Pete replied. "I coulda took that bullet outta your leg myself, but I'm gonna take you to the doctor. So stop your bellyaching."

Pulling up before the two men loading the wagon, Pete called them over. "You two ain't gonna mend no fences today," he told them. "I've got somethin' better for you to do."

"What the hell happened to you?" Lou George asked, looking at Brownie.

"That's what I want you and Jack to take care of," Pete answered for Brownie. He then gave them the order to eliminate Drummond's problem.

Lou looked at Brownie and grinned. "So, you and Lon tried to kill a snake and got yourself bit," he jeered.

"You'd best watch yourself," Brownie groaned. "He's a mean one."

"Is that so?" Lou sneered. "We'll see how mean this sidewinder is. Hell, me and Jack here, why, that's what we specialize in—pullin' the fangs outta rattlesnakes like McCrae. Ain't that right, Jack?" Jack Teach grinned wide and nodded.

"Well, make damn sure you get the job done. Mr.

Drummond already sent Brownie and Lon to take care of it. Lon came back across his saddle and Brownie, here, shot up, and the job ain't done yet." He looked back at Brownie seated on the buckboard and added, "And Mr. Drummond ain't too happy about it."

Chapter 5

J. D. Townsend leaned back in his chair, using an open desk drawer for a footstool. Having just consumed a plate of fried potatoes and biscuits spiced with sawmill gravy from the Whiskey Hill Kitchen, he was resting his stomach, his head already nodding. His chin was almost ready to settle on his chest when the door was suddenly flung open. "Dammit, Stoney," he started, thinking it was his deputy. But when he jerked his head up, it was to see Frank Drummond striding into his office, followed closely by Deputy Stoney Yates.

Almost asleep moments before, J.D. was wide-awake now. Barely avoiding catching his boot heel in the open drawer, the sheriff lurched to his feet. "Mr. Drummond," he stammered, "what can I do for you, sir?" He aimed one quick glance in his deputy's direction and received a helpless look in return.

"Sheriff." Drummond's booming voice filled the modest office. "We've got a helluva problem in Whiskey Hill, and I need to know what you're going to do about it."

"Why, of course, Mr. Drummond," J.D. replied nervously. "I'll sure look into it." He hesitated a moment. "What is it?"

"We've got a murdering renegade shooting and killing like a wild Injun," he charged. The sheriff's eyes grew large as saucers. Drummond continued. "My foreman just took one of my men to Dr. Taylor's office with a gunshot wound. And Lon Branch is dead, shot down on my range by that murdering convict, Colt McCrae."

"Damn!" J.D. exclaimed, at a loss for words. He glanced again at his deputy, who stared back with the same mystified expression. "We'll certainly look into it," he repeated. The sheriff knew what everybody else in town knew, that he held that office for only as long as Frank Drummond permitted. Drummond owned most of the town, and almost all the land surrounding it. The sheriff, the mayor, and the town council answered to Drummond.

"I want you to do more than look into it," Drummond remarked. "I want you to ride out to McCrae's ranch and arrest him. I'm a law-abiding man, so I've told my boys to let the law handle the murdering son of a bitch. But they're gonna stay alert in case he tries to bushwhack somebody else. I will protect my property."

"Yes, sir," J.D. said, "that's just what I was thinkin'." He motioned to his deputy. "Stoney, get on your horse and bring the bastard in."

Stoney Yates stood motionless, not sure which way to jump. "Where do I go to look for him?" he finally asked.

"Hell, I don't know," the sheriff answered. "His uncle came to town to pick him up. I expect that's as good a place as any to look."

Although his face was absent of expression, Drummond watched the uncertainty between sheriff and deputy with amused satisfaction. He felt he had successfully planted the image of Colt McCrae as a reckless killer, and as long as the law was actively looking to arrest McCrae, any action taken by his men would seem justified by the citizens of Whiskey Hill. Although ruthless in his drive to own the territory, Drummond was smart enough to know the importance of keeping a facade of legitimacy for the people to see. There was no value in owning a town if there were no people to run it.

There had been a modest swell of concern from the townsfolk when Sam McCrae had been killed, and word had gotten back to Drummond that some thought he might have had something to do with it. Drummond had felt it necessary to call on Mayor Roy Whitworth to assure the folks that he not only had nothing to do with the killing, but had sent his men out to hunt for the killer. After all, Drummond had suggested, Sam was his neighbor, and would be missed. Now, if his men did the job they were sent to do today, the thorny problem of Colt McCrae should be settled. Afterward, Drummond expected Vance McCrae to turn tail and run. That would leave only Burt McCrae to stand against him, and the old man would soon wilt under Drummond's constant pressure, especially with no way to get to water. *I couldn't have planned it better*, he thought as he left the sheriff's office. *If I'd known it was going to work out this well, I'd have shot Lon and Brownie myself.* He walked down the street to see if the mayor was in his office.

Bill Wilkes sat up straight, listening. He motioned for Tom Mosley to keep quiet. Something, a sound or smell, had caused the horses to blow and snort. Bill put his coffee cup down beside the fire and got up to take a look. Peering out at the darkness surrounding the campfire, he said, "Somethin's spooked the horses, maybe a coyote sniffin' around. I think I'll have a look."

Tom nodded and remained where he was seated. He and Bill had ridden winter nighthawk for many years for Sam McCrae, and now for his son, Vance. There was always something prowling around out there in the darkness, but most of the time it wasn't worth worrying about. He and Bill had rounded up eleven strays late that afternoon, and since they were close to Rocking-D range, Bill was probably worrying about the number of cattle that had been shot over this way. *I'm getting too damn old for this,* Tom thought. *My bones are getting so they feel the cold more than they used to.* He had no sooner had the thought than he heard a voice behind him.

"Well, lookee here, Lou, ain't nobody guardin' these cows but two old men." Jack Teach walked into the circle of firelight, an insolent sneer upon his stubbled face. Tom tried to scramble to his feet, but was shoved firmly back down on his behind. "You just set there, old man, if you don't want your head cracked open."

He called back over his shoulder, "Hey, Lou, where are you?"

His question was answered in the next moment when Lou George emerged from the darkness dragging the limp body of Bill Wilkes. "He fell and bumped his head on somethin'," Lou said. "I think it was my gun butt." His comment caused the two Rocking-D riders to roar with laughter while he dragged Bill over by the fire and dropped him.

"You two low-down skunks." Tom sneered. "Get the hell offa Bar-M range." He crawled over to his partner, whose head was split beside his eye and blood covered half his face. "What's the matter?" he spat. "Couldn't you find no cattle to shoot? Damn Rocking-D scum."

"Shut your mouth, you old fart," Lou snorted, "before I knock you in the head." He turned to grin at his partner then. "Besides, I believe we found about a dozen right here." He whirled around and started shooting blindly into the cows gathered in the small ravine, laughing at the resulting panic among the bawling cows. Tom tried to charge him, but was knocked down again by Jack Teach. When Lou had emptied his pistol, he turned back to Tom while he reloaded. "All right, old man, where's Colt McCrae? We got some business with him."

"Is that what you two snakes come ridin' in here for?" Tom replied. "Well, he ain't hereabouts, and I don't know where he is." For his answer, he received a sharp rap across his cheek with Lou's pistol barrel.

"Old man, I know damn well he's ridin' for Burt

McCrae. Now, suppose you start givin' me some straight answers."

"You go to hell," Tom spat. "I'm too damn old to be bulldogged by trash like you."

"Wrong answer again," Lou said. He aimed his pistol at Tom's foot and pulled the trigger. Tom screamed in pain. Lou looked up at his partner and grinned. "I bet he starts rememberin' pretty soon."

While Tom writhed in pain, Jack Teach, his pistol drawn, stood over Bill Wilkes as the dazed old man began to show signs of consciousness. Aware of Tom's groans, Bill started to get up on his hands and knees, only to feel the cold hard steel of Teach's revolver barrel against his skull. "You just stay right there," he was warned. With little choice, Bill was forced to do as he was told.

"I'm gonna lay it out plain and simple," Lou said, his patience draining. "If one of you don't tell me where we can find Colt McCrae, and pretty damn quick, then there ain't no use in keepin' you alive." He reached down and grabbed a handful of Tom's hair. Jerking his head back, he stuck his gun barrel up against the wounded man's cheek. "Now, where is he?"

"I don't know," Tom gasped. "I swear I don't know."

"I don't believe they know where he is," Jack said. "We might as well clean up this mess and head over to the Broken-M."

Lou nodded his agreement and released his hold on Tom. He stepped back in preparation to execute the witnesses, but suddenly staggered drunkenly when the sharp crack of a rifle rang out. Shot in the gut, Lou doubled over in pain and collapsed. Stunned by the sight of his partner sprawled upon the ground, Jack Teach stood motionless, his mouth agape, when a second shot smacked into his chest, backing him up a few steps before he fell to the ground beside the fire.

A ghostly figure astride a big buckskin horse slowly emerged from the darkness and slow-walked into the fire-lit circle, the only sound that of a Winchester cranking a new round into the chamber. His rifle ready, Colt watched the two bodies carefully as he dismounted. Before checking on his friends, he kicked the pistol away from Jack Teach. With the toe of his boot, he then rolled him over to confirm that he was dead. When he got to Lou George, the wounded man gasped painfully, "You gut-shot me, you son of a bitch."

"I reckon so," Colt replied calmly. "I'm still gettin' used to this rifle. It shoots a mite low." Anticipating Lou's next move, he put a bullet into the belligerent bully's forehead when he suddenly made a move for the pistol beside him. His grim work done, he then turned to help his friends.

"Boy, am I glad to see you!" Bill said. "We was as good as dead." When Colt knelt down to look at him, he said, "I ain't as bad as I look. Just a bump on the head. Tom needs lookin' after. The son of a bitch shot him."

Although he was seemingly calm and unhurried in his execution of Drummond's two men, the tide of anger that had washed over Colt when he arrived at the brow of the ravine was slow in receding from his mind. When he saw Drummond's paid gun hands preparing to murder the two innocent men, men who had worked for his father since Colt and Vance were boys, he was overcome with rage. There were no guilt feelings over the disposal of these two predators. "I'm sorry I didn't get here sooner, Tom," he said. "I was about a mile away when I heard the shots."

"You got here," Tom said, grunting as Colt removed his boot. "And you were the best sight these old eyes had ever seen. Me and Bill was about to go under, and that's a fact. I ain't worried about my foot. It ain't that bad, just hurts like hell."

"Maybe so," Colt said, examining the bloody foot. "But it looks like you ain't gonna be doin' a lot of walkin' for a spell. Looks like the bullet went clean through, but we'd best have the doctor tend to it." Tom was about to protest that it wasn't necessary, but Colt interrupted him. "I'll take you into town. Bill, it might be a good idea if you went back to the house in case some more of Drummond's men are snoopin' about. Tell Vance to keep a sharp eye about him."

"They was lookin' for you," Bill said.

"I figured," Colt replied. "Like I said, I'll take Tom to the doctor, and I'll drop these two off on the way."

With Bill's help, he caught the Rocking-D horses and loaded the bodies across their saddles. After he got Tom settled comfortably on his horse, he turned to Bill Wilkes. "You gonna be all right?"

"Hell yeah. Don't worry about me. I ain't afraid of Drummond's men, now that I know what's goin' on. They ain't likely to surprise me again."

• • •

It was still a good two hours before sunup when a lone rider, leading two horses behind him, walked his mount slowly past the garden fence and up to the wide front porch. Dismounting, the rider tied the reins of the two horses he had been leading to the hitching post. Stepping up in the saddle again, he turned and rode away at an unhurried lope, unnoticed by anyone in the sleeping bunkhouse and generating only casual interest from the horses milling around in the corral.

Dr. Henry Taylor pulled the curtain back to peer out his front window to see who was seeking his services at such an early hour. There were two riders. One he recognized as Tom Mosley; the other was a stranger. "I ain't even had my coffee yet," he complained to his wife. He pulled up his suspenders and went to the door. "Tom, what in the world have you gotten into?" he asked when he saw the rag wrapped around Tom's foot. "You cut your foot or something?"

"Howdy, Doc," Tom replied. "I got shot."

Dr. Taylor walked out on the short porch and stood watching while Colt helped Tom down. "Bring him on in here," he directed. "Gunshot, you say? You shoot yourself in the foot?" He looked hard at the silent man helping Tom, wondering if he had anything to do with it.

"Nope," Tom answered, "one of Drummond's trash did it."

"You don't mean it," the doctor exclaimed. "How'd it happen? He didn't do it on purpose, did he?" Remaining a quiet observer, Colt let Tom do the talking. After Tom had told of the late night visit from two of Drummond's men, Dr. Taylor shook his head and sighed, "I reckon I'd better get ready to patch up a few more crazy cowhands. You're already the second gunshot I've seen this week. Frank Drummond sent one of his boys in yesterday." He glanced up, his gaze focusing on Colt. "I don't reckon you boys had anything to do with that?" When there was no response from either, he held the door to his examining room open and waited for Colt to help Tom inside. "Sit down on the table, there, Tom." When Tom was settled, Dr. Taylor said, "Who's your friend, here? I don't recollect seeing him around town before."

"Colt McCrae," Colt answered.

"Oh, so you can talk. I figured that's who you might be. As a matter of fact, some folks were predicting the shooting would start since you've come back to town. I guess they were right."

Tom quickly interceded on Colt's behalf. "It ain't Colt that started the shootin'. If it weren't for him, I reckon me and Bill Wilkes would both be dead. Them Drummond coyotes jumped us in the middle of the night."

"Bad business," Dr. Taylor muttered as he removed the rag from Tom's foot. "We haven't had any serious gunfighting around Whiskey Hill for quite a spell. I'd hate to see it start again."

"Except for my father," Colt quietly reminded him.

"Well, yes, young fellow, I'm sorry about that. Still, we don't need any more, and that's a fact." He looked at Tom again. "Have you told the sheriff about this? He might wanna go after them two that jumped you."

"Ain't no hurry," Tom said. "They ain't likely to go nowhere."

Dr. Taylor shifted his gaze up to fix on Colt's eyes. "Oh," he said, getting Tom's meaning. "I suppose I'm going to be busier than I thought." Turning his attention back to the injured foot, he said, "Looks like a pretty clean wound to me. Went in the top and out the bottom. As long as it bled out pretty good, and it looks like it did, it oughta be all right. Hard to say if you broke any bones or not—be damn lucky if you didn't. I'll dress the wounds and you can see how it goes. You'll be able to tell after a few days if the swelling doesn't go down."

"What do I do if there is a broke bone and the swellin' don't go down?" Tom asked.

"Limp," Dr. Taylor replied. Then, after a long pause, with Tom looking obviously astonished, the doctor laughed. "I'll take a look at it after a day or two. Then we'll see. Now get on outta here. I ain't even had my coffee yet."

"How much I owe you?" Tom asked.

"Never mind, I'll give Vance my bill." He held the door open for them again, and as they passed him, he spoke to Colt. "You'd better be real careful, young fellow. You ain't the most popular man around this town. I'm sorry about your father. Sam McCrae was a damn good man." Colt nodded in reply.

Outside, Colt helped Tom up in the saddle, then stepped up on Buck and wheeled the big horse around. "Well, since the good doctor's gonna save the bill for Vance, I figure I've got enough money to buy us a breakfast. I don't know about you, but I'm hungry."

"That suits me just fine," Tom said.

• • •

For the second morning in a row, Frank Drummond was awakened by the sound of someone pounding on his front door. Already irritated, he listened for the sound of Alice Flynn's unhurried footsteps in the front hall. After a few moments, he could hear some excited talk from one of his cowhands. Who it was or what he was saying was not discernible, but Drummond knew it was not good news. Feeling his bile rising, he threw back the heavy quilts he had been sleeping under and got up. Throwing a long robe over his nightshirt, he stormed out of the room to see what trouble awaited.

"Mr. Drummond . . ." Pete Tyler started, but stepped quickly out of the way when Drummond pushed on by him, having looked past his foreman's shoulder at the two corpses lying across their saddles.

Livid, Drummond sputtered, "Where'd you find them?"

"Right where they are," Tyler answered. "They were tied right there at the rail when I came out this mornin'."

Clucking her disgust, Alice returned to her kitchen, leaving the men to their foolish business. She never questioned her employer's methods of acquiring his many holdings, although she never disguised her disapproval. A woman of her status—a widow for more than twelve years and no family to fall back on—had little choice but to do whatever was necessary to survive. Keeping house and cooking for Frank Drummond was not difficult. He had no family, so there was just the two of them to clean up after, and he seemed indifferent to her perpetual frown and sharp tongue.

The saddle trash Drummond hired soon learned to stay clear of the cranky old witch that ran the house. Alice preferred it that way.

Turning to direct his rage toward Tyler, Drummond demanded, "How in hell can someone just ride right in here and nobody see him?" Drummond didn't have to be told that these stiffening corpses were the two men Pete had selected to take care of Colt McCrae.

"I don't know," Tyler started. "I noticed them tied up here before sunup when I started to—" That was as far as he got before being interrupted again.

"War!" Drummond roared. "If it's war he wants, then by God, I'll see he gets it!" His face a maelstrom of fury, he glowered at his foreman as if seeing right through the man. The image in his mind's eye was that of the insolent face of Colt McCrae sitting on his horse where the two horses of his men now stood, a rifle aimed at his gut. In the ten years since he had come to this valley, he had never been openly challenged. His gang of ruthless gunmen, loosely called cowhands, ensured his acquisition of most of the open range in the wild young territory, and led to his dominance of the town itself. And now to be seemingly stalemated by one insolent man, a troublemaker the town had gotten rid of years ago, was more than Drummond intended to tolerate. His first thought was to call out his entire crew, now minus three dead, and hunt this menace down, and in the process, clean out the hangers-on at Bar-M and Broken-M.

Accurately reading his boss' thinking, Tyler asked, "Want me to round up the men?"

On the verge of saying yes, Drummond checked

himself with a calmer thought. Though ruthless, he was not a foolish man. His empire had been built under a guise of legitimacy. Even the vigilance committee that had rid the town of undesirables when the railroad was being built was heavily made up from Drummond's men. In recent years, he had even given thought to the possibility of running for governor of the territory. A vigilante-like response to this one man might turn the town's citizens against him. In control of his emotions now, he answered his foreman's question. "No, not yet, I'll talk to the men tonight. I'm going in to talk to the sheriff first." With that, he dismissed Tyler to take care of the bodies.

At approximately the same time Drummond discovered the bodies of Lou George and Jack Teach parked at his front door, the man responsible walked into the Whiskey Hill Kitchen. In the kitchen, Mary Simmons turned to peer through the pass-through window behind the counter when she heard the door close. "Well, look who's back," she murmured, causing Pearl Murray to sidle over to have a look. So intense was their concentration upon Colt that they failed to notice Tom Mosley's bandaged foot, covered only by his sock.

"He's got plenty of brass," Pearl commented. "I didn't think he'd show his face in town again." She nudged Mary and grinned. "It ain't gonna make ol' Oscar any too happy, is it?"

There had been a great deal of talk about the return of Colt McCrae during the last couple of days, a lot of discussion about what, if anything should be done about him. Waiting the table in the back room, Mary usually overheard most of what went on in town, and the talk the day before was of the shooting of two of Frank Drummond's men—one of them, Lon Branch, was dead. In Mary's mind, that wasn't much of a loss to the world in general. The discussion at the table was whether it was a gunfight or a murder. J.D. sent Stoney Yates out to Burt McCrae's ranch to bring Colt in, but Stoney came back without him. He said Burt told him that Colt didn't stay at the ranch. Mary wondered what J.D. would do if he knew Colt McCrae had just walked into the dining room.

"Well, are you gonna wait on 'em?" Pearl broke into Mary's thoughts.

"Of course I am," Mary replied, and started toward the kitchen door.

"You know Oscar was talkin' about not servin' him if he ever came in again," Pearl reminded her, then waited for Mary's reaction, a big smile painting her face.

"Oscar's full of hot air. He talks pretty big, but I'd like to see if he's got the guts to tell him to get out when he comes back from the store." She looked at Pearl and winked. "Besides, I still think he's nice looking. I'll wait on him."

"Atta girl," Pearl laughed. "Lady loves an outlaw."

"Well, I see you came back to see us," Mary greeted her two early customers cheerfully. Then, noticing Tom's bloodstained sock, she asked, "What happened to your foot, Tom?" While he went into detail about the incident that resulted in his gunshot wound, her eyes remained fixed upon the dark brooding gaze of his younger companion, almost missing the point that there were two more dead. When it registered with her, she suddenly recoiled. Directing her question to Colt, she exclaimed, "You shot two more of Drummond's men?"

Uncomfortable with the position in which Tom had placed him, Colt could only explain, "I reckon I didn't have much choice."

"Mister, for somebody who's been away for a while, you sure didn't slip back into town quietly. Have you got a death wish or something? That's a rough bunch you're taking on by yourself."

"He ain't exactly by hisself," Tom spoke up.

Mary gave the remark only a sideways glance, her eyes still locked on Colt's. "All the same, you'd better watch yourself." She glanced around as if to see if anyone else could hear. "Why are you sitting in here? Don't you know J.D. might come in here any minute?"

Tiring of the questions, although touched by her obvious concern, he favored her with a faint smile. "I'm sittin' in here because I want some breakfast, and I haven't done anything but defend myself and my friends. Now, do you think Pearl can fix me some more of those eggs?"

She shook her head, exasperated. "All right, but I'd really hate to see you hauled off to jail if J.D. comes in."

"I appreciate that, but I'll take my chances."

"Me, too," Tom piped up. "We'll take our chances."

"I'll get you some coffee," she said, and turned to go to the kitchen.

Pearl looked up expectedly when Mary breezed through the kitchen door. "Well?" she asked.

"Two orders of bacon and scrambled eggs," Mary replied, making an effort to sound businesslike, then went directly to the coffeepot.

"Yeah, two orders of bacon and eggs," Pearl shot back sarcastically. "What's he doin' back in here? I bet it's because you were blinkin' your eyes at him the last time he was here."

"Why, Pearl Murray," Mary replied, a mock look of offense upon her face. "I'm ashamed of you for even thinking such a thing. I guess he's back in here because he's hungry, and your breakfast didn't kill him last time."

Serious then, Pearl warned her young friend, "I wouldn't get too interested in that boy, honey. I don't think he'll be around for very long, especially if he's takin' to shootin' Frank Drummond's men."

Mary, herself serious at that point, said, "According to what Tom just told me, he shot two more of Drummond's men last night." She went on to relay Tom's telling of the attack upon him and Bill Wilkes.

"Damn," Pearl exhaled. "Like I said, you're battin' your eyes at a dead man." Then, her mischievous side never far away, she grinned. "Let me cook some breakfast for those two. I wanna make sure they're still here when Oscar gets back. He's been talkin' about how he might throw Colt McCrae out if he showed his face in here again."

"I swear, you're bad," Mary said, shaking her head as she left the kitchen with two cups of coffee. Though she would never admit it to Pearl, she did find herself interested in the broad-shouldered brother of Vance McCrae. Pearl had reminded her several times that the quiet young man was an ex-convict, and she knew it unwise to even toy with thoughts toward him. Still, she told herself there was no harm in entertaining thoughts. She would never act upon them. It was just something to speculate on. There was no harm in that. "Here you go, gents," she sang out cheerfully as she set the cups down on the table. "Pearl's scrambling up some eggs right now."

Colt and Tom were just starting on their breakfast when Oscar returned from the store. Coming in the back door to the kitchen, he was met by Pearl, a wicked smile on her face. "Look who's settin' in the front booth, Oscar."

"Who?" he asked, and when Pearl didn't answer, he walked over to the pass-through window. "Damn," he muttered under his breath. He stood there, staring at the two men eating breakfast, for a long moment before suddenly turning around and retracing his steps toward the back door. "I'll be back in a bit," he mumbled as he closed the door behind him.

Pearl couldn't suppress a devilish giggle. "He musta forgot he was aimin' to toss him out."

Mary was not as amused as her friend. "Damn, Pearl, I'll bet he's gone to get the sheriff." What appeared to be a joke to Pearl seemed likely to spell trouble for Colt. J.D. was already looking for him. Feeling she should at least warn Colt, Mary hurried back out to the booth.

Tom Mosley was properly concerned when Mary told them that Oscar was probably going to fetch the sheriff. His bravado of a few minutes before rapidly dissipated. He looked at Colt anxiously, but the news appeared to have little effect on the calm exterior of Sam McCrae's younger son. "Maybe we oughta finish up real quick and get the hell outta here," Tom suggested.

"I don't get a good breakfast like this every day," Colt replied while he casually buttered up a biscuit. "I don't figure on rushin' through it." Then giving Tom an understanding glance, he said, "Maybe you should go, Tom. There's no sense you gettin' tangled up in my troubles."

"Colt," Mary insisted, "he'll throw you in jail."

"I haven't done anything to go to jail for," Colt said. He was thinking about the town that had railroaded him off to prison nine years before. He had no intention of submitting to J. D. Townsend, even if it resulted in a shoot-out. Maybe he was pushing his luck to show his face in town, but he was determined not to be intimidated by the town council again. He would deal with J. D. Townsend when it came to that. The war was already started. He had no intention of letting the sheriff get in his way. He glanced up again to catch Mary's eye. "I could use another cup of that coffee," he said calmly.

"Me, too," Tom announced in a show of renewed courage.

Mary shook her head, perplexed by their stubbornness, and left to get the coffeepot. Before she had time to return with it, the front door opened, and in walked J. D. Townsend, followed a few paces behind by Oscar Anderson.

Without hesitation, J.D. walked straight over to the booth. With his hand resting on the butt of his pistol, he addressed the placid man gazing back at him. "I'm placin' you under arrest," he blurted, albeit somewhat nervously. He glanced at the Winchester rifle propped in the corner of the booth opposite Colt, out of easy reach.

"Is that a fact?" Colt's response was calm and unhurried, his cold unblinking gaze locked on the sheriff's eyes. "What's the charge?"

"Murder, for one thing," the sheriff responded, "the murder of Lon Branch." He stood nervously shifting from one foot to the other, his hand gripping and regripping the handle of the revolver in his holster. "Now get your hands up on the table where I can see them."

"Before you take a notion to pull that pistol, I'd better warn you that I've got a pistol layin' in my lap. So I reckon I'll keep my hands right where they are." He nodded toward Mary Simmons standing paralyzed in the middle of the room, holding the coffeepot. "We were just about to have another cup of coffee. Why don't you sit down and have a cup, and we'll talk about this mistake you were about to make."

When J.D. hesitated, not sure what to do, Tom spoke up. "Dammit, J.D., Colt ain't murdered nobody. You oughta be ridin' out to the Rocking-D to arrest Frank Drummond. Two of his men jumped me and Bill Wilkes last night, and if Colt hadn't come along, we'd both be dead." He held his wounded foot up for J.D. to see.

Clearly surprised by this new piece of news, J.D.

nevertheless attempted to regain the air of authority he had borne when he first entered the room. "I don't know nothin' about that. Right now, I'm talkin' about the murder of Lon Branch."

"You people have got a habit of arrestin' folks for somethin' they didn't do. I killed Lon Branch, but it wasn't murder," Colt said, his voice still showing no sign of emotion. "He came to kill me in my camp on McCrae land. He was shot in self-defense, and no man has ever gone to jail in this territory for that. I'm not gonna be the first."

The sheriff took a step backward, and squared up his stance, making a show of his authority. "Mr. Drummond says you were on *his* range." His hand tightened on his pistol handle.

"Drummond's a damn liar if he said that," Colt replied. "And if he didn't, then you're a damn liar. Now I think we're about finished with this little conversation. Tom and I are gonna get on our horses and ride outta town real peaceful. At least, that's the way I want it. But if you draw that weapon, I'm gonna cut loose with this one under the table. I expect it'll catch you right about your balls, since I can't raise it any higher. You might be able to kill me, but you ain't gonna be siring any calves for a helluva long time."

Oscar Anderson backed away from the sheriff until he bumped into the counter. "Move over!" Pearl whispered from the pass-through window behind him when Oscar's body blocked her view.

J.D. was stunned. He had not expected to be faced down with an open challenge, and the look in Colt's eyes told him it was no bluff. He hesitated, reluctant to back down in front of witnesses, but also knowing he couldn't get his gun out of the holster in time to avoid being shot. "All right," he finally said, and removed his hand from the pistol. "There's too many folks in here to risk somebody innocent gettin' shot." Trying to save what reputation he could, he turned to Tom. "Tom, you're sayin' this man was not on Rocking-D range when he shot Branch?"

"He sure as hell weren't," Tom replied. "And it was Drummond's men that started the shootin'."

"All right, then," J.D. said. "I'm gonna let you go now, but I'll be lookin' into all this to see who's tellin' the straight of things." In a final attempt to assert his authority, he added, "Now I think you both better get mounted and get on outta town before I change my mind."

Although there was no change in the stoic expression on Colt's face, he was greatly relieved by the sheriff's decision. He had no use for J. D. Townsend, but he had no desire to gun down the sheriff or anyone else who was not involved in his personal war. Aside from that, he had nothing in his lap but a napkin. His pistol and holster were in his saddlebag. As the sheriff moved over to stand beside a dazed Mary Simmons, Colt waited a moment to let Tom get up first. Then he laid the napkin on the table and reached over to pick the Winchester up from the corner of the booth. As he rose from the booth, he cocked the rifle just in case. It was unnecessary as the sheriff blanched when he realized he wasn't wearing a gun belt.

Standing to face the mortified lawman, Colt reached in his pocket and put some money on the table. He smiled briefly at Mary and said, "I think there's enough there to cover our bill. We'll be goin' now." Backing all the way to the door, he followed Tom, who was already limping toward the horses.

J.D. made no move to go after them, knowing it would only soil his reputation further. Oscar looked at the sheriff in disbelief, but decided to remain mute. Pearl, however, was never a person to stifle her cynical sense of humor. Striding through the kitchen door, she broke the stunned silence left in Colt's wake. "Damn if that weren't somethin'. For a minute there I thought we were gonna have us a real shoot-out." Enjoying the scene, she looked at Mary. "Mary, you'd better clean off that table, and be careful of that napkin. It might go off in your hand."

"Shut your mouth, Pearl," Oscar snapped, all too aware that he and the sheriff had both been exposed as lacking in backbone. Pearl looked at Mary with a wink and a smile.

Chapter 6

J. D. Townsend had been sheriff in Whiskey Hill for six years after serving as a deputy for five years prior to that. It had not been a hard job since the town had been cleaned up after the railroad crews moved out of Cheyenne. Almost all the bad elements had been eliminated thanks to Frank Drummond's crew of gun-toting cowhands acting as a vigilance committee. Had he been inclined, the sheriff might have looked a little deeper into Drummond's methods for handling troublemakers. Some in the town council had made comments in the past that most of the banished troublemakers had been competition to Drummond. Those members had short careers as council members. J.D. was well aware of Drummond's control of the town, and knew his job was courtesy of the man. Back in his office after the encounter in the Whiskey Hill Kitchen, he sat and worried about his future as sheriff.

It had been some time since J.D. had experienced the uncertainty—he was reluctant to call it fear—that had caused him to back down that morning. Up to now, his bulk and bluster had been sufficient to cower most of the two-bit saddle tramps that wandered through town from time to time. But this morning had been different. When he had looked into the eyes of Colt McCrae, he had seen a cool fury burning deep inside that told of a lack of fear and a sense of nothing to lose. It had been a bluff, but the man had not hesitated to bet his life on it. The thought of future confrontations with Colt McCrae troubled him, but there were other things that worried him. Frank Drummond would want to know the reason Colt was not in jail. The thought had no sooner left his mind than Stoney Yates walked in.

"Just met Mr. Drummond and a couple of his boys comin' in," Stoney announced. "He said to tell you to come on over to Coolidge's. He wants to talk to ya."

"Did he say what about?" J.D. asked, although he had a pretty good idea. He wondered if Drummond had seen McCrae riding out of town when he came in.

"Nah, just said he wanted to talk to ya."

"All right," J.D. sighed and rose to his feet. "I reckon I could use a drink this mornin', anyway."

Although it was still over an hour before noon, Turk Coolidge's saloon had been open for a couple of hours in order to feed the few patrons who were dependent upon a liquid breakfast. Turk nodded and offered a good morning to the sheriff when J.D. walked in. "Turk," J.D. acknowledged and went directly to a table in the back where Frank Drummond sat nursing a cup of coffee. Two of his men flanked him on either side, each working on a glass of beer. "You wanted to see me, Mr. Drummond?"

Drummond looked up from his coffee cup and forced a thin smile that quickly faded away. "Yeah, Sheriff," he said and pulled a vacant chair back from the table. "Sit down and have something to drink—a glass of beer, or something stronger. I'm having coffee myself. I like to keep a clear head when I'm talking business."

J.D. glanced briefly at the two surly-looking men flanking Drummond. He had not seen them before, but it was not unusual for the owner of the Rocking-D to hire on new men during the time of year when most ranches were letting men go. "Thank you just the same," J.D. said. "I don't reckon I need anythin' right now." He sat down in the chair indicated.

Drummond fixed a steady gaze upon the uncomfortable sheriff for a long moment before continuing. When he spoke, his tone was almost fatherly. "When me and the boys rode in a little while ago, I almost thought I caught sight of Colt McCrae riding out the other end of town." He glanced at one of the men seated across from him and received an amused snort in reply. Drummond went on. "I told 'em that couldn't be McCrae because McCrae was most likely cooling his heels in your jail." He nailed J.D. with an intense gaze. "Now, tell me that ain't so." When the sheriff flushed and hesitated, Drummond continued. " 'Cause I know that was what we agreed on. Wasn't it, J.D.?"

"Yessir," J.D. stammered. "That was what I was aimin' to do, all right, but there was some complications that come up."

"Complications?" Drummond responded, his voice still calm. "What complications could there be? The man's a murderer. All you had to do was arrest him and throw him in jail. Then we would hang him, like we do with all murderers."

"That's right," the sheriff quickly replied, plainly flustered. "That's exactly right. But he had a witness that said he was on his own land and shot in self-defense."

"What witness?" Drummond fumed, beginning to lose control of his emotions.

"Tom Mosley," J.D. replied.

"Tom Mosley?" Drummond roared. "Goddammit, Sheriff, that's one of his own men. What did you expect the lying bastard to say? The only witness there was Brownie Brooks, and he's lying up at my ranch with a gunshot wound." He pounded the table with his fist, causing his two men to grab their beer glasses to avoid losing the contents. "Now, I'll tell you something else. That murdering convict shot two more of my men last night! He's got to be stopped."

J.D. looked stunned, at that moment realizing that he had failed to question Tom about how he got shot in the foot. He didn't have to be told now why Drummond lost two more men. His rational mind told him that Drummond had sent them to jump Tom and Bill, but Colt must have come along in time to catch them in the act. Then if what Drummond just said was true, Tom Mosley might not have been witness to Lon Branch's shooting. He should have questioned him more thoroughly. Deep down, he knew that Drummond was behind all the trouble with Colt McCrae, but he forced himself to think that he was acting for the good of the town. He had cast his lot with

Drummond long ago, and he knew he was going to look the other way as usual. "Maybe I'd best ride over to Fort Russell and get some help from the army," he finally suggested.

"It's past time for that," Drummond quickly replied. The last thing he wanted was to involve soldiers from nearby Fort D.A. Russell. "I've got a better idea. We've always handled our own problems in this town. We don't need the army coming in here telling us how to run things. You just stay close to town. Go over to the dining room and sit down with Roy Whitworth and the others. Drink your coffee and swap your tales about the old days. Leave the job of running down Colt McCrae to me and my boys. You can deputize Rafe and Slim, here, if it'll make you feel better. Just stay outta our way." He paused to watch J.D.'s reaction. When the sheriff just sat there looking dazed, Drummond softened his tone. "I'll take care of our problem. The town will go back to being peaceful again, and your job will be a helluva lot easier. Ain't that right, J.D.?"

"Yessir," the sheriff drawled obediently. "I reckon you know best."

"Good," Drummond said and patted J.D. on the shoulder. "Now you don't have to worry about a thing."

"I changed my mind," J.D. said wearily, "I believe I will have that drink." Drummond was correct in saying the town had handled crises in the past without the army's help. Back in the winter of '67, when J.D. was a deputy, it was so cold and icy that the Union Pacific had to stop construction of the railroad halfway up

Sherman Hill after several attempts to lay the tracks over the top. Stymied by the weather, the railroad reluctantly told all the workers to go home and come back in the spring, which was hardly practical for most of the men. As a consequence, they had all descended upon the town of Cheyenne. It was a wild time. J.D. remembered it well. Over ten thousand souls poured into Cheyenne with a considerable number spilling over into Whiskey Hill, which was ill-equipped to handle the strain. There was no one to keep the peace but the sheriff and J.D., his single deputy. That was the time when Frank Drummond really came into power, when the vigilance committee was formed. Drummond already had a payroll of half a dozen, all hardened gun hands, and he was only too happy to volunteer their services. They soon became known as the Gunnysack Gang, and for the next six months they kept the peace in Whiskey Hill. It was the only period in Frank Drummond's life when he had operated on the side of the law. Back then J.D., as well as Roy Whitworth and the town council, welcomed Drummond's support in the taming-down of Whiskey Hill's undesirables. The land-hungry cattle baron's cold-blooded ways were accepted as good for the community. J.D. wasn't really sure exactly when Drummond came to own such complete power over the little town, but it had happened almost without anyone taking particular notice until it was too late to do anything about it. J.D. wasn't proud of the fact that he was afraid to question anything the ruthless owner of the Rocking-D did, but he felt helpless to stand up to him now.

• • •

Colt covered the distance between his uncle's ranch and Cheyenne in less than half a day without pushing the buckskin excessively. He knew that it might be a waste of his time, but he was bound to make the effort for the sake of justice if nothing else. Bailey's Saloon was not hard to find—a run-down building that was little more than a one-room shack, on the north edge of town. Colt paused at the door to look the place over before entering a room lit only by the flame from the fireplace. Glancing at the bar, he saw a short balding man with an eye patch. At the one table in a back corner of the room, three men were playing cards. Colt walked in.

Rufus Bailey looked up when Colt approached the bar. He placed the knife he had been cleaning his fingernails with on the bar and regarded the stranger with a bored expression. "What'll it be, mister?"

Colt gave the bartender a brief glance before shifting his gaze to the men at the table. "I could use a glass of beer," he said without looking back at Bailey. One of the men playing cards looked a lot like the man he had come to find. "I heard Ronnie Skinner hangs around here," Colt said, turning back to the bartender then.

"Yeah, that's him back there at the table," Bailey replied. "Are you a lawman?" he asked. Not waiting for a reply, he went on. "I hope to hell you are. That damn no-account drunk hangs around here damn near all day, panhandling for drinks."

Colt considered that for a moment before commenting, "Looks like he's got enough money to play cards."

"He ain't got a cent to his name," Bailey scoffed. "They're usin' chips. If he's losin', he'll run out on 'em before they try to collect their winnings. Hell, if he had any money, he'd be drinkin'."

Colt finished his beer, nodded to the bartender, then walked back to the table to stand opposite Skinner. All three players looked up to appraise the somber stranger. "Lookin' to play some cards?" one of them asked.

"Nope," Colt replied, locking his gaze upon his former friend. "I just stopped by to say hello to Ronnie."

Ronnie returned the steely gaze with one dulled by excessive use of alcohol. Failing to recognize the stranger at first, he squinted his eyes, straining to see when something about the face suddenly sparked his memory. "Colt?" he asked, unsure. Then realizing it was him, indeed, he exclaimed, "Colt!" He jumped to his feet, almost upsetting the table. Ignoring his playing partners' protests, he rushed around the table. "Gawdamn, Colt, you're a sight for sore eyes. When did you get out? Gawdamn, I really felt bad about them haulin' you off to prison for that damn robbery. Hell, I wanted to tell 'em you didn't have nothin' to do with it, but you know, hell, I couldn't hardly tell 'em it was me. I'da been a damn fool to do that, wouldn't I?" He grabbed Colt by the hand, shaking it wildly. "Damn, this calls for a drink. I'm a little short right now, but if you'll buy, I'll pay you back later." Colt stood passively studying his former friend as he rambled through his wild discourse. His cool response caused Ronnie to hesitate. "They ain't no hard feelin's, is there? I mean, there weren't nothin' I could do to help you. Hell, you gotta figure you was lucky they didn't hang you, like they did ol' Tucker. Right?"

A jumble of thoughts were swirling around inside Colt's mind as he witnessed the foolish ramblings of the obviously worried man. It was apparent that Ronnie wasn't sure what Colt's frame of mind was, and he was doing his best to talk him out of thoughts of revenge for letting him take the rap. Seeing the sorry state Ronnie had progressed to, he wasn't sure he cared enough after all the years to think about vengeance. At the same time, he figured that Ronnie should receive some form of punishment for his part in the robbery and killing. Finally, he acted. "Nah, no hard feelin's," he said, then planted a right fist flush on Ronnie's nose, putting his shoulder and upper body behind it. Ronnie was driven back against the wall, where he slid down to the floor and fell over on his side, out cold.

It was scant compensation for over nine years in prison, but it gave him some satisfaction. He turned and left the saloon, stopping at the bar on his way out. "Here," he said, slapping some money on the counter, "buy him a drink when he comes to."

Satisfied that the law would not interfere, Drummond was now ready to launch his war against Colt McCrae. Like a commanding general, he formed his plans to not only rid the town of the ex-convict, but to finally capture the land that separated his vast range from the water he desperately wanted. He had exhausted his patience waiting for Burt and Vance McCrae to accept his offers to buy their land. It was now time to take the land. If they stood and fought, their deaths would simply be an unfortunate tragedy caused by their interference with a deputized posse in the process of capturing a murderer. Since his men had been deputized by the sheriff, none in the town council should question the killings that were bound to happen.

Back at his ranch, Drummond called his army of thugs together to give them their marching orders. Colt had reduced their number to ten gun hands, counting Brownie, who was still limping around with a bullet wound. In Drummond's opinion, this was ample strength to effectively do the job. "Now you're gonna get the chance to earn the money I've been paying you," he told them. He singled out three men. "You three are gonna ride over to the Bar-M." He parted out three more. "You three, Broken-M," he said. "Me and the other three are gonna scout the creek that runs between the two. That son of a bitch is hiding out somewhere on that creek."

"Whaddaya want me to do, Mr. Drummond?" Brownie Brooks spoke up.

Drummond cocked his head to glare at the wounded man. "I want you to sit here on your ass in case that jailbird shows up here again. If you'd done the job I sent you to do, we wouldn't have to go after Colt McCrae, would we?" Properly contrite, Brownie limped back to a corner of the bunkhouse. Drummond continued his instructions. "Make no mistake, the McCraes will fight, and I don't want a one of them left standing. Do your job and you'll all get a fifty-dollar bonus, and the man whose bullet stops Colt McCrae gets an extra two hundred dollars." He paused to let that soak in, gratified by the nodding and grins of his *soldiers*. "Sunup tomorrow," he said.

Vance McCrae was a man with a troubled mind as he drove his buckboard along the rutted road between his ranch and his uncle's. Sitting stiffly beside him, Susan remained sternly silent, having already spoken her piece about the meeting at Burt McCrae's house. She had at first refused to accompany him, but Vance insisted, saying it was too dangerous to leave her and their son at home, even with Tom and Bill keeping an eye on the place.

Things had been bad before, but now there was bound to be real trouble. His world had been effectively turned upside down since the return of his brother. Colt had killed three of Drummond's men in the span of two nights. Drummond would never stand for that. They were all in danger now. Maybe Susan was right to damn Colt for igniting a range war. Vance wished with all his heart that the bloodshed could have been avoided. Now, facing the certain prospect of more, he wasn't sure he had the stomach to stand up to Drummond's gang of outlaws. Thinking back, he remembered his father warning that one day Drummond would make a move to overrun him and Uncle Burt. *Then, by God, we'll have to stand and fight for what's ours*, he had said. Two short weeks after making that statement, Sam McCrae was cut down by a bushwhacker's bullet. Vance still bore the heavy guilt for not avenging his father's murder.

Breaking her silence, Susan asked, "Will he be there?"

"Colt?" Vance replied. "Why, I expect so. Nobody's more involved in this than him."

"I just don't see that this trouble has anything to do with us," she said sharply. "He shot those men. This business should be between him and the sheriff."

Even though he wished they were not involved, Vance could not understand his wife's refusal to see the right and wrong of the recent trouble. "Lon Branch tried to kill him, honey. You can't much blame him for protecting himself. And Tom and Bill were jumped by Drummond's men. If Colt hadn't come along when he did, they both might be dead."

"Maybe," she admitted, "but maybe they might have just been meaning to scare them."

"I doubt that," Vance said, shaking his head in frustration. "Bill said they were just gettin' ready to shoot both of them when Colt cut them down."

"I still think your uncle should go over and talk to Frank Drummond and straighten this whole mess out, instead of letting an ex-convict ride around like a wild Indian, shooting everybody."

"Uncle Burt's already tried to talk to him, and you know I've tried to talk to Drummond. After Daddy died, I went over there. There's no talkin' to that man. Colt's doin' what I oughta be doin'." He paused to think about what he had just said, then added, "I ain't sure Colt was in on that bank guard shootin' they sent him to prison for." Susan did not comment, returning to her silence of before.

It was a somber gathering that greeted Colt when he walked into the front room of his uncle's house that evening, effectively causing a pause in the conversation. Standing in the doorway, he looked around the room, nodding to each face he saw. Everyone there had known Colt to be an untamed boy before he was sent away. His transformation into the imposing figure that now filled the doorway was something some were not sure boded them good or evil. The silence was broken when Burt stood and pulled an empty chair over next to him. "Come on in, Colt. We was just gettin' started."

Rena came in from the kitchen and handed Colt a cup of coffee, never bothering to ask if he wanted one. He smiled at the ever-silent woman and nodded his thanks. Never changing her expression from the stone face she always wore, she returned to her kitchen. Aware of the eyes fixed upon him, he sat down next to Burt and cautiously sipped the scalding black liquid. He knew from recent experience that Rena kept the coffeepot to a near-boil on the stove until it was empty.

It was a small gathering, he noted, as he scanned the faces: his uncle, Vance, Susan, little Sammy, his uncle's two hired hands, known only to him as Jesse and Tuck, and Tom Mosley and Bill Wilkes. It was an unimpressive army to fight a range war against Drummond's hired killers. As he shifted his gaze, it lingered upon the face of Susan Sessions McCrae, now his sister-in-law. She did not meet his gaze, her eyes concentrating on the coffee cup held in her lap. Though she was an older, mature woman now, he could still picture her as a young girl, precocious and sassy—until she glanced up from her lap. Her expression was hard and defiant, but also exhibited a hint of fear. It was natural under such circumstances, he decided.

As expected, the topic of discussion, and the purpose of the meeting, was what steps they should take to defend their homes and livestock. The talk didn't go far before someone voiced the obvious. "Look at us," Tuck blurted, "a few old men against them gunmen that ride for Drummond. Sure, Vance and Colt are young enough, but they ain't but two, and they're gonna be after Colt for sure." He glanced apologetically in Colt's direction. "No hard feelings, but you're the one that started this war, and your life ain't worth much more than a plugged nickel." Like Jesse, Tuck was not convinced that there would be such a serious situation were it not for the ex-convict's aggression. He and Tuck were too old to be fighting range wars. They had worked for Burt McCrae for many years, and they both felt they had hired on to tend cattle, not to fight bushwhackers.

"Now, hold on a minute, Tuck," Burt protested. "Let's get one thing straight. Colt never started anything. This trouble was brewing long before he came back. Let's not forget my brother was shot in the back. Colt's here because I asked him to come back and help. We all know what the cause of this is, Drummond's plan to run us out of our homes. The question we have to decide is what we're gonna do about it."

"Burt's right," Tom Mosley said. "Them two that jumped me and Bill was meanin' to kill us both. If Colt hadn't come along when he did, there'd be two less of us here tonight."

Colt chose not to defend his actions, preferring to remain a silent nonparticipant in the meeting. The discussion that filled the next hour and a half hinged mainly upon whether they should all concentrate their defenses in one spot. This would mean abandoning either Vance's house or Burt's, and neither party was inclined to do so. As the evening wore on, it became apparent that there was little they could do beyond what they were already doing. Burt and Vance would each try to defend their homes as best they could with the men they had, and hope for the best. They agreed that Colt was best used on horseback, helping wherever he could. Someone suggested taking their problem to the sheriff, but the suggestion was not given much consideration, since J.D. was owned lock, stock, and barrel by Drummond. It was late in the evening when Vance carried a sleeping Sammy to the buckboard and headed back to the Bar-M, flanked by his two hired hands. Seated beside her husband, Susan turned to watch the dark figure of her brother-in-law as it faded into the blackness of the night toward the north ridge.

Like a troop of cavalry, the gang of hired killers filed out of the Rocking D gate, led by the imposing figure of their captain. Frank Drummond sat erect in the saddle, his spine as straight as a flagpole. There was no sound save that of the creaking of leather saddles and the soft occasional snort of the horses. The first rays of the morning sun crept over the line of rolling hills to the east, illuminating the frosty breath of horses and riders, creating a ghostly procession.

Riding directly into the rising sun, Drummond led his column of bushwhackers for a distance of four miles to the junction of two small streams. Holding his horse back, he dispatched his men to their assigned targets, and watched for a few moments as the two groups of three disappeared over the ridge to the south. Satisfied, he kicked his horse again, and headed toward the creek that ran between Bar-M and Broken-M range. It was a day that had been too long in coming.

Drummond had given his foreman the job of calling on Burt McCrae's ranch because, in Drummond's mind, that was the most likely place to find Colt. Pete Tyler was a capable man. He had been with Drummond from the early days and had never questioned an order, regardless of the nature. Drummond was confident that Pete would run McCrae to ground, and take care of his uncle in the process. Although Drummond had taken three of the men with him to search the creek, supposedly to find Colt's camp, he felt certain that Colt would be found at the ranch. It couldn't hurt to be somewhere else when the troublesome ex-convict was killed, just in case there was some talk about it in town.

"What about them two that work for McCrae?" Jake White asked as the three men approached the Broken-M ranch house.

"Those two old coots?" Tyler replied. "I ain't worried about them. You just do what I tell you. Those two ain't gonna cause no trouble. We'll just ride right in like we was the law."

"I don't see that big buckskin he's been ridin'," Jake replied. "It don't look like he's here."

"Maybe not," Tyler said. "We'll have us a look-see, anyway." There was a hint of disappointment in Tyler's tone. He badly wanted to be the one who found Colt McCrae. "You two take a look in the barn—see if those two old buzzards are in there. Check the bunkhouse, too. I'm goin' to the house, and I don't want them sneakin' up my back."

Jake and his partner, a man named Blanton, peeled off and headed for the barn. Had they known, they could have saved themselves the trouble. Jesse and Tuck, after talking it over the night before, decided it was not worth risking their lives to stand up to Drummond. They had ridden out before dawn that morning, heading for Laramie.

Burt McCrae paused when he heard someone calling his name. He had been splitting firewood since coming out that morning to find that his help had fled. Still holding his ax in one hand, he walked around the house to find Frank Drummond's foreman sitting on his horse at the edge of his front porch. He silently cursed himself for not having his rifle with him. "What do you want, Tyler?" he demanded.

Seeing the defiant old man holding nothing more than an ax, Tyler permitted a crooked smile to play across his ruthless features. "I've come for that murderin' son of a bitch, Colt McCrae," he spat. "Where is he, old man?"

"You got your damn nerve, ridin' in here like that. Sorry to disappoint you, but Colt ain't here. Now get your sorry ass off my property."

At that moment, Jake and Blanton rode up behind

Tyler. "Ain't nobody down there, Pete, and from the looks of it, it looks like they lit out for good. Ain't nothin' in the bunkhouse."

Tyler's grin returned as he shifted his gaze back to Burt. "Is that right, old man? Did your help light out on you? Maybe they've got more sense than you have." He threw a leg over and stepped down. "Now we'll have a look inside to make sure Colt ain't hidin' under the bed or somewhere."

"The hell you will," Burt replied evenly.

Tyler chuckled, enjoying the confrontation. "You aimin' to stop me with that ax? We'll cut you down before you get close enough to swing it."

"You'll be next," a voice from the door announced.

Tyler jerked his head around to discover a rifle barrel protruding through the partially opened door. It was aimed right at his belly with Rena's steady hand on the trigger. "What the . . . ?" he blurted, too surprised to finish, his hand automatically dropping to the pistol he wore.

"I wouldn't if I was you," Rena warned, her tone dead serious enough to make Tyler hesitate. He played with the notion of pulling the weapon, but only for a moment, as Rena pushed the door open wider so as not to encumber her aim.

The two men with him were startled at first by the sudden appearance of the stone-faced woman with the rifle. While Tyler hesitated, they began to shuffle around, not certain what to do. It was plain to Tyler, however, that one move from one of them and he was the one who would receive a belly full of lead. "Hold on, boys, we don't wanna do nothin' crazy right now."

Holding his hand well away from his gun, he returned his attention to Burt, changing his tone considerably. "Listen, McCrae, we've been deputized by the sheriff to find Colt. You'd best tell your housekeeper to put that rifle down before somebody gets hurt."

A thin smile parted Burt's lips as he replied, "Rena's been with me for over twenty-five years and I ain't never been able to order her to do anything. I ain't never seen her aim a rifle at somethin' unless she was of a mind to shoot it. If you take one step toward the house, I expect, she aims to shoot you." He waited, watching Tyler's nervous indecision, Drummond's foreman wondering if he could pull his pistol before the stoic woman cut him down. "I already told you Colt ain't here," Burt said.

Still Tyler hesitated, his frustration over the ridiculous situation turning rapidly to anger over being held at bay by an old woman. Rena's hand was steady, the barrel of the rifle never wavering, the expressionless face of the woman as impassive as granite. Her resolute demeanor only served to infuriate him further until it became too much for his pride to contend with. In a moment of senseless defiance, he suddenly reached for his pistol. The stillness that had descended over the tense confrontation long moments before was ripped apart by the immediate bark of Rena's rifle, causing Blanton, Jake, and Burt to jump, startled, and Tyler to double up in pain as the bullet tore into his stomach. Without hesitation, Rena calmly ejected the spent cartridge, and swung her rifle around to bear on the other two men.

Both Jake and his partner, although stunned for a

split second, reacted almost immediately. Seeing this, Burt hurled his ax at the closest man. The deadly missile narrowly missed hitting Jake, causing him to recoil—the ax flying by his face to land solidly against Blanton's horse. The resulting blow on the horse's withers caused the animal to buck and sidestep away, leaving neither man the opportunity to get off a steady shot. Rena's second shot knocked Jake out of the saddle. In a panic now, Blanton did not discourage his horse's desire to run. Lying low on the galloping animal's neck, he retreated. Chasing after him on foot, Burt picked up his ax and flung it again in the fleeing man's direction, the missile falling far short of its target. "Run, you bastard!" Burt yelled after him.

His anger fully aroused by then, he returned to stand over the two wounded men lying before his front porch. Writhing in agony, Tyler moaned woefully, "That old witch shot me in the gut. I need a doctor. I'm bleedin' bad."

Taking the rifle from Rena's hand, Burt looked down at the suffering man. "I ain't got no doctor, but I've got some medicine that'll make you feel better." He aimed the rifle at Tyler's head and pulled the trigger. Without a pause, he stepped over the body and finished Jake as well.

Watching the executions, her face still expressionless, Rena stood at the edge of the porch after the final shot was fired. "Will you be wantin' your breakfast now?"

"I reckon," Burt replied.

Chapter 7

He led his horse down below the brow of the ridge and dropped the reins onto the ground, knowing that Buck would not wander. Then he climbed back to the ridgetop and looked out across the frosty prairie. He wondered what the new day would bring, unaware that by that time, Drummond's men were already on the way.

Led by Red Wiggins, the three riders made their way through the cottonwoods that lined the creek and rode up the rise toward the house. Confident that they well understood Drummond's intentions, they planned to spend little time in negotiations. Looking foremost for Colt, they were determined to rub out his brother and lay waste to the ranch house and outbuildings as well.

Vance McCrae paused midway between the barn and the house when a movement beyond the creek caught his eye. Squinting against the sun still climbing up the eastern ridges, he focused on the rise behind the cottonwoods, realizing then what had attracted his attention. There were three riders approaching the creek at a brisk walk. Although they were still too far away to identify, he had a feeling he knew who they were. "Sammy," he called to his son, who was coming from the chicken house behind the barn, "go in the house." While his son did as he was told, Vance turned to stare out again toward the creek. He feared the moment he had dreaded had finally come. It was poor timing for him, since Bill and Tom had already left to round up some strays on the south range. There was no one but him to defend his home. The riders had almost reached the creek now. He turned and followed his son into the house.

"What is it, Vance?" Susan asked when her husband walked straight to the mantel and took his rifle down from the pegs above it.

"I don't know," Vance replied. "There's three men I don't recognize ridin' up in the yard. You and Sammy better go in the pantry and close the door till I see what they want." He tried to keep his voice calm, but could not disguise his apprehension.

Susan's face immediately paled with anxiety, the discussion of the prior night's meeting still fresh in her mind. Within seconds, however, her face flushed in anger. "I told you," she cried. "They've come looking for Colt. He's brought those killers down on us. I told you this was going to happen."

Vance stiffened as his fingers fumbled with the cartridges for his rifle. He gave his wife a forlorn glance. "I ain't got time for this now, Susan. Take Sammy and hide in the pantry." Though possessing little stomach for it, Vance was determined to defend his home and protect his family. Rifle in hand, he went to the front door and stood in the open doorway, waiting. In a few minutes, the three pulled up before the house.

Seeing Vance standing in the doorway, Red demanded, "Where's your brother?"

"My brother ain't here," Vance answered. "What's your business here?"

"What's my business here?" Red slurred sarcastically. "I'll tell you what my business is. My business is to clean out all the lilly-livered bastards like you and your brother squattin' on Rocking-D range." Without warning, he drew his pistol and started shooting.

Taken by surprise, Vance was just able to duck inside the door as several .44 slugs ripped into the door frame, sending splinters flying. Taking the cue from their partner, Red's friends drew their weapons and joined in the barrage, their bullets splintering the wooden door. Vance hit the floor and rolled away from the door. Susan screamed in alarm at the sudden eruption of gunfire, but Vance was too occupied to hear her. He crawled to a window and knocked the shutter aside with his rifle barrel.

Outside, Red swore when he missed the opportunity to kill Vance before he ducked inside. "Look out!" he yelled when he saw the shutter open, but one of the other two was not quick enough to escape the rifle blast that knocked him out of the saddle. Red and the other man immediately concentrated their fire on the window, causing Vance to flatten himself on the floor while lead flew over his head in a deadly hailstorm. Confident that Vance was effectively pinned down for the moment, the two intruders made a hasty retreat to the barn for cover.

Once safely inside the barn, they jumped from their saddles, drawing their rifles as they dismounted. "Nate!" Red ordered. "Keep him busy at that window. I'm gonna sneak around behind the house. He's all by hisself in there. He can't watch front and back." Nate acknowledged with a nod of his head and took a position by the barn door. He began to spray the window with rifle shot while Red slipped out the back of the barn.

Making a wide circle around the corral, Red came up behind the house to the kitchen door. He paused there to listen until he heard Vance's rifle firing from the front room. Confident that Vance was totally occupied with Nate, he cautiously pushed the door open and peered inside. There was no one to be seen. He slipped quietly past the door, his rifle ready, and tiptoed across the kitchen floor, heading for the parlor where he could hear Vance reloading. Almost to the door between the kitchen and parlor, he hesitated when he heard a rustling sound. His attention was immediately jerked toward the pantry door. It took a second to register, but then a thin grin spread slowly across his whiskered face as he remembered that he had heard that Vance had a pretty young wife. *I'll be back for you in a minute, sweetheart*, he thought. *Soon as I take care of your husband.*

With thoughts now of mixing in a little pleasure with business, Red inched up to the parlor door and cautiously peered past the door frame. There lying prone before the front window, Vance hurriedly fed cartridges into his rifle's magazine, unaware of the danger behind him. Red grinned broadly. It was too easy. He raised his rifle and pumped a bullet into the unsuspecting man's back. Vance grunted and lay still.

Mindful of being hit by one of his partner's bullets, Red opened the front door a crack and yelled out, "Come on in, Nate! He's done for!" He waited only a second longer until he saw Nate coming from the barn, and then he went straight to the pantry. Standing to one side in case the lady might be holding a gun, he slowly opened the pantry door. When he was not greeted with buckshot, he pulled the door fully open and peered in. "Lookee here, lookee here." He smirked softly as he leered at his discovery. "By God, they wasn't lying. You're a pretty little thing." The terrified woman huddled in the corner, clutching her young son tightly to her. "Come on outta there, missy, so's I can get a better look at you." He reached out to her.

"Get away from me!" she screamed. "Vance! Vance!" she called out desperately.

"Ain't no use in callin' for him," Red said. "He ain't gonna be able to help you." He grabbed Sammy by the arm. "Come on, boy," he said as he dragged the reluctant youngster from his mother's clutches.

Fearing the worst, she screamed out for her husband again, and tried to push by the frightening intruder blocking her pantry door. Red easily caught her, imprisoning her roughly with one arm, chuckling at her frantic efforts to escape. "I told you, Vance can't do you no good right now." He thrust his face nose to nose with hers and sneered. "But I can. I expect ol' Nate can, too," he added when his partner came in the door. "Can't you, Nate?" he tossed at the grinning gunman now openly leering at the terrified woman. "Course, Nate's gonna have to be satisfied with seconds after me and you have our little go-round."

"How come you get her first?" Nate asked. "I say we flip for it. That's the fair thing to do."

"My ass," Red responded. "I get her first 'cause I caught her. Here, take this young'un." He shoved the struggling boy toward Nate, so he could use both hands to subdue the child's mother. "Let's go to your bedroom, darlin'," he teased as he dragged her toward the hallway.

Fighting helplessly against her abductor, Susan caught a glimpse of her husband lying facedown by the front window and cried out to him as Red pulled her down the hall. Her struggling hopeless, she nevertheless continued to try to break free, the horror of what awaited her clearly pictured in her mind. Her outcry upon seeing Vance lying there caused Red to glance in that direction also. Thinking that he saw a slight motion in the body, he called back to Nate in the kitchen, "Nate, put another bullet in that son of a bitch. Make sure he's dead."

Upon hearing Red's instructions, Susan cried out, "No!" But it was too late. Before she was dragged through her bedroom door, she heard the shot. The impact of the sound on her frantic brain was enough to almost render her unconscious, and left her hanging in a state of mental confusion. Her will to fight was paralyzed in a fearful stupor, causing her to abandon all hope.

Sensing a sudden relaxation of his victim, Red

looked down into eyes wide and glazed with fear, and
chuckled, pleased that she had given up her resistance.
He threw her roughly on the bed and stood leering
over her while he unbuckled his belt and let his
trousers drop around his boots. Unbuttoning his dingy
underwear, he hesitated when he detected a change in
her eyes as if she had seen a ghost. Sensing something
wrong, he turned to look back at the door. At first, he
was not sure if what he saw was real or not. The apparition standing in the bedroom door was almost as
tall as the door frame, and the morning sun rising over
the corral shone through the open front door to illuminate the figure, casting a fiery shield around him. In a
dreadful moment of realization, Red reached for his
pistol, forgetting that his gun belt lay gathered around
his boots. His death cry was like the bellow of a bull
elk as Colt hammered him with three shots, cranked
out in quick succession from the Winchester, the bullets thudding against his chest with the hollow sound
of a drum. He was dead before he collapsed to the
floor.

Colt walked into the room, grabbed Red's corpse by
one foot, and dragged it from in front of the bed. "It's
all over now, Susan," he said. "You're all right." He
could see that she was still in a state of shock, but she
had not been physically harmed. "I've got to see about
Vance." He turned and left the room, leaving her to
gather her wits. Seeing Sammy standing wide-eyed
and confused in the hall, he said, "Go to your mama,
boy." He took him by the arm and gently started him
toward the bedroom.

Kneeling beside his brother, Colt was not sure if

Vance was dead or alive, but as he started to turn him over on his side, Vance's eyes fluttered open. "Colt?" he whispered painfully.

"Yeah, it's me," Colt replied. "I thought you had gone under for a minute there."

"I'm shot bad," Vance forced, his voice weak and hoarse. "I ain't sure I'm gonna make it."

"You're gonna make it. It ain't as bad as you think." He lied. It looked real bad. A single gunshot wound in the back, but there was blood all over the floor. He wasn't sure what he should do, but it was obvious that he had to stop the bleeding before his brother bled out completely. Looking around him, he searched for something to use as bandage. Seeing nothing in the parlor, he hurried back to the bedroom to find Susan sitting on the side of the bed, holding Sammy in her arms. "I need you to help me with Vance," he told her as he grabbed a sheet and ripped it from the bed.

"Vance?" she replied, bewildered, thinking her husband dead.

"Yeah," Colt answered impatiently. "He's hurt bad, and I need your help, so pull yourself together and get up from there."

Jolted from her stupor, she got to her feet and followed him out of the room. Her brain was swirling now with confusing thoughts. He had said that Vance was still alive. The shot she had heard before was not her husband's fatal shot, but was fired by Colt instead. The very man she had tried so hard to turn Vance against had saved both their lives. It was too much for her to handle at this point, so she tried to concentrate on tending to her husband.

As she followed Colt back to the parlor, they heard the sound of horses approaching the house at a gallop. Turning to Susan, Colt ordered, "Get that shirt off of him, and wrap this sheet around him." Picking up his rifle again, he hurried to the front door in time to see Vance's two ranch hands approaching.

"We heard the shootin'!" Bill Wilkes exclaimed when he and Tom pulled their horses up before the porch. They both stared down at the corpse lying in the dust by the front steps. "Is ever'body all right?"

"Vance has been shot," Colt said, then wasted no time in giving them instructions. "Hitch up the buckboard. I want you to take Vance and Susan and the young'un over to Uncle Burt's. It'll be safer for everybody to stay in one place. I'm goin' into town to get the doctor."

After seeing the aftermath of the executions that took place inside the house, Tom and Bill were both visibly shaken, but still committed to the cause. "Tom can take Vance over to Burt's place," Bill volunteered. "I'll stay here and clean up this mess." There was the matter of what to do with three bodies and three horses.

"I'll help you load 'em on their horses, and I'll leave 'em at the sheriff's office," Colt decided. "Drummond can take care of 'em from there."

It was past noon when Colt turned the buckskin up the narrow lane that led to Dr. Henry Taylor's house after leaving the three horses and their grim cargo tied to the hitching rail in front of the jail. No one had come out to question him when he left the bodies, although there were several people on the street who stopped to gape at the grave rider as he passed. He figured that J.D. was probably eating his noon meal at the Whiskey Hill Kitchen. *It'll give him something to help digest his dinner*, he thought.

"Ma'am," Colt acknowledged respectfully when greeted at the door by the doctor's wife, indifferent to the disapproving scowl on the woman's face. "I need to see the doctor."

"The doctor's having his dinner right now," Mrs. Taylor replied. "You'll have to come back later."

"No, ma'am, I need to see him now. My brother's been bad hurt, gunshot wound, and Dr. Taylor needs to see him right away."

"I'm sorry, but—" Mrs. Taylor started before being interrupted by her husband.

"What is it, Marjorie?" Dr. Taylor asked as he came from the hallway.

"My brother's been shot," Colt said. "It looks bad, and he needs a doctor right away."

"Well, where is he? Bring him in," Taylor replied.

"He's at my uncle Burt's place. He looked too bad hurt to haul him all the way to town."

"Hell," Taylor replied, "if you want him treated, you'll have to bring him here. I'm not going to ride out in the middle of that shooting war between you and Drummond's folks." He took a step back, expecting that to be the end of it.

Colt didn't reply at once as he calmly studied the doctor's face. When he spoke, it was without emotion, stating a simple fact that he knew to be true. "You'll have to go to Vance. I don't think you understand. You ain't got no choice in the matter, so if you'll get your bag, we'll get started."

Taken aback by the quiet man's audacity, Taylor was speechless for a moment, a void filled by his wife. "How dare you talk to the doctor that way?" Mrs. Taylor exclaimed. She was not accustomed to hearing anyone dictate to her husband in such a manner.

"Never mind, Marjorie," Taylor said, his demeanor returning to calm, matching that of Colt's. To Colt, he asked, "Is it your intention to force me to go with you?"

"I reckon so," Colt replied, still with no outward emotion. "I was hopin' you'd come on your own, but whatever it takes, my brother needs doctorin'."

Dr. Taylor shook his head as if amazed. Gazing at the resolute face before him, he had no doubt that this determined young man meant what he said. "All right," he conceded. "Marjorie, get my bag, please. I'm going with Mr. McCrae, here, as soon as I saddle my horse."

"I'd be glad to handle that chore for you," Colt said.

"By God, we showed that old buzzard," Tom Mosley crowed. "I think we've done won this war. Drummond ain't got more'n three or four men left." Upon finding out what had happened in the failed raid on Burt's ranch, they counted five men that Drummond had lost on that day alone. "Hell, he ain't got enough men left to take care of all them cattle he's got."

"Drummond ain't the kinda man to take a whippin' lightly," Burt said. He took the cup of coffee that Rena held out to him and sat down at the table with Vance's two cowhands. "I'm afraid he ain't gonna quit as long as he's standin'. And he's got a craw full of Colt now that he can't swallow or spit out. He ain't gonna be satisfied until one of 'em's dead."

"How come we ain't seen hide nor hair of J. D. Townsend?" Tom Mosley wondered.

"Shit," Burt grunted in disgust. "Because J.D.'s on Drummond's payroll, same as Tyler or Red or any of them others. Same reason he ain't gone to the army for help. He was most likely ordered to keep the table clear for Drummond's move to own the whole valley."

The discussion was interrupted briefly when Susan came in from the back bedroom. As one, they all turned to face her. "He's sleeping now," she said, "but he's breathing awfully hard." Exhausted, she sat down at the table beside Burt. Moments later, Rena placed a cup of coffee down before her. "Thank you, Rena," she said, trying to form a smile for the solemn old woman. She gazed out the window at the fading light and said, "I hope Colt gets here with the doctor soon."

The conversation had not yet picked up again when Rena said, "Horses comin'." The men scrambled from the table.

"It's Colt and Dr. Taylor," Bill announced.

The doctor nodded a brisk hello to everyone, then followed Susan back to the bedroom. The others remained at the table to await the prognosis. Without waiting to be asked, Rena set a plate of food before Colt and poured the dregs of the coffeepot in his cup. "I'll make more," she said and went to the pump to refill the pot. It was down to less than half-full when the doctor finally came out again, followed by Susan. Rena dutifully did the honors.

"How is he, Doc?" Burt was the first to ask.

"He was lucky. He's got a serious wound through the upper chest, but it didn't appear to hit his heart or lungs. I can't say much more than it's up to him, I guess—how bad he wants to live, I suppose. Anyway, these next twenty-four hours will tell the tale. I've done all I can. I've told Susan what to do for him." When offered food, he refused, taking only a cup of Rena's coffee. Looking out the window, he commented, "Getting dark already. Days are getting mighty short this time of year. I expect I'd better be getting along. Marjorie will be worried."

"I'll see you back to town," Colt said, getting up from the table. "You drink your coffee. I'll get your horse outta the barn." He pulled on his coat and went outside.

Still suffering with indecision, Susan watched the quiet man as he walked out the door. She hesitated for a moment more before making up her mind, then got to her feet, wrapped a shawl around her shoulders against the cold night air, and followed him. She met him leading the horses out of the barn. Surprised, he greeted her, "Susan."

"Colt," she started, uncertain how to say what she wanted to say. "I just wanted to thank you for saving our lives."

"I'm just glad I was close enough to hear the shootin'," he said. "Sorry I wasn't closer. Maybe Vance wouldn't have been shot." He started to walk again.

"Wait," she said, deciding to say what really bothered her. He turned to face her, holding the reins of the two horses, their breath frosty plumes in the crisp night air. She hesitated, reluctant to go through with it. He was about to question her when she said her piece. "I owe you an apology, a debt I can't really repay—"

"It's all right," he interrupted. "Hell, it's my fault Vance is wounded. They were comin' after me."

"No," she insisted. "I'm not talking about that. I'm talking about how you really saved my life, and after I failed you so terribly. You would not have gone to prison if I had come forward at your trial. I'm the one other person who knew where you were that day. I could have saved you, but I was so afraid it would have killed my father if he found out what we did that day." She looked down at her feet, preferring not to look in his eyes as she poured out her guilt. "And you never said a word. Vance has no idea that he was not the first, and when you came back, I was sure you hated me so much that you would tell everybody. But you never said a word!" She started to cry, unable to hold back the shame she felt.

He did not know what to say. Her apology brought back years of bitterness that he had suffered in prison, knowing that had she come forward, she could have saved him. His so-called trial had happened so fast that he was on his way to Kansas, it seemed, before there was any thought of a defense. Wild as he may have been at that age, he had still felt reluctant to destroy a young girl's virtue, so he kept their secret. In the beginning, he had hope that his innocence would surely be proven when his father had pleaded for a new trial. After a few years with no results, he finally gave up hope and resigned himself to serve his time. Learning that Susan and Vance had been wed, he resolved that the secret would die with him. *What's done is done*, he thought. *What good would it do anyone to bring it out now?* The years he had spent behind bars could not be returned to him. At this moment, he would have preferred that she had not opened that old wound. But since she had, what could he tell her? Forgiveness, he supposed, was what she sought. *Well, for what it's worth, I'll give it to her.* "Those days are long gone, Susan. I don't think about them anymore. You might as well forget them, too." Mercifully, Dr. Taylor walked out on the porch at that moment.

Chapter 8

Frank Drummond was furious. His troop of ten self-proclaimed gunfighters had been thoroughly defeated at every attempt to wipe out a puny force of five, three of whom were old men. The most infuriating aspect of the defeat was that those ten had been pared down to five. He had never before been so defeated, and the anger in him threatened to burst the blood vessels in his neck as he berated the remnants of his gang. He might have enlisted the services of J. D. Townsend and his deputies to go after Colt McCrae, but he was concerned that the sheriff might send word of the war to Fort Russell. He couldn't afford to involve the army in his private conquest. There might be too many questions asked.

Drummond was totally convinced that the one catalyst that had put backbone into Burt and Vance McCrae was the return of Colt McCrae. The thought of the broad-shouldered man with his rifle cradled casually in his arms so infuriated him that he picked up a lamp from a side table and smashed it against the wall. It did not serve to vent the rage that was eating him up inside. His five remaining men cowered before his wrath. Even Alice Flynn, his ill-tempered housekeeper, and usually the only person with backbone enough to stand up to him, made no remark as she looked at the broken lamp and the puddle of kerosene on the floor. Without a word, she turned and left the room to fetch some rags.

Drummond paused in his tirade for a few moments, perhaps calmed by the sight of the acid-tongued woman dutifully mopping up the spilled kerosene. He stood looking out the window, his mind on a man he had heard about from Pete Tyler, his recently departed foreman. Maybe it was time he met the man. After a long moment, he turned to the five seated there. "Brownie, I'm sending you to Denver to find a man for me," he said.

Drummond only knew the man by one name, *Bone*. Tyler had said that was all anybody knew him by, but every outlaw in Colorado Territory knew of him. He worked out of Denver because he wasn't wanted for anything there. Tyler had described Bone as a hunter and tracker, a killer as deadly as a rattlesnake. It had been rumored that Bone had once taken a contract to track down and kill his own brother. Pete had said he had no reason to doubt the validity of it. It galled Drummond to have to resort to calling in a killer like Bone, but Colt McCrae had proven to be a dangerous man to trap. Tyler had said that the only way to contact Bone was to leave a message for him at the Palace Saloon on Cherry Creek.

"What if he don't wanna come?" Brownie asked, not really enthusiastic about riding south to Denver, especially since there had been some talk of a few recent isolated raids by a band of renegade Cheyenne warriors.

"You tell him there's a hundred dollars in it for him if he'll just come over and talk to me," Drummond said.

"Most of them men like that want their money up front," Brownie said. "Maybe I'd better have the money with me, since he don't know you."

"You think I'm a damn fool?" Drummond came back. "I'm not about to send your worthless ass off with a hundred dollars." Brownie cringed under the verbal assault. "You just deliver my message. Tell him Pete Tyler recommended him. He'll come."

"Yessir," Brownie slurred. "You're the boss. I'll fetch him."

"You'd better," Drummond snapped. "I don't wanna see you back here without him."

It was a little more than a good day's ride to Denver, but it took Brownie more than half of the following day to find the Palace Saloon. When he did, it was somewhat of a disappointment. Hardly a palace, it turned out to be a small log structure with no sign to identify it, built on an old mining claim by the creek. There was a smaller shack behind it with a lean-to attached. He would not have found it at all had it not been for the directions given him by a local miner.

With a slight limp, favoring his wounded leg, Brownie pushed the door of the saloon open and peered into the dark interior. It took a few moments for his eyes to adjust to the poor light. When objects began to take definite shape, he could see only a single table near a door in the rear, and a roughly built bar facing him. Behind the bar, a huge man with a full beard and a bald head stood staring at him in stoic unconcern.

A slight opening appeared in the brushy beard allowing a few disinterested words to escape. "What'll it be?"

"Whiskey," Brownie responded and watched while the massive barkeep blew the dust from a shot glass and poured his drink. "I'm lookin' for a feller name of Bone," he said.

"What fer?"

"I got a message for him from my boss."

"Who's your boss?"

"Mr. Frank Drummond, up at Whiskey Hill. Maybe you heard of him," Brownie said as he tossed his whiskey back.

"Nope," the bartender replied, recorking the bottle. "I ain't never heard of him. Bone don't come in here no more."

At once dismayed to hear this, Brownie almost forgot, but then said, "Pete Tyler said to look for Bone here."

This seemed to make a difference. The bartender uncorked the bottle again and refilled Brownie's glass. "You know Pete?"

Gratified to see the change in the big man's attitude, Brownie responded immediately. "I sure do. Me and Pete's been ridin' for Mr. Drummond for more'n a few years. Sorry thing, though, Pete's dead, shot by a no-good ex-convict. That's why Mr. Drummond sent me to find Bone."

"Well, I'll be . . ." the barkeep drawled. "Pete Tyler dead—that's bad news sure enough." He shook his head slowly as he thought about it. "Bone ain't hereabouts right now, but he said he'd most likely be back tomorrow."

"Well, then, I reckon I'll come back tomorrow to see if I can catch him."

"If you want to, you can sleep in that shed out back. You can build you a fire in the open end—keep you warm enough—there's wood stacked against the wall."

"Why, that's mighty neighborly," Brownie replied. "I just might take you up on that."

"Not a'tall," the bartender said. "Here, let's have another drink on the house to ol' Pete Tyler. He was a good'un." He took the bottle from the bar and replaced it with another. Had Brownie been a man of average intelligence, he might have surmised that he was no longer drinking watered-down whiskey.

It didn't take long for the full-strength spirits to addle Brownie's brains, and after a couple of free drinks, he spent what money he had to continue into the evening. Dead broke, and barely able to stand on his feet, he managed to build a fire in the lean-to before wrapping his blanket around him and passing out.

Gradually aware of his pounding head, Brownie was reluctant to open his eyes, praying earnestly that he would go back to sleep and wake up again without the feeling that he was going to throw up. He knew the chances were not good. He was going to be sick, just like every other time he'd had too much to drink, and he uttered a low moan as he felt the familiar churning in the pit of his stomach. To add to his discomfort, his face felt hot, and it seemed to get hotter by the second until it actually felt like it was burning. Unable to tolerate it any longer, he opened his eyes. Startled, he recoiled. His face was barely inches from the fire. Had he somehow crawled up to it while still asleep? He was dumbfounded. To further confuse him, the flames were building higher and higher. Then he jerked back in a panic when a sizable stick of wood fell on the roaring fire, sending sparks and ashes flying.

Struggling to clear his groggy brain from his alcohol-induced sleep, he became aware of a pair of boots on the opposite side of the fire. His gaze immediately drifted up from the boots to a black coat, open to reveal a gun belt with two pistols, butts forward. Quickly tracing upward, his focus settled on a pair of piercing eyes, glowering out from under bushy black eyebrows like two dark orbs set in a pitiless countenance of weathered rawhide. Certain that he was gazing upon Lucifer himself, Brownie cringed before the frightening apparition, fearful that he may have awakened to find himself in hell.

"I'm Bone," the specter said, his voice hoarse and rasping as if echoing from the bottom of a gravel pit. "What do you want?"

Totally sober now, Brownie experienced an irresistible urge to empty his bladder, but he was too nervous to move. Trying his best to disguise his stunned reaction to his frightful awakening, he said, "Mr. Drummond sent me to fetch you. He's got a job for you."

"Mr. Drummond? I don't know no Mr. Drummond. What does he want?"

Grimacing as his need to urinate became more and more intense, Brownie explained as quickly as he could relate the problems that Drummond wanted eliminated. "The main job he wants for you is to take care of one man, Colt McCrae," Brownie strained, his condition now becoming excruciating, so much so that Bone finally took notice.

"What in hell's the matter with you?"

"I gotta pee," Brownie admitted sheepishly.

"Well, get up from there and go piss," Bone growled, disgusted. "I reckon I can see why your boss sent for me."

The ride back to Whiskey Hill was an uncomfortable one for Brownie Brooks. The man called Bone did not ride beside him, preferring to follow along behind. Brownie could feel the man's piercing gaze upon his back. With his long black coat and his dark hair in a long greasy ponytail, adorned with one eagle feather, hanging from a wide-brimmed leather hat—Bone bore the perfect image for one of Satan's lieutenants. He never seemed to have thirst or hunger, and might not have stopped all the way back had it not been necessary to rest the horses. He uttered no more than a handful of words, only those absolutely necessary. Brownie likened it to riding with a corpse. He had ridden with quite a few bad men in his life. Pete Tyler, Lou George, and Jack Teach came to mind. Buck and Jack were not only bad—they were crazy-bad. But none compared to the eerie manner of Bone. Brownie was damn glad to see the front gate of the Rocking-D when they crested the final ridge before riding down into the valley.

Brownie, as was customary among the hired hands, dismounted, walked to the edge of the front porch, and knocked respectfully on the porch floor. Casting a curious glance in his direction, Bone walked up the steps and headed straight for the door. It opened before he reached it, and Frank Drummond came forward to meet him. "You'll be Mr. Bone, I presume," Drummond said, looking the reputed tracker up and down.

"Just Bone," his sinister visitor replied.

"Right. Well, Bone, looks like you got here just in time for supper. Come on in the house and we can discuss some business while we eat." He gave Brownie a dismissal glance. "Alice just took some chuck down to the bunkhouse. You'd best hurry if you want to eat. And take care of Bone's horse for him." He turned, held the door open, and indicated for Bone to enter.

Bone did not move, his deadpan expression never changing. "Your man promised a hundred dollars if I came," he said.

"You'll get it," Drummond replied. "We'll eat supper first."

"I wanna see the hundred dollars first," Bone responded, still standing firm.

Drummond saw at once that he was dealing with a man accustomed to having the upper hand. He didn't like it. When he gave an order, he expected an immediate *yes, sir*. He started to tell him that he would decide when he got paid, but something about those cold, lifeless eyes told him that this was a man who cowered to no one. They stood gazing eye to eye for several moments, a lion trying to stare down a cobra, before Drummond decided to give in. "Fine," he finally muttered, "let's go inside and I'll get your money out of the safe." Bone nodded and followed him inside.

Without being told, Alice Flynn set another place at the huge table, then stood back and waited while Bone stood in the dining room door, counting the hundred dollars. "Supper's gettin' cold," she said, and graced him with a disapproving scowl when he sat down, never bothering to remove the leather hat he wore. Wearing a look of disgust, she returned to her kitchen. Of all the villains, killers, and saddle bums she had seen pass through the Rocking-D, this new face possessed the most potential for raw-cut evil. She hoped Drummond's business with him would not take long.

"Who is he, and whaddaya want done?" Bone asked point-blank as he greedily devoured his supper, assaulting the plate of food like a man who had not eaten for days.

Drummond glanced toward the door to make sure Alice was not within earshot before answering. The cantankerous woman was not that naive. She most likely knew why Bone had been sent for, but Drummond saw no reason to have witnesses to the conversation. "Colt McCrae," he replied. "I want him dead."

Bone studied Drummond's face for a few moments before responding. "One man? What's so special about him? How come you have to send for me to take care of one man?"

Drummond explained. "I've lost eight men trying to kill that son of a bitch. He's a little more wildcat than you expect, and he doesn't stay in one place long enough for anybody to get to him. That's why I need somebody who's a tracker. By God, I'm running out of men."

"What's he worth," Bone asked, "this son of a bitch who's so hard to run down?"

"Two hundred dollars," Drummond replied, "not counting the one hundred I already gave you."

"Shit," Bone shot back. "That's what I get for goin' after somebody like Brownie out there. Four hundred, not countin' the hundred you already gave me. Take it or leave it."

"That's a helluva lot of money for killing one man." Drummond hesitated, but he knew it was worth it to get rid of the main key to his problems. Without Colt, he anticipated the resistance would crumble. "All right, we've got a deal." He extended his hand.

Bone ignored it. "What about the law?" he asked.

"Don't worry about the law. I'll take care of that. The sheriff won't get in your way. As long as you don't do anything in town to upset the citizens of Whiskey Hill, the sheriff doesn't care what happens out on the range."

Chapter 9

Intending to ride quietly into town, buy the ammunition and supplies he needed, and leave as quickly as possible, Colt pulled the buckboard to a stop by the hitching rail at Raymond Fletcher's dry goods store. His uncle had volunteered to make the trip into town, but had to make a choice between that and riding over to Vance's ranch to tend to his nephew's stock. Several quiet days had passed since the shoot-outs at both ranches had occurred, and Vance was encouraged that maybe the trouble was over. Both Colt and Burt saw it differently, knowing that Drummond was not going to accept his apparent defeat. But since there was a lull in the action, Colt suggested that his uncle had better take advantage of it and make sure the stock was taken care of.

"What if that puffed-up excuse for a sheriff tries to arrest you?" Burt had asked.

"For what?" Colt replied. "I haven't done anything but defend myself. I haven't broken any laws."

"That didn't stop 'em from sendin' you off to prison for nine years," Burt had reminded his nephew.

"That ain't gonna happen again," Colt had promised. "You can count on it." That thought was on his mind as he got down from the buckboard.

Taking but a moment to look up and down the empty street, Colt stepped up on the board walkway and entered the store. Eunice Fletcher glanced up from the counter where she was sorting some new material that had just come in. She immediately spun on her heel and retreated to the back room where her husband was busy repairing a shelf. "Raymond!" she gasped. "That murderer is out there in the store."

Raymond dropped his hammer on the shelf and stepped down from the chair he had been using as a ladder. He, like his wife, had no desire to deal with the ex-convict. But unlike her, he was burdened with the role of man of the family. "I'll see what he wants," he told his wife.

"Tell him he's not welcome in this store," Eunice directed. "We don't have to cater to his kind."

"I'll tend to it. You just stay back here until he's gone." *Mighty damn easy for you to say*, he thought, remembering the formidable image of the man just returned from prison.

Colt turned as Fletcher walked in from the back. Mindful of his wife's instructions, the nervous storekeeper was hesitant to pass on her sentiments, but he was also reluctant to greet him with the courtesy usually accorded a regular customer. Consequently, he was left in a quandary, the result of which caused him to say not a word, but to gape openmouthed. Colt seemed not to notice, and handed him a scrap of paper with a list of items his uncle needed.

"Uncle Burt will be needin' these," Colt said as he passed the note to Fletcher.

"All right," Fletcher replied, relieved to have an explanation for his wife as to why he didn't order Colt out of his store. The supplies were for Burt, and Burt was a valued customer. That made a difference. Gathering up the items on the list, Fletcher wasted little time in filling his customer's order, and within minutes of his arrival, Colt was loading the supplies onto the buckboard.

Deputy Stoney Yates craned his neck to stare at the driver of the buckboard pulling away from Fletcher's store. Certain then that it was who he thought it was, he turned around and went back inside the office. "Sheriff, you ain't gonna believe who's drivin' a buckboard down the middle of the street."

"Who?" J.D. asked.

"Colt McCrae," Stoney answered.

"Are you sure?" the sheriff questioned, and got up from his chair. Going to the window, he stared out. "Why, that son of a bitch . . ." was all he uttered at the moment. He had figured that he would hardly see the likes of Colt McCrae in Whiskey Hill again, and if he did, it would more than likely be on a slab at the undertaker's. "I reckon I'd best have a word with him," he said, feeling that he was called upon to do something.

It was not an easy decision for J.D. at this juncture. In spite of Frank Drummond's efforts to keep the battle between him and the McCraes a private affair, some of the town's citizens knew there was a range war going on. The mayor had asked J.D. point-blank why he was not taking action against one or both of the parties involved. J.D. had tried to sidestep the issue by insisting that it had been blown out of proportion, and besides that, it was not affecting the citizens of Whiskey Hill. It didn't help matters when the bodies of three of Drummond's men were found tied to the hitching rail in front of the jail. Roy Whitworth had suggested contacting the army, and J.D. had lied to the mayor when he said he had sent word to Fort Russell. *I wish to hell Drummond would end this thing*, he thought as he put his hat on and started for the door.

"Hold up, there, McCrae," J.D. sang out as he walked out onto the dusty street.

Colt drew back on the reins, pulling the horse to a stop. He picked up the Winchester behind the seat and propped it beside him—a move the sheriff did not fail to notice. "What can I do for you, Sheriff?"

"Maybe you can start by tellin' me about them three dead men you left tied up in front of the jail the other day," J.D. said in a tone as authoritative as he could manage.

"Who said I left them there?" Colt responded.

"There was two or three folks that saw you leadin' 'em down the street," the sheriff insisted.

"Maybe I found 'em outside of town and just dropped 'em off at the jail—figured you'd let Drummond know they were his men. How do you figure they got shot, Sheriff? I figured they musta been out huntin' and surrounded a bunch of antelope, and wound up shootin' each other."

J.D. didn't respond for a few moments while he absorbed Colt's sarcasm. "Mister," the sheriff finally warned, "you might think you can buffalo me, but you just might find yourself a guest in my jail."

"For breakin' what law?" Colt demanded. "Oh, I forgot, you don't have to break a law to get locked up in Whiskey Hill." He glared at the obviously irritated lawman for a moment. "Now, can I be on my way?"

Frustrated, but not to the point of challenging the steady hand resting on the rifle barrel, J.D. stepped back from the buckboard. "I think it's best if you just ride on outta town now. You ain't welcome in Whiskey Hill."

Although his intention had been to do just that, the sheriff's warning struck an irritating chord in Colt's mind and he responded defiantly. "I expect I might fancy a cup of coffee before I make the trip back to Broken-M." He popped the reins sharply across the horse's back and left the sheriff standing in the street. He had no particular desire for coffee, but he was damn tired of people telling him to get out of town. When he came to the Whiskey Hill Kitchen, he had just about cooled his temper enough to forget the spiteful cup of coffee, but something changed his mind.

"Colt!" Someone called and he turned to see Mary Simmons standing in the doorway of the dining room. He pulled up before the door. She walked out to the edge of the board sidewalk, a broad smile across her face. "Well," she said, "I see they haven't run you out of the territory yet."

"No, but it ain't been for lack of tryin'," Colt replied,

a grin slowly forming on the face that was so defiant moments before.

"You must be as ornery as they all say. Pearl and I have been telling 'em you didn't seem the kind to cut and run." She didn't mention the fact that Pearl also said he'd be a damn fool if he didn't. It was an ill-kept secret that Frank Drummond wanted him gone, and J.D. was usually quick to do Drummond's bidding.

"Is that a fact?" Colt replied. His decision made then, he guided the buckboard out of the street and climbed down. "I expect I could use a cup of that stuff you folks pass off as coffee."

"Well, come on in," she invited grandly. "I just made a fresh pot not more'n fifteen minutes ago." She opened the door wide for him. "Pearl might even be persuaded to scramble some eggs for you."

"Just coffee'll do," Colt said.

"Well, look who's here," Pearl Murray sang out when Colt took a seat at the counter. "Thought you'd be dead by now."

"Is that so? Sorry to disappoint you."

Pearl laughed. "You got more'n your share of sand. Ain't he, Mary?"

"That's a fact," Mary agreed while she filled a cup from the pot on the stove. Noticing a wide grin on Pearl's face, accompanied by an impish nod toward the kitchen, Mary glanced in that direction in time to see the back door closing. She almost laughed, knowing Oscar had ducked out the back, heading for the sheriff's office. To Colt she said, "We might be seeing J.D. any minute."

"He's already seen me," Colt said. "He told me to

get outta town. That's the main reason I stopped here for coffee."

"Well, I like that," Mary replied as though insulted. "I thought you just wanted to see me and Pearl."

"That, too, I reckon," he said with a sheepish smile.

Pearl walked over to stand directly in front of him while he sipped the hot coffee. "Colt, what in hell's goin' on out there? All they've been talkin' about in the back room is some kinda range war goin' on—dead men showin' up at the sheriff's office, one of Drummond's men with a bullet in his leg, you bringin' Tom Mosley in with a gunshot—and now I hear your brother, Vance, was shot. What the hell's goin' on? J.D. says it ain't nothin' that concerns Whiskey Hill."

Colt took another long sip of coffee while he decided how to answer her question. "It's kinda simple," he said. "Somebody's tryin' to take land that belongs to other folks, and those folks ain't inclined to let him have it."

Whether or not it was explanation enough to suit her, it was obvious that it was all she was likely to receive, so she just shook her head and said, "It ain't right. J.D. oughta do somethin' about it."

"I'd just as soon he didn't," Colt replied, " 'cause I know which side he'd be on." He gulped the last of his coffee down. "I'd best be goin'. It's already gonna be after dark by the time I get back. How much I owe you?" Pearl waved off his attempt to pay.

Mary walked him to the door. "Colt, you be careful," she said. "They're out to get you." Then lightening her tone, she added, "Don't stay away so long."

He glanced down to look directly into her eyes.

Smiling, he promised, "I'll get back to see you. You can count on that."

Pearl came from behind the counter and walked over to stand in the door with Mary. They watched him until he turned at the end of the street and disappeared from their view. "Honey," Pearl warned, "you're lookin' to find yourself some trouble if you keep givin' him those sheep eyes. That man attracts trouble like a horse turd attracts flies."

"I was not," Mary protested. "But I still think he's a lot nicer than everybody makes him out to be."

Pearl was about to say more, but couldn't help but giggle when they heard the sound of the back door closing. "Oscar's back," she whispered. "Came back to throw Colt out." They both laughed at that.

He set the horse's nose on the trail leading back toward the Broken-M and Bar-M ranges, thoughts of Mary Simmons filling his mind. The young woman had a way about her. He couldn't decide if she was pretty or not—certainly attractive, with those dark eyes that so easily captured his attention—and hair as dark as her eyes. *This ain't the time to be thinking about a woman*, he lectured himself. *Get your mind back on the business at hand.* But he found that was not so easily done. Already he had lingered in town longer than he had intended. *I just hope this horse of Uncle Burt's knows his way home in the dark,* he thought. Had he been aware that Stoney Yates had ridden out of town on a fast horse while he was drinking coffee, he might have been more alert for trouble.

• • •

Stoney galloped in through the front gate of the Rocking-D Ranch and slid to a stop at the porch, his horse lathered and wheezing. Halfway up the steps, he heard someone call. Turning, he saw Drummond and two men coming from the barn. He immediately ran to meet them. When Drummond heard that Colt McCrae was driving a buckboard back from town, he knew he had been given an opportunity to settle with him once and for all. "Rafe," he ordered, "you and Slim get mounted right away. If you hurry, you might catch McCrae before he gets to the other side of Pronghorn Canyon." Knowing their mission well, they didn't have to ask questions, and were off and running before many minutes had passed.

"Is that the man you hired me to kill?" Bone asked, surprised that Drummond had sent two of his men to do the job.

"It is," Drummond replied evenly.

More confused, Bone said, "Them two are most likely to get in my way." He started to head back to the barn to get his horse.

"Hold on," Drummond said. "Things have changed."

"Changed?" Bone questioned, his dark face twisted in a scowl as he began to get the gist of things. "I thought we had a deal."

"I was gonna hire you to track McCrae and kill him. I don't need you to track him when he's riding down the road on a buckboard. My boys can take care of a simple bushwhacking job."

"We had a deal," Bone said, his scowl deepening into anger.

Remembering then, Drummond reminded him,

"We never shook on it. You ain't lost nothin', anyway. You got a hundred dollars just for taking a ride up from Denver." Seeing the anger building up in the brutal face, Drummond decided it wise to offer a settlement. "I'll give you an extra fifty for your trouble. It's too late to start back tonight, so you're welcome to stay here for supper—start back in the morning."

Hardly appeased, Bone shrugged nonetheless, and without another word, turned and went to the bunkhouse. Drummond grinned, pleased that he had saved the cost of the notorious killer's fee.

Pronghorn Canyon was not really a canyon at all. In reality, it was a shallow ravine almost a mile long that served as a buffer between Crooked Creek and the open range beyond. In fact, no one knew from whence the name had come. As far as anyone could remember, there had been no abundance of pronghorn there, either. Colt drove the buckboard along the center of the ravine, intending to veer off to the east at the end. To remain on a straight course would take him to the Rocking-D range.

He had traveled approximately halfway through Pronghorn Canyon when a big, almost full moon rose over the distant hills, bathing the ravine floor with moonlight. *Uncle Burt will start to worry about me*, he thought. He didn't have time for other thoughts along that line, for in the next instance, a bullet gouged out a strip of wood from the floorboard, followed almost at once by the bark of a rifle.

His reaction was automatic. Lashing the horse with the reins, he crouched down in front of the seat, calling

for all the speed the sorrel could give him. More shots
rang out, sending lead slugs slithering through the
frosty air all around him. A fist-sized chunk of wood
flew over his shoulder, knocked out of the seat back.
Suddenly he felt a solid blow against his side that
caused him to sprawl sideways on the floor, losing the
reins as he fell. In the next instance, the horse screamed
as a bullet found fatal purchase, and the sorrel tumbled, throwing the buckboard upside down, spilling
the contents, including the man. By miracle or instinct,
he was able to hang on to his rifle as he sailed through
the air, landing hard on the canyon floor.

Still with no idea of how many or from where, he
lay on the ground trying to regain the breath that the
fall had pounded from his lungs. The numbness in his
side began to sting and he grabbed his side, only to
pull it away again covered with blood. Off to one side,
the buckboard lay smashed, the dead horse still in the
traces. He had his rifle, but no extra cartridges. There
were cartridges somewhere in the parcels that had
been scattered, but he could not see them. After a few
agonizing minutes, he regained his breath. Now, with
nothing but the pain in his side, which seemed to be
getting progressively worse, he struggled to get to his
feet.

He had taken no more than a few steps when the
riders charged down from the dark side of the ravine.
Dropping to one knee, he opened fire with his rifle.
With no time to aim properly, his shots failed to hit a
target, but they served to halt the charge. He could see
now that there were two of them. Taking advantage of
their hesitation, he retreated as quickly as he could up

the opposite slope. Soon bullets were whistling all around him, forcing him to seek cover in a shallow gully. Bolder now that their quarry was on the run, the two riders urged their horses up the slope after him. Taking time to aim, Colt cranked three shots into the foremost rider, knocking him off his horse. The remaining assailant wheeled his horse around at this and retreated to the ravine floor where he continued to spray the slope with rifle shot.

Certain that if he stayed put, he was bound to get hit again, Colt opened up with his rifle, causing the gunman to back even farther away. He pulled the trigger again, only to hear the dull click of the hammer against an empty chamber. With no other option, he forced himself to scramble up over the side of the ravine. Unknown to him, the rider he had left behind was not willing to follow him to finish the job, afraid that he would meet the same fate as his partner. While Colt made his painful way back in the direction of Crooked Creek, Rafe paused only long enough to throw Slim's body over the saddle before hurrying back to the Rocking-D to report the results.

Supper being long since finished, Drummond got up from his chair beside the massive stone fireplace. Alice Flynn had cleaned up the kitchen and retired to her room although the evening was still young. Placing another log on the fire, he paused when he thought he heard the sound of hoofbeats outside. Hurrying to the front porch, he arrived in time to see Rafe slide to a stop from a full gallop. He was leading Slim's horse with a body across the saddle.

Drummond's first thought upon seeing the body was gratification that they had been quick enough to cut McCrae off. Slim was obviously dead, but Drummond was willing to lose a man in exchange for the elimination of his main source of irritation. Rafe's report upon seeing his boss on the porch only served to send Drummond into a frustrated rage. "Damn you!" he roared. "You let him get away?"

"Couldn't help it," Rafe pleaded in his defense. "He's too damn good with that rifle. We almost got him—killed his horse, and I'm pretty sure I hit him once. He's on foot and wounded—oughta be dead by now."

"Why in hell didn't you follow him to make sure?" Drummond stormed. "I told you to make sure he was dead."

"Well, sir," Rafe fumbled, "it was dark and he had the high ground up on that ridge, and him and that rifle—"

"Shit!" Drummond cut him off in disgust. Then in a moment of urgency, he ordered, "Go to the bunkhouse and get Bone." Then he had a second thought. "Never mind, I'll fetch him myself. You get rid of that body and get ready to take Bone to where you lost McCrae."

Storming down the steps, he strode across the yard, at a furious pace, worried that the smug gunman might have decided to leave. Charging in the door of the bunkhouse, he was met by Brownie, who had also heard Rafe ride in. "Where is he?" Drummond demanded. "Bone, where is he?"

"Yonder," Brownie answered and pointed to the back corner of the bunkhouse. "He's asleep."

"Well, wake him up," Drummond said.

Brownie cast a quick nervous glance in Bone's direction. "We pretty much been lettin' him be. He said anybody that woke him up was liable to get shot."

Brownie's reply only served to deepen Drummond's disgust with his cautious gunman. He started toward the back of the building. "Turn that lantern up," he said. Approaching the sleeping man, he stopped several feet short. "Hell," he snorted, surprised, "he's awake."

"No, sir," Brownie countered. "He's asleep."

Drummond stared at the menacing figure, his back propped up, almost in a sitting position, his arms crossed before his chest with a pistol in each hand. "His eyes are open," Drummond insisted.

"That's the way he sleeps, with his eyes open," Brownie said. As far as he was concerned, that alone was evidence enough that the dark gunman was in league with the devil.

Drummond looked from his obviously frightened ranch hand back to the sleeping man. Sure enough, Bone's eyes were really only half open. The man was asleep. Not in the mood for any more frustration, Drummond began calling out Bone's name. "Bone! Bone! Wake up, man!" Just to be safe, he took a couple of steps back.

Finally there was a flicker in the drooping eyelids. Then instead of the violent reaction they expected, he slowly rolled his eyes upward, his arms slowly unfolding to point the pistols in front of him. The awakening was mindful of a possum coming out of its defensive sleep, instead of a lion suddenly awakened. "What the hell do you want?" he growled, irritated to have been awakened.

Drummond hurriedly told him of the unsuccessful attempt on Colt's life by his men, and the necessity to find him before he was able to escape. Bone listened with no sense of urgency. In fact, boredom was the more obvious reaction. When Drummond finished talking, Bone commented, "So now you want me to go after this jasper. Well, the price just went up a hundred dollars."

"Whoa!" Drummond protested. "Why in hell would it? If anything, the job's a helluva lot easier. Rafe says McCrae's wounded, and he's on foot. He oughta be easy enough to follow."

"Then why didn't he bring him back?" Bone replied. "Fact is, a wounded man can be more dangerous, like runnin' down a wounded bear or elk. That's why the price went up. And trackin' a man on foot is harder than trackin' a horse, especially at night."

Drummond felt the pressure of time, so he couldn't afford to dicker if he was to rid himself of Colt McCrae. "All right," he conceded. "You'll get your extra money, but you've got to get going before the trail gets colder than it already is. Rafe can take you to pick up his track. Brownie, you go with them."

Chapter 10

Colt's eyes flickered open and he awakened, blinking several times to focus, alarmed that he had been asleep. It was still dark. He had stopped to rest for a few moments, not intending to sleep. He could not guess how long he had been out, but the moon was still high, so it could not have been long. He started to roll over on his side, but stopped short when the pain in his ribs caused him to reconsider. In a rush of confusion, his memory returned to alert him, and he listened for sounds of pursuit. Surely they knew he had been hit, so they wouldn't quit until they found him. *Where the hell am I?* he thought. He wasn't sure— somewhere on the east side of Crooked Creek, he guessed. He couldn't have gotten far from Pronghorn Canyon. *Can't stay here*, he thought, and struggled to get on his feet, one hand clutching his bloody side. He realized then that his rifle was gone. He must have lost it somewhere before he blacked out.

Pausing a moment to steady himself, he was trying to remember which way he had come when suddenly he heard the sound of horses splashing across the shallow creek some thirty or forty yards behind him. With no hope of finding the rifle now, he took the first likely avenue of escape. Forcing himself to ignore the pain that screamed out at him with each step he took, he plunged into the head-high brush that rimmed the crest of a deep gully. Straining to remain on his feet, he pushed through the branches that snatched at him and caught in his clothing until finally he lost his footing on the steep slope and tumbled head over heels to the bottom.

Unable to move for a moment, he lay there and listened. Within seconds, he heard them above him. With his empty rifle far behind him on the ridge and no chance of outrunning their horses, he could only lie there and wait, hoping the darkness hid his trail down the side of the gully. They were now so close above him that he could hear them talking.

"He can't be far ahead of us. Hell, he's bleedin' like a stuck hog," one voice said. "Judging by the blood all over that rock back yonder, I'd say he can't get much farther."

Another voice commented, "The son of a bitch has likely just crawled off and died. We're most likely followin' a dead man—might as well go on back."

"The hell we will," a third voice said. "I'm gettin' paid to drag his dead ass back to your boss. We'll keep followin' this ridge. He's bound to be along here somewhere. The man's bleedin' out. He won't last much longer."

Thinking the same thing, the wounded man below them breathed a sigh of relief, albeit temporary, when he heard them move off along the ridge. Reaching once again for strength in a well that was rapidly running dry, Colt forced himself to his feet. Following what appeared to be a small game trail, he made his way painfully down the gully, carefully placing each foot in the darkness.

Nearing the mouth of the gully, he began to stagger drunkenly. He knew he had little strength left and was making his way on determination alone. Soon his mind began to reel and his head began to swirl, and he thought for a moment he heard angels singing. *Strange,* he thought just before everything went black. *Angels singing.*

"Some of you fellers give me a hand," Dewey Jenkins exclaimed as he burst through the door of the tiny church by the creek. "There's a man out here hurt bad—or dead. I ain't sure which."

His sudden interruption effectively stopped the singing, and the small congregation turned as one. There were only five men in the church, but all five immediately responded to Dewey's call for help. Pearl Murray placed her hymnal on the bench beside her and turned to talk to the other women while their menfolk followed Dewey out the door.

Outside, Dewey led the other men back beyond the buckboards and wagons to the narrow wagon trace that led up from the creek. "I dang near run over him," Dewey said when they reached the prone body in the road. "If my horse hadn'ta drawed back, I reckon I would have."

"Is he dead?" John Tasker wondered aloud.

"He's still breathin'," Dewey declared as he knelt beside the man, "but he's awful bloody."

"Who is it?" one of the others asked.

"Don't know," Dewey replied. "Let's get him inside where we can see." Responding to Dewey's suggestion, they picked up the wounded man and carried him inside the church amid a flurry of whispered comments from the women. "Lay him on the bench, there," Dewey directed. Turning to his wife, he said, "Bring that lantern over here so we can see what's what."

"Looks to me like he's been shot," John Tasker said. His comment caused a wave of concern among the others as they crowded in closer in an effort to see for themselves.

"He's running from somebody," someone said. "Probably the law," someone else suggested. "Maybe we'd better send somebody to town to fetch the sheriff," still another said. "He might be an outlaw."

"Get outta the way, Dewey," Pearl Murray said as she shouldered a couple of the men aside and bent close over the victim. "That's Colt McCrae," she stated. The name meant nothing to these simple settlers, whose contact with Whiskey Hill consisted of infrequent visits to town for supplies.

Before there was time to question, someone by the door announced, "There's riders comin'."

"Maybe the sheriff," Tasker speculated, "huntin' this feller. I thought he might be an outlaw."

"He ain't no outlaw," Pearl said emphatically, "and most likely them's Drummond's hired killers you hear out there. We've got to help him."

•   •   •

Bone reined his horse up to a halt and stopped to listen when he came to the creek. "What the hell is that?" he asked.

"Church meetin'," Brownie answered. "There's a church down the road a piece."

"A church!" Bone snorted, exhibiting his contempt for all churches. "Well, he's got to have come this way somewhere, so let's go have a look in that church."

In the midst of the second verse of "Jordan's Golden Shore," the small congregation fell suddenly silent as the church door was flung open and slammed noisily against the wall. Fearful faces turned to meet their rough visitors as Drummond's gunmen swaggered into the church. Led by the menacing figure of Bone, they stood inside the door, leering at the handful of worshippers who stared wide-eyed at the intruders.

"Come on in and join us, brother," Dewey Jenkins nervously greeted Bone.

Bone did not reply at once, but stood smirking as he scanned the small group of settlers. When he spoke, it was with a sneer of contempt. "You the preacher?" He directed the question toward Dewey, who was standing up front.

"No, sir," Dewey replied. "We don't have a regular preacher. I'm just leadin' the singin'. You and your friends are welcome to join in our worshippin' service."

Ignoring the invitation, Bone said, "We're lookin' for somebody. He's got a bullet hole in him and he mighta come this way."

"Well, we ain't seen nobody," Dewey answered.

Bone continued to glare at Dewey for a long

moment, the smile of contempt prominently in place upon his narrow features. He was thinking the man seemed considerably nervous in spite of his efforts to appear hospitable. Maybe he was hiding something, he thought. Maybe not. Bone was aware that he was usually met with nervous precaution. "You wouldn't be lyin' to me, now, would you, preacher?" His lips parted slightly to form a suspicious smile. Before Dewey could answer, Bone suddenly whirled around to confront a frail little woman near the front bench. "What about you, sweet pea? Have you seen a wounded man come in here?" The woman, too frightened to answer, simply drew away terrified. "Well?" Bone demanded, thrusting his face inches from hers.

"Get your sorry ass outta here!" Startled, Bone looked up to find Pearl Murray standing and pointing a threatening finger at him. "There ain't nobody here you're lookin' for. We're tryin' to hold a prayer meetin'. So get on outta here and let us get on with it. I'd like to get home sometime tonight. I got to go to work in the mornin', and I ain't got time to waste on your foolishness."

Lying helpless under her bench, Colt strained to remain still, knowing that he was bound to be discovered if they decided to search the pews. Bone remained silent for a few moments while he fixed the gutsy woman with a sarcastic grin. Amused by her bluster, he failed to notice a slight nervous waver as she stole a quick glance down at the thin trickle of blood on the plank floor, slowly making its way toward the front of the room.

After a long pause while all parties stood uneasy,

watching each other, Bone spoke. "You're a mouthy bitch, ain't you?" He hesitated a moment more, then decided. "All right, go on back to your caterwauling. Let's go, boys."

Not one of the modest gathering moved a muscle until the sound of horses reached their ears. When it was evident that their visitors had indeed departed, a general sigh of relief filled the small building, and people began to stir again.

"Somebody help me get him out from under my feet," Pearl said. "We'll put him in my buggy."

"What are you aimin' to do?" Dewey asked. "Take him to Dr. Taylor's?"

Pearl hesitated, considering that option. "I reckon that's what he needs, all right," she replied. "But that would be the same as handin' him over to Drummond's gang of outlaws."

The prayer meeting effectively over, the congregation scattered to return to their homes. Pearl drove her buggy with the wounded man back toward town to the simple cabin her husband had built two years before he died. Henry Murray had built a stout cabin that was intended to be a temporary home until he could clear the land around it, hoping to someday have a prosperous farm and a bigger house. It was not to be. The Good Lord called Henry home six years ago with a case of pneumonia. Pearl had some relatives back East, but no desire to return there, so she remained in the little cabin Henry had built and supported herself by cooking for the patrons of the Whiskey Hill Kitchen. A woman of lesser fortitude and determination might have succumbed to the temptation to seek refuge with kin back East, or at the least, sought out another husband. As Pearl explained to Mary Simmons, "I've had one man in my life, Henry Murray. He sure as hell wasn't perfect, but I doubt I could find one as good as he was. He wasn't gettin' a ravin' beauty when we got married, and I always appreciated him for that. He was a good man, worked hard, and I don't care to fool with breakin' in another one.

"I guess Drummond's wolves finally caught up with you," she said as she helped him from the buggy. "What happened?" Grimacing with the pain that seared his side like a hot branding iron, he explained that he was bushwhacked on his way back from town. "How bad are you hurt?" she asked. When he replied that he wasn't sure, she said, "Well, we'll see if we can patch you up. I'd take you to see Dr. Taylor, but that might not be the best thing for you. As soon as J.D. found out, you'd most likely get a visit from that trash that came in the church lookin' for you. That one that did all the talkin' is a new face to me. I ain't ever seen him before. He looks like a mean one. I think Drummond musta bought himself a professional killer."

Inside the cabin, she helped him in on the bed, where he lay back and breathed an exhausted sigh of relief. Looking up into her eyes as she spread a blanket over him, he gave her his thanks. "I appreciate what you're doin' for me. I just need a little time to get my strength back. Then I'll move on. I don't wanna bring any bad luck down on you."

"Don't worry about that. Don't nobody know where you are. Those folks at the church ain't gonna say nothin', so you just rest up and get yourself well. The first thing we're gonna have to do is clean you up a little and then maybe we can see how bad you're wounded."

"I don't think I'm torn up inside," he said. "At least I ain't spittin' up no blood, but somethin's awful wrong in my side. I think I mighta busted a rib or somethin'."

"Just lie back," she told him when he started to sit up. "Let me clean up some of that blood so I can see the wound." The words were unnecessary, for as soon as he attempted to rise from the pillow, the room began to spin, and he sank back. She shook her head like a mother chiding a child. "You've lost a helluva lot of blood. Ain't no sense in gettin' frisky till you build up your strength again."

After removing his shirt and cleaning the wound, she held the lantern close to his side while she examined the seriousness of it. Then she rocked him halfway over on his side and took a look at his back. Her diagnosis confirmed, she told him, "You got two holes in you. I guess that's good news unless you got shot twice." He shook his head. "Well," she continued, "it looks like the bullet went clear through." After a few moments more with a washcloth and a basin of water, she said, "Now I reckon we need a little drink." She went to a cupboard in the kitchen and returned with a bottle of rye whiskey. She offered it to him, but he declined, thinking whiskey wouldn't sit too well on his stomach under the circumstances. She turned the bottle up and took a short drag. "That's powerful stuff," she allowed, then splashed it liberally over the two bullet holes.

"Damn!" Colt swore. "That's worse than gettin' shot."

"My late husband said whiskey was good for a wound. Maybe he's right." She chuckled. "His belly musta been plumb full of wounds, 'cause he sure treated 'em regularly." She put the bottle aside. "I'll just wrap a bandage around you now. Then I'll scare you up somethin' to eat."

"Pearl, I can't tell you how much I appreciate . . ." He paused and stumbled for words. She cut him off.

"Don't waste your breath. You just get yourself rested up." She stood gazing down at him for a few moments, then shook her head as if exasperated. "I reckon I've got a weakness for wounded critters," she said, and went into the kitchen to fix him something to eat.

"Somethin's gone wrong," Burt McCrae said. "He shoulda been back long ago." He stood on the porch peering out into the darkness. His worry was justified. Colt should have returned from town hours before this. He looked down at Bill Wilkes, who was standing at the foot of the porch steps. "Bill, saddle up. You and I better go see what happened to Colt." Bill immediately turned to comply. Burt called after him, "Tell Tom to keep a sharp eye while we're gone." Going back inside, Burt told Susan of his concerns for Colt. "Me and Bill are goin' back to see if we can find him. Tom'll stay here to look after things. How's Vance doin'? Any change?"

"I think he's doing a little better now that he's finally been able to sleep a little," Susan replied. "Do you think something bad has happened to Colt?"

"Well, he oughta been back by now," was all Burt would offer. "We might be gone awhile. Ask Rena if you need anything."

Even in the dark, it was hard to miss the upturned buckboard and dead horse near the midpoint of Pronghorn Canyon. The moon, still high overhead, shone a faint light upon the scene of the ambush with the supplies Colt had picked up scattered about the canyon floor. "I was afraid of that," Burt said. "They jumped him, all right." After searching a wide area around the wreckage, they found no trace of his nephew.

"I reckon that's good we didn't find no body," Bill offered. "You don't suppose we coulda missed him on the way, him being on foot?"

"I don't see how we coulda," Burt replied. "Nah, he got away, but where did he go? He might be hurt."

"Maybe Drummond's men carried him off," Bill suggested.

"They'da shot him right here. Nah, he's out there somewhere on foot. No tellin' where." Burt looked around him again, trying to pierce the darkness.

They searched both sides of the ravine in the shadows, but to no avail. It was too dark to pick up any hint of a trail. Finally, when the moon began its descent beyond the foothills, they admitted defeat. "We'll have to come back in the mornin'," Burt said. They managed to unhitch the buckboard from the carcass of the sorrel. Although it had suffered some damage, they were able to hitch Bill's horse to it and haul the supplies back to the Broken-M.

"You're looking a little more ornery than usual this morning," Mary Simmons greeted her friend when she arrived for work.

"Do I?" Pearl replied. "Well, might be there's a reason. For one thing, though, I'm sure tired as hell this mornin'." She gave Mary a little wink. "I've got a man in my bed for the first time since Henry died."

"Pearl Murray!" Mary exclaimed. "Shut your mouth!" She giggled mischievously. "Maybe I oughta start going to that church of yours."

With little time before Oscar might join them in the kitchen, Pearl didn't carry on with her little joke. "It ain't as good as you think. I slept on a blanket on the floor." Mary's smile turned to a look of puzzlement. Pearl glanced out the kitchen door to make sure they were alone before whispering, "Colt McCrae is lying in my bed, shot through the side."

Mary was stunned. She took a step backward as if jolted off balance. "Who . . . ? How . . . ?" she started, scarcely believing her ears.

"Drummond," Pearl whispered, "at least some of Drummond's hired killers." She went on to relate the happenings of the night before when they had hidden Colt under her feet in the church.

"Oh, my Lord in heaven," Mary gasped. "How bad is he hurt?"

"I ain't really sure," Pearl replied, "but I don't think he's gonna die. At least he looked some better this mornin'. I reckon he needs a doctor, but I didn't think it was a good idea to try to get Dr. Taylor to come see him."

Mary stood there frowning for a long moment, still trying to absorb the disturbing news. "No," she then agreed. "You're right. We can't take a chance on Oscar or J.D. finding out where he is. I'll come over to help you after work. I'll have to help Mama with supper first, but I'll slip out and get over to your place as soon as I can."

"I figured you would," Pearl said, then winked as Oscar walked into the room. She had expected Mary to volunteer her help, knowing she had a weakness when it came to Colt McCrae, even though she refused to admit it.

"Figured you would what?" Oscar asked, overhearing Pearl's last remark.

"Put an extra cup of cow shit in the coffeepot," Pearl shot back, causing Mary to giggle.

"I swear, Pearl," Oscar said, shaking his head in wonder, "you've got a worse mouth on you than some of them gals down at the bawdy house."

"Hell, if I was a little younger, and a whole lot prettier, that's where I'd be," Pearl said. "Probably make a whole lot more money."

The fever of the hunt was developing in the fearsome man known only as Bone. A keen-eyed tracker and a hunter of men, he prided himself on his unfailing ability to run his prey to ground, and his pleasure was the brutal execution of the victim. Over the years, his passion had become a game to him in which he was pitted against his quarry, winner take all, and the stakes were a man's life.

On this morning, he was more than a little irritable. It was galling to him that he had not been successful in tracking down a wounded man on foot. Even though it had been at night, he should have run him to ground easily. Working alone now in the early morning light, he followed the obvious tracks that led away from the rim of the ravine. Here and there, he discovered smudges of dried blood where Colt had placed a hand on a rock or bush for support. So far, the trail was easy to follow as it led down toward a shallow creek running parallel to a deep gully rimmed with thick brush.

Crossing the creek, Bone dismounted when he reached the edge of the gully. This was the place where he had effectively lost the trail the night before. In the light of day, small patterns of blood were detected in the grass, telling Bone's experienced eye that his man had stopped there for a while. "Colt McCrae," he pronounced softly, trying to picture the wounded man as he had rested there. Bone liked to know everything about the prey he hunted. He had questioned Drummond extensively about the uncompromising ex-convict, and from what he had been told, he couldn't understand why McCrae had chosen to run instead of standing to fight. "He was out of cartridges," Bone suddenly surmised. As he knelt beside the blood-stained grass, he scanned the wall of brush that lined the rim of the gully, looking for signs that might tell him McCrae had pushed through. Something caught his eye as it skimmed past, causing him to stop and look more closely. The sun had reflected off something metallic. Bone hurried to the spot. A slow smile formed on his whiskered face as he reached down and pulled a Winchester '73 rifle from under a serviceberry bush. "Well, now, there's a nice little bonus," he said, checking the rifle over. The discovery of the weapon also told him that his quarry was hurt badly. Otherwise, he would hardly have knowingly left his rifle.

Pushing through the brush, Bone led his horse carefully down the steep slope to the bottom of the gully, where he found more blood. Looking toward the end of the gully, he could see that it came out to a narrow road and the church beyond. "Son of a bitch," he growled, for it occurred to him then that McCrae had in all likelihood made his way to the church, and may have been hiding there after all. "That son of a bitch," he uttered, thinking of Dewey Jenkins. "Lying, Bible-thumpin' son of a bitch." He got on his horse and followed the gully out to the road and on to the church.

Pushing the door open, he strode inside the empty building. As it was little more than a one-room cabin, there seemed to be no place to hide. *Maybe he didn't come here*, he thought, hesitating. Walking toward the back of the room, he looked down the rows until his gaze stopped on a thin dark streak running under the benches. Moving quickly down the row to get a closer look, he immediately confirmed his suspicion. It was dried blood. He traced it back two rows to its origin. Standing up straight again, he paused to re-create the scene in his mind. *That was just about where that mouthy bitch stood up and told me to get the hell out of here*, he thought. He was not immediately angry. Instead, he almost chuckled at the irony of having been buffaloed by the woman, knowing that, in the end, he would have the last laugh.

Outside the church, he looked around, searching for anything that might give him a clue as to where McCrae went from there. In the small churchyard were many tracks from hooves, wagons, and buggies. It was a simple task to determine fresh tracks from old ones for a tracker of Bone's skill, the job made considerably easier because the ground was not yet frozen. He was left to decide which might have been McCrae's conveyance away from there, for he was sure he didn't walk. All vehicles went the same way from the churchyard, so he got on his horse and followed the narrow lane back to the road. It was there that he had to make another decision, which he knew could be no more than a guess.

Stepping down from the saddle again, he examined the clear tracks he was able to distinguish from the multitude left there—old and new, some going in one direction on the road, some the opposite. Finally, he decided upon the tracks cut by what he guessed to be a farm wagon, reasoning that it would be the natural thing to lay a wounded man in a wagon bed. Climbing back in the saddle again, he followed the wagon tracks, leaning low on the side of his saddle to keep his eyes sharply focused on the impression left by the wheels.

In less than a half mile, several of the various tracks split, and the wagon tracks forked off on a narrow trail, making them much easier to follow. After approximately another mile, Bone topped a rise to discover a modest farmhouse tucked between a brace of cottonwoods on the opposite side of a narrow creek. He pulled his horse to a stop while he took a few moments to look the place over before riding in.

At first glance, there appeared to be no one about, but while he watched, a woman came to the door and called out to someone that breakfast was on the table. Seconds later, a man appeared in the entrance to the barn and walked toward the house. Recognizing the man as the one he had called preacher the night before, Bone cracked a satisfied smile and nudged his horse with his heels. Entering the yard at a fast walk, Bone looked right and left to make sure there was no one else to be accounted for as he rode up to the tiny porch.

Dewey Jenkins paused when he heard his dog barking at something in the front yard. Hearing a horse snort then, he turned and went back to the front door. The shock he had experienced the night before, when the dark intruder had suddenly stalked into the church, returned to freeze his heartbeat again. As sinister in morning light as he had been in the dim lantern light of the church, the man looked to be the devil's special lieutenant. Dewey was stunned speechless.

His lip curled into a sneer, Bone casually threw a leg over and stepped down from the saddle. Standing before the porch steps, his long black coat open to reveal two pistols, he peered out from under his leather hat brim with eyes black as coal. "Hello, Preacher," he said softly. "I believe you've got somethin' that belongs to me."

Finding his voice, but stumbling over his words,

Dewey was at a loss as to how he should respond. "I'm sorry, sir. I don't rightly know what you mean."

"Don't make me get nasty with you, Preacher," Bone said, pulling his coattails apart to clear his gun butts. The gesture was not lost upon Dewey, who swallowed hard. "That wounded coyote you hid under the bench last night, where is he?" Bone insisted.

"There ain't no wounded man here," Dewey replied.

"Is that a fact?" Bone responded. He stepped up on the porch. "I reckon I'll have to see for myself." He pushed the frightened man ahead of him as he forced his way inside. "Where is he?"

Hearing the confrontation at her front door, Vera Jenkins was now aware that something was wrong. Coming from the kitchen, she almost fell when her husband was shoved into her. Recognizing the evil specter from the incident at the church, she shrieked in horror. Determined to find what he was convinced was there, Bone pushed her aside so he could peer into the bedroom. Finding no one there, he shoved Dewey aside and thrust his head inside the parlor door. "Where the hell is he?" he demanded, his anger mounting.

"Who?" Vera cried, terrified.

Bone shot a quick sneer in her direction. "You know damn well who," he snarled. "And I better find him gawdamn quick. You're wastin' my time." He started toward the kitchen, only to be confronted by Dewey's fourteen-year-old son. The boy, hearing the commotion in the hallway, had quickly run to fetch the shotgun over the fireplace. Like unbridled lightning, Bone reacted. Before the startled boy could raise the shotgun, Bone drew both pistols and pumped four slugs into the unfortunate young man's chest.

Screaming hysterically, Vera Jenkins rushed to her fallen son. A widening stain of dark red blood spread across his woolen shirt as she cradled his head in her arms, screaming his name over and over. Bone turned a casual head toward Dewey to judge his reaction to the slaying. The stunned father had bellowed out involuntarily in response to the sudden explosion of gunshots. His eyes blind now with rage and grief, he charged toward the merciless killer. Prepared for just such a move, Bone stepped deftly aside and struck Dewey on the back of his head with his pistol butt. The defenseless farmer went down hard. Bone stood over him for a few moments until he was sure Dewey wasn't going to get up right away. When he was sure there was no immediate threat from that quarter, he walked over beside the sobbing woman and picked up the shotgun. Spotting a cake of corn bread on the table, he reached over and broke off half of it. He stood watching the woman cry for a few minutes, while he casually ate the corn bread. When he thought she had cried enough, he bent low, his mouth scant inches from her ear. "Where is he?" Bone whispered. "Is he in the barn?" When she was unable to reply, he said, "I'll go have a look." His visit ended, he turned and walked out the door, calling back over his shoulder, "He brought it on hisself. He shouldn'ta come at me with that damn shotgun."

In the saddle again, Bone rode into the barn. Quickly checking the stalls, he saw there was no one there. Realizing then that he had wasted the morning by following the wagon tracks, he swore in disgust and flung Dewey's shotgun over into one of the stalls. Although it was he who had guessed wrong in tracking Dewey, he nevertheless blamed the unfortunate farmer for leading him astray. Wheeling his horse angrily, he headed back to the house.

Storming back into the kitchen, he found the devastated parents kneeling on either side of their dead son, grieving hysterically. Bone hesitated for only a moment before stalking over and with his foot, kicked Dewey over on the floor. "You've wasted enough of my time, damn you. Now I want some answers. Who carried Colt·McCrae away from that church?"

Dewey looked up at the grim executioner, his eyes dazed and streaming tears. Suddenly overcome with rage, the likes of which he had never known before, he roared through clenched teeth, "You murderin' son of a bitch!" Charging up from the floor, he went for the insolent devil that had taken his son's life. Unaccustomed to dealing with gunmen like Bone, he received a sharp rap across his temple from Bone's pistol barrel, knocking him to the floor again.

"You don't never learn, do you, sodbuster?" Bone hissed in contempt for the man's feeble attempts to retaliate. The act caused Vera to scream hysterically. With a look of total disgust, Bone reached down and grabbed the sobbing woman by her hair. Dragging her away from her son's body, he stuck his pistol barrel against her cheek. "Now, by God, I'm fixin' to send you to hell with your son if you don't tell me what I wanna know."

"Pearl!" the terrified woman cried. "Pearl Murray. Pearl took him!"

"Who the hell is Pearl?" Bone demanded. "Took him where?"

Dewey answered. On all fours, with his head hanging almost touching the floor, he was a beaten man. "She's the woman who told you to get out of the church," he uttered painfully. Ashamed to have told, he lied, "She took him to the doctor," hoping to save Pearl a visit from the savage killer.

Satisfied that he had a straight answer, he released the crazed woman. "The doctor, huh? Hell, I shoulda known to look there in the first place."

Chapter II

"Sheriff!" Barney Samuels yelled as he charged in the front door of the Whiskey Hill Kitchen. Running straight to the back room where the sheriff and Roy Whitworth were seated at the table, he called out excitedly, "One of them folks from over near Long Creek is driving a wagon down the middle of town lookin' for you. He's haulin' a dead man in the back of his wagon."

"Well, hell," J.D. replied, irritated that his noon meal was being interrupted. He scowled up at Barney. "Did he go to the office? Stoney oughta be there."

Barney shook his head vehemently. "He don't wanna talk to Stoney. He wants the sheriff."

J.D. sighed reluctantly and got up from the table. Following Barney out to the street, he called to Mary to set his plate on the edge of the stove until he returned. "I hope this won't take long."

Joined by Pearl then, Mary went to the window to see what the commotion was about. "Why, that's Dewey Jenkins," Pearl said. Concerned then, she went out the door after J.D. and Barney.

Mary ran to the back room to get the sheriff's plate, almost bumping into Roy Whitworth on his way out to the front. "Take my plate, too," the mayor said as he hurried past. After setting the two plates on the edge of the stove, she ran out to join the other spectators, arriving just in time to hear the stricken father's outcry.

"Sheriff!" Dewey cried out upon seeing the bulky lawman approaching. "He shot my boy! He came into my home and killed my son!"

"Who did?" J.D. replied as a small gathering of spectators crowded up to the wagon to peer at the boy's body.

"One of that murderin' scum that works for Frank Drummond," Dewey cried. "I don't know his name. He just walked in my house and murdered Jeremy— threatened my wife." He held his hand up to a nasty gash beside his head. "He pistol-whipped me till I couldn't see straight." Spotting Pearl in the crowd, he made an attempt to apologize. "He was lookin' for that Colt McCrae feller. I'm sorry, Pearl, but he might come lookin' for you."

This was not good news for the sheriff. Drummond had assured him that no one outside the Broken-M and the Bar-M would be involved in the elimination of Colt McCrae. He had gotten word about the hired killer Drummond had brought in, and he had feared he might have to answer some questions from the mayor and the council if some of the trouble spilled over into their little town. He glanced over at Pearl, a questioning look in his eye, wondering what she had to do with it. Before he could ask, he was forced to respond to Dewey's demand.

"I wanna know what you're gonna do about it, Sheriff!"

"Why, I'll look into it," J.D. responded weakly, not really knowing what he could or should do about it until he talked to Drummond.

Pearl moved up to stand beside the wagon seat. "Dewey, I'm awful sorry. Is Vera all right?"

"Well, her son is dead," Dewey replied sarcastically. "How do you reckon she is?" After having grieved over their tragedy, he and his wife could not help but place a lot of the blame on Pearl for their loss. "I had to tell him you hauled him away from the church. He was gonna kill Vera if I didn't. But I told him you took him to the doctor."

"I guess you couldn't help it," Pearl said, feeling her share of guilt for causing Dewey to become involved. Turning to look at Mary, whose worried expression told her they were both thinking the same thing, she whispered, "I've got to get him outta my house. They're sure to find out where my place is." They both turned to glance in the direction of Dr. Taylor's house, half expecting to see the killer coming.

Her emotions sufficiently tangled, Mary made some quick decisions. Pulling Pearl a few steps away from the wagon, she said, "I'll go to your house and get Colt outta there." When Pearl started to protest, she interrupted. "It's best if you stay here where you won't be alone. He doesn't know anything about me, and we can't let him find Colt in your house. You can tell Oscar I got sick and had to go home."

"It's my fault for hidin' him," Pearl insisted. "I

don't wanna get you involved. Dammit, I've already got Dewey's son killed."

"I'm already involved," Mary said. "I better get going. I can walk to your place in an hour."

"Hell, you can't walk. Take my buggy, and I'll walk home later. You're gonna need the buggy, anyway, if you're aimin' to take him someplace, 'cause I don't think he can walk."

Unnoticed by the others gathered around the wagon, Mary slipped away toward the stables where Pearl kept her buggy when she was in town. Meanwhile, J.D. made noises toward taking charge of the situation. "Everybody just settle down and let the man take his son to the undertaker," he ordered in as official a tone as he could muster.

"What are you gonna do about my son's murderer?" Dewey wanted to know.

"I'm gonna look into it," J.D. said. "You just go along and take care of your boy."

"Look into it?" Dewey exploded. "Goddammit, Sheriff, there's a mad-dog killer loose out there. And you're gonna look into it? Why don't you get up a posse and run the murderer to ground?"

"The man's right, J.D.," Roy Whitworth said. "We can't have this sort of killer running loose in our town. You need to form a posse and go after this man."

"Dammit, Roy," J.D. protested, "let me see what's what before we talk about a posse. We don't even know where to look for him." He didn't like the picture of Frank Drummond he already had in his mind if he came riding onto his range with a posse looking for Bone.

"I expect you wouldn't have to look no farther than the Rocking-D," Barney Samuels grunted.

"Now, see," J.D. quickly remarked, "we don't know any such thing. That's why I wanna make sure we don't go off half-cocked. We don't know if Drummond had anything to do with the killin'."

"The hell we don't," Barney shot back. "Anybody that don't think Drummond's behind all the killin' around here is dumber than a fence post."

"Barney's right," Roy Whitworth said. "We've all knuckled under to Frank Drummond for years, but I think this time he's gone too far."

"Ain't that the God's honest truth," Pearl spoke up. "It took a long time in comin', Mr. Mayor, but damned if you ain't finally said somethin' that makes sense."

Ignoring the acid-tongued woman's insult, the mayor continued to press the sheriff for action. "I think it's time to confront Drummond about this wave of killings, J.D.—and this business about a war with the McCraes. I'm ashamed to admit that we've become so blind about Drummond that we're afraid to travel far outside of town to see what's really going on."

J. D. Townsend's worst fears were suddenly being realized. Deathly afraid of crossing Frank Drummond, he had never deceived himself that he was anything but Drummond's man. At the same time, he coveted his position as sheriff of Whiskey Hill, a position that afforded him some measure of authority. Now this latest escalation of killing had caught him right in the middle, and the town council expected him to do something. Of the two sides pressing him, he knew that he was a hell of a lot more frightened by

Drummond than the town council. Still hoping, however, to appease the mayor and his fellow citizens, he tried to reassure the faces now staring at him and awaiting answers. "Now, Roy, we don't wanna make more of this than it really is. Like I said, I'm gonna look into it. We don't need to get up a posse just yet. I'll ride out to talk to Drummond about it." The response he read in their faces was not encouraging. "Now, you folks go on about your business, and let this poor man take his son to the undertaker." His appetite totally destroyed, he turned and headed for his office.

Colt McCrae grunted with the pain caused by his torturous walk from the bedroom to the kitchen. The wound stung with each step he took, but it was his rib cage that caused him to flinch. He was convinced now that he had landed so hard when thrown from the buckboard that he had cracked some ribs. But painful or not, when he heard the buggy coming up the lane, he forced himself to move to the kitchen to get the double-barreled shotgun he had seen there.

With the shotgun in hand, he checked to make sure it was loaded before letting his body collapse onto a chair at the table. With the weapon lying on the table before him, he sat facing the door.

"Colt!" Mary cried out in alarm upon opening the door, startled to see the wounded man seated at the table.

"What are you doin' here?" Colt responded.

"I've got to get you out of here," she replied. "The man trying to kill you knows that Pearl brought you from the church. It's just a matter of time before he finds out you're here."

"What about Pearl?" Colt asked. "Is she all right?"

"I think so. She's gonna go over to my house when she finishes work today. I think as long as she's in town, she'll be all right. So far, none of Drummond's crowd knows I'm involved, so let's get you out of here to someplace safe." Though she did not voice it, she felt reasonably sure that they would not think to look for Pearl in her parents' house since her mother was a full-blood Cheyenne, and her father, a white man, was the town drunk.

"I need to get back to my uncle's—my horse, my rifle," Colt started, then shook his head, bewildered. "I ain't much good without a horse and rifle."

"You wouldn't be much good even with them from the looks of you right now," Mary stated. "Pearl said you've lost a lot of blood, and we need to get you someplace where you can heal."

"I guess you're right," he confessed. "I can hardly keep myself sittin' up in this chair. Do you know a place I can hole up for a spell?"

"I do," she said as she moved to help him up from the chair. "My grandmother's."

It was the second time Colt had ridden in Pearl Murray's buggy. On this occasion, it seemed more painful than the first, when he was barely conscious of the trip from the church to Pearl's little cabin. On this day, however, he felt every stone or rut that jolted his ribs as Mary drove the horse up through the foothills, at times when there was barely enough trail for the buggy to pass. It took most of his depleted strength just to remain in the seat beside her. To his relief, the rough journey finally ended when they crossed over a long tree-covered ridge that formed one side of a gentle basin and descended into a small gathering of a dozen tipis.

Their arrival sparked an immediate alarm among the inhabitants of the village when the buggy was sighted. Women screamed excitedly *"Vi ho ah I!"* as they ran about, gathering their children. Men ran to their tipis to get their weapons, for the appearance of a buggy meant *white man*. Mary stopped the horse and stood up. To Colt's surprise, she called out to them. Speaking in their tongue, she identified herself by the name her grandmother had always called her, Little Star. Then she pointed to Colt and said, *"Ehaomohtahe.* He is sick." Her words seemed to calm the concerned Cheyenne.

Near the center of the small gathering of Indians, an old woman made her way to the forefront. She stood looking at the young white woman for a long moment before finally her leathery old face broke into a wide smile and she called out, "Little Star."

Mary drove the buggy into the camp and they were quickly surrounded by curious men, women, and children. Mary stepped down to receive the warm embrace of her grandmother. The old woman's smile was as wide as her wrinkled face, revealing gums with more gaps than teeth. It had been more than two years since Mary had visited the tiny village of her grandmother, Walking Woman, and it was obvious by the glow in the old woman's face that she had been missed. When Mary explained why she had brought the wounded white man to their village, her grandmother did not disappoint her.

"Take him to my lodge," she said. "There he can rest, and I will make him strong again." While two of the men helped Colt down from the buggy, Walking Woman asked Mary, "He is a good white man?"

Understanding, Mary at once assured her grandmother that Colt was a good white man. Rightly concerned, Walking Woman was still sad that Mary's mother had married a white man who was not good. "How is your mother?" she asked. Mary replied that her mother was getting along as well as could be expected. "She is still with that man, your father?" Mary nodded. Walking Woman shook her head sadly. "She should come back to her people." Finished with the subject then, she spun on her heel and followed after the men carrying Colt. "Come, we will see about this white man. He is important to you?"

Mary blushed. "Well, kinda, but some bad men are looking for him. I didn't know where else to take him."

"I'll take care of him," Walking Woman said. Inside her tipi, she fashioned a bed with several blankets on one side of the lodge. Feeling helpless in a strange world, Colt lay quietly while the old woman took the bandage off and looked at his wound. "Bullet go in, bullet come out," she announced.

"I think he's got some broken ribs," Mary said.

Walking Woman placed her hand on Colt's side and pressed gently, causing him to grunt with the pain. She nodded. "I'll put some medicine on the wound, heal him up. We'll bind his ribs." She pulled her head back as if seeing him for the first time. "He's a strong man. He'll heal quick." She left to search for the roots she needed.

"What did she say?" Colt asked as soon as the old woman disappeared. The entire consultation between the two women had been conducted in Cheyenne, so he was lost and anxious. Mary repeated everything that they had said. "Where the hell am I?" Colt asked impatiently. "I've got to let my uncle know where I am."

Mary knelt down beside him. "You're not in any shape to do anything right now but get well," she told him. "You're in Red Moon's village. He is one of the men who carried you in here. He's my uncle. You'll be safe here. This camp is well hidden. Nobody bothers these people."

"I thought the Cheyenne fought with the Sioux at Little Big Horn, and were on the run from the army. How come these people are here so close to Fort Russell?"

"When you were outside, did you see any young men?" she replied. "The young men are with Little Wolf. There is no one left here but the women and old men, and some children. The soldiers at Fort Russell know that Red Moon's village is still here, but they don't know exactly where—and they don't care. These people are not threats to anyone."

"I've got to hurry up and get outta here," Colt said. "I need a horse and my rifle. There's a lot of unfinished business that needs to be taken care of." He was concerned about the hired gunman who was stalking him, but his main worry was for Vance and his uncle Burt.

They needed his gun to stand up to Drummond. "What about that sorry excuse for a sheriff? Is he doin' anything about Drummond?"

"J.D.'s too scared of Drummond to interfere. You know that."

"Damn, I've got to get outta here," he moaned.

"You've got to get well before anything else," she informed him. "I'll get word to your uncle that you're all right." She got up to leave. "I've got to get Pearl's buggy back to her. You'll be all right here. Walking Woman will take good care of you. She knows a few words of English."

"Mary," he started, not sure how to express it, "I don't know how to tell you how much I appreciate what you've done for me—you and Pearl."

"You're the first man who's ever really stood up to Drummond," she said with a smile. "I don't want anything to happen to you." She started toward the entrance. "I'll try to get up here tomorrow if I can."

"Mary, wait." He stopped her, his voice with a hint of urgency. She paused and waited, puzzled by his apparent inability to choose his words. "What if . . . A man has to . . . I mean, what if I have to . . . ?"

"Pee?" she mercifully came to his aid.

"Yeah, pee," he said, blushing.

"You go out behind the tipi like everybody else. I think most of the men go in the willows on the other side of the creek. If you can't make it on your own, Grandma will help you."

"Oh, I'll make it on my own," he assured her. He could still hear her laughing as she walked to the buggy. Left alone in this new, strange environment, he felt more helpless than before. His contact with Indians had been limited at best, and he was left to wonder why this village of Cheyenne would so willingly take him, a white man, in. If the reason was totally due to the fact that Mary was Walking Woman's granddaughter, it still wouldn't explain the cordial reception by the rest of the village. After all, the very land that his uncle and his father had claimed for themselves was once Cheyenne hunting ground. *I'll be lucky if one of them doesn't cut my throat while I'm asleep,* he thought as he lay back to ease the pain in his ribs.

Outside, Mary paused by Pearl's buggy to wait to say good-bye to her grandmother, who was already coming up from the creek with a handful of roots. "This white man," Walking Woman said, "maybe he is a special white man." She smiled knowingly with a mischievous twinkle in her eye. Her granddaughter's concern for the wounded man did not escape the old woman.

Mary smiled with a slight blush. "He is a special man. Take good care of him."

"I will, little one," Walking Woman assured her. "You will come back soon?"

"I will."

"That can't be nobody that's up to any good," Tom Mosley muttered under his breath. He reached down and picked up his rifle, then edged over to the end of the swale he had taken a position behind. It was mighty late at night for honest visitors, so Tom was not willing to show himself before he could determine what manner of rider was approaching Burt McCrae's ranch.

Watching intently as the rider gradually materialized in the darkness, Tom nervously touched the trigger of his rifle with his fingertip, wondering if he should alert the others back at the house. Seconds passed, and he could now see that it was only a single rider for certain, a fact that made him feel better about not sounding an alarm. Maybe it was Colt, he thought, but as the rider neared him, he could tell that it was not big enough to be Colt. He waited a few seconds longer before calling out. "Just hold it right there," he said forcefully, still crouching low behind the swale. The rider stopped at once. "Who are you?" Tom demanded.

"Mary Simmons," the voice came back.

Tom got up immediately and walked out to meet her. "Mary," he exclaimed, "what in the world are you doin' out here this time of night?"

"I've come about Colt," she answered.

It was a greatly relieved brother and uncle to learn that Colt was still alive although seriously wounded. Burt and Vance had speculated on the possibility that he might be holed up somewhere, wounded, but they had found no clues that might tell them for sure. As each day passed without his appearance, it was difficult to avoid the conclusion that he might be dead.

Mary told them of Colt's concealment in the church by Pearl Murray and his subsequent escape to Pearl's house—the events that followed resulting in the killing of young Jeremy Jenkins, and Colt's removal to Red Moon's village on Willow Creek.

"I knew he was alive somewhere," Burt exclaimed. "They'da damn sure let us know about it if he was dead." The news was welcome, indeed, to Colt's uncle, who was feeling the pressure of trying to defend two ranches at the same time. He desperately needed Colt's help since there was very little he could do to stop Drummond from driving off his cattle. Vance's healing was coming along very slowly, and Burt didn't have the heart to tell him his cattle were scattered all over the prairie. He had sent Tom and Bill over to Vance's ranch that morning, and they reported back that most of the stock was gone, and the house had been ransacked. At least they didn't burn it down, but Burt was afraid it probably hadn't occurred to them. They might be back.

"I was there again yesterday," Mary said. "He is getting much better, but it may be some time before he is fully strong again." She paused to smile at Rena when the Cheyenne woman brought her a cup of coffee. The somber-faced Rena asked her about her mother, speaking in the Cheyenne tongue. Mary answered that her mother was well.

Impatient with the exchange between the two women, since he had no understanding of Cheyenne, Burt interrupted. "I better go get him. Can you lead me to Red Moon's camp?"

"I think it would be better if you leave him where he is," Mary replied. "My grandmother is taking care of him, and not many people know where Red Moon's village is. He's safer there."

"Little Star is right," Rena said, calling Mary by her

childhood name. "When he is strong enough, he will come."

"She's probably right," Tom said. "Them devils would most likely follow you if you went after him."

Burt nodded, reconsidering his first impulse. For the last two days, there had always been at least one rider spotted along the high ridge east of the ranch, watching for anyone coming or going. On the two occasions when Burt and Bill Wilkes rode out to confront him, the rider disappeared only to reappear after they returned to the house. "Anybody see you come in?" he suddenly thought to ask. He wasn't really sure if there was anyone watching at night.

"I don't think so," Mary replied. "It's awfully dark out tonight, no moon, and I was pretty careful."

"I'll see you back home," Burt said. "It ain't safe for a young lady to be ridin' through these hills alone at night."

"I'll be all right," Mary insisted, "but thanks for the offer. One thing, though, Colt needs his horse and a rifle. He lost his when he was wounded."

Burt sent Tom to saddle Colt's horse, then turned to question Mary. "You plannin' to take him his horse tonight?"

"No," she replied. "I wouldn't have time before morning. I'll take his horse to my mother's tonight, and take it to Colt tomorrow night."

Burt thought about that for a moment, still uneasy with the young woman alone on the prairie at night, but Mary seemed sure of herself. "All right, but you be mighty careful, young lady. I'll send him one of the rifles we picked up from Drummond's men. And it wouldn't hurt to slap a pistol belt around that dainty little waist of yours while we're at it."

With Colt's horse saddled and tied on behind Mary's, they walked outside with her. Burt wanted to know if the sheriff was doing anything at all to stop Drummond's hired killers. Mary had to tell him that J.D. seemed to want nothing to do with the war that was going on. She also told him that Roy Whitworth and some members of the town council were growing impatient with the sheriff's lack of response. "I reckon there ain't no doubt which side J. D. Townsend's on," Burt said.

"Nobody doubts that," Mary said, "but I think maybe the town's getting tired of it." She turned then to climb up in the saddle.

Watching without comment until then, Rena stepped up beside her and asked softly so no one else could hear, "Is your mother still living with that man Simmons?" When Mary nodded, Rena said, "He is a bad man. Tell your mother to go back to her people." Mary could only respond with a sad smile. Her father was a brutal man, but alcohol had rendered him harmless, except for verbal abuse, and her mother felt an obligation to take care of him, choosing to forget the years of physical abuse. "Take care, Little Star," Rena whispered as Mary turned her horse toward the ridge.

Chapter 12

Marjorie Taylor was startled for a few moments when she opened the door to confront the sinister figure standing there. The tall, gaunt man wearing a long black coat stood smirking at her. His dark, menacing eyes peered out from under the wide brim of a leather hat, seeming to penetrate her brain as he glared at her.

"The doctor's with a patient right now," Marjorie said, closing the door partway. "You can wait on the porch. It shouldn't be very long." With most of the doctor's patients, she would invite them to wait in the parlor, but she was reluctant to let this ominous-looking individual into her home.

Her apparent concern amused Bone. His smirk widened into a large grin. He shoved the door open again, pushed past the astonished woman, and walked into the parlor. "I'll just have me a look around," he told her, then proceeded to walk through the house, looking into every room. Ignoring the shocked woman's protests, he opened any doors he found closed to peer around inside the room before moving to the next. When he opened the last door, he discovered a speechless Dr. Taylor in the midst of lancing a boil on the backside of one of the town's citizens.

"What the hell . . . ?" Dr. Taylor blurted when he found his voice.

About two steps behind the rude intruder, Marjorie tried to explain. "I tried to tell him—" was as far as she got before Bone walked over to the examining table, grabbed the unsuspecting patient by his hair, and jerked his head back sharply.

Taking a hard look at the wide-eyed patient, Bone shoved his head back down on the table. "This ain't Colt McCrae," he charged. "Where is he?" Bone had never laid eyes on Colt, but it was fairly obvious that the frightened little store clerk on the table was not the man he hunted.

Flustered for a few moments only, Dr. Taylor recovered his professional dignity to demand, "What do you mean, busting in here like this? I'm with a patient. Now get out of here!"

The doctor's haughty response tended to amuse Bone immensely. "You're a feisty one, ain't you?" he said, suddenly thrusting a pistol into Taylor's face. "I asked you a question. Now, where's Colt McCrae?"

The defiant attitude rapidly drained from the doctor's face, leaving him a good deal more contrite. "Colt McCrae?" he stammered. "I don't know where Colt McCrae is."

"He was here," Bone insisted. "Some woman named Pearl brought him here with a gunshot wound."

"No," Taylor pleaded, "not here. I haven't seen McCrae or Pearl. I didn't even know he was shot."

Bone looked uncertain. "You sure you ain't just lost

your memory? Night before last, woman named Pearl brought him here late."

"Not here, she didn't," the doctor insisted. "Tell him, Marjorie. Have I treated Colt McCrae for anything?"

Bone jerked his head around to glare at the woman while she confirmed her husband's claims with a nervous shaking of her head. He looked back at Taylor, glowering at him for a few moments more before deciding the doctor was probably telling him the truth. "That lying son of a bitch," he mumbled, thinking of Dewey Jenkins. "I shoulda shot him instead of that whelp son of his." Now a sliver of doubt crept into his mind about the rest of Dewey's tale. Maybe this Pearl woman hadn't been the one who took McCrae away from the church. *Well, we'll find out if she did or not*, he thought.

Done with the doctor, he holstered his pistol and turned toward the door. As he walked by the table, he delivered a hard smack with his open palm on the shivering patient's bare backside. "Go on back to work, Doc, before this jasper freezes his ass off," then chuckled when Marjorie stepped quickly back, aghast, shocked by his crudeness.

Figuring that this was as good a time as any to pay a visit to the town of Whiskey Hill, Bone headed his horse toward the little gathering of rough buildings a few hundred yards away. Drummond had requested that Bone stay away from the town so as not to upset the citizens who lived there. But this hunt for McCrae had gone on long enough to start to eat at Bone's pride, and he was determined to end it as quickly as possible. The next step in his search was to tail the woman named Pearl, since she obviously did not take the wounded man to the doctor. Drummond's man, Brownie, said Pearl was the cook at the Whiskey Hill Kitchen. *So I reckon I'll go find her*, he thought.

There were only two customers in Oscar Anderson's place when Bone walked in. Both turned to gape at the man in the long black coat. With his hat brim pulled low over his forehead, and the long ponytail of greasy black hair, with one eagle feather dangling against his back, he walked casually over to the counter and sat down.

Mary almost dropped the stack of plates she was carrying from the back room when she saw him. She knew at once this was the killer who was hunting Colt. Pulling her wits together as quickly as she could manage, she took a deep breath to calm her nerves, then went to the counter. "Can I help you?" she asked.

Bone looked her up and down for a long moment before answering. "Yeah, gimme a cup of coffee."

She turned about and went into the kitchen where Pearl was still bending over a tub of dirty dishes. "It's him!" Mary whispered. "That killer hired by Drummond. He's out there at the counter!" She glanced anxiously at her friend while she hurriedly poured a cup of coffee from the pot on the edge of the stove. Pearl said nothing in reply, but Mary could see that she was properly shaken. "He's bound to recognize you," Mary said. "You better stay back here in the kitchen till he's gone." Pearl nodded, still not speaking. Her mind was racing, however, and looking around for something with which to protect herself, she settled for a large butcher knife.

About to deliver Bone's coffee, Mary stopped when Oscar came in the kitchen door. "Who's that settin' at the counter?" Oscar asked. "I ain't ever seen him before."

"That's the son of a bitch that shot Dewey Jenkins' son," Pearl volunteered. "Maybe you oughta slip out the back and fetch J.D."

The news sobered Oscar in a second. "Damn, he's a mean-lookin' feller, all right. Maybe I had better get the sheriff." Wasting no time, he went out the back door. Mary looked at Pearl and shook her head with a gesture of dismay, then proceeded through the door with the coffee.

"Took you long enough," Bone growled when Mary set the cup down before him. She could feel his eyes roaming up and down her body. Dumping several heaping spoonfuls of sugar in the black coffee, he took a sip, then asked, "You ain't the cook, are you?"

Not sure how she should answer, she said, "Sometimes I cook."

"Yeah, but your name ain't Pearl, is it?" She didn't have to answer. He was certain that she was not the woman he had words with in the church. It had been fairly dark in the little church, but he was sure that the woman who had sassed him was a good bit older than this one.

"I'm busy in the kitchen," Mary said. "Just holler if you want something else." She left him then to drink his coffee, hoping that Oscar would show up at any minute with the sheriff.

Joining Pearl in the kitchen, Mary whispered, "That's the most evil-looking man I've ever seen in my life." She was about to relate Bone's questions to Pearl when the door suddenly opened, and both women froze.

"That's what I thought," Bone grunted with a wicked grin. "Hello, Pearl. Me and you got a little somethin' to talk about."

"Hold on there, mister," a voice commanded from behind him.

Bone spun around to see Stoney Yates standing squarely behind him. "Who the hell are you?" he demanded.

"I'm the law," Stoney replied. "I need to talk to you about that killin' over at Dewey Jenkins' place the other day."

"What killin'?" Bone replied. "Who's Dewey Jenkins?"

"You know damn well what I'm talkin' about. You shot Dewey's son, Jeremy."

Bone didn't answer at once, looking the young deputy over, measuring the adversary facing him. "Was that his name? Yeah, I shot him. I reckon it broke him of the habit of comin' after somebody with a shotgun. What are you aimin' to do about it?" A spiteful smile crept slowly across his dark face as he waited for the lawman's response. He was in a killing mood. He hoped the deputy would push him.

Oscar, who had been standing behind Stoney, backed away toward the door, but stopped dead still when Bone shot a warning glance in his direction. The only two customers in the diner were both struck like statues, afraid to move. Stoney sensed at that moment that perhaps he had gone too far. J.D. should have been the one to confront Bone, but J.D. was not in the office when Oscar came for help. He was not sure at this point if he should arrest the self-admitted killer or not. Maybe Bone *had* simply fired in self-defense. On the other hand, he thought, this might be an opportunity to show the people of Whiskey Hill that he might be the man to replace an aging J.D. He made up his mind. "I'm gonna have to take you in," he said and dropped his hand to rest on the handle of his revolver.

He might have walked away from the confrontation had he not reached for the pistol. A fatal mistake— Bone whipped out both of his pistols and pumped four slugs into Stoney's chest before the deputy's even cleared the holster. At such close range, the shots backed the startled lawman a couple of steps before he crumpled to the floor.

The sudden explosion of the two .45s shocked the already frozen spectators in the establishment. The room was now clutched by an eerie silence as a thin blue cloud of gun smoke floated waist-high over Stoney's body. Bone, pistols still drawn, slowly scanned the room, making direct contact with every horrified eye. "Everybody in here saw him go for his gun," he said softly. His voice, low and absolute, carried an obvious threat. Thinking it best never to linger too long at the scene of a killing, however, he holstered his weapons and walked to the door, pausing for a second only to cast a warning threat in Pearl's direction.

When he was gone, no one dared to move for many long seconds until Mary rushed to Stoney's side, releasing the room from the killer's icy grip. "Somebody go get Dr. Taylor," Oscar said, his hands still shaking from the ordeal.

"No use goin' for the doctor," Pearl said, shaking her head woefully. "He was dead when he hit the floor." She looked up to meet Mary's eyes, both women harboring the terrible thought that Pearl might be next on the killer's list. "Has anybody seen J.D.?" Pearl asked. No one knew where he was.

At the moment of his deputy's death, J. D. Townsend was seated in the parlor of Frank Drummond's ranch house. He quickly got to his feet when Drummond entered the room. "Sit down, Sheriff," Drummond said as he walked across the room to select a cigar from a box on his desk. Without bothering to offer one to his visitor, he lit up, then asked, "What brings you all the way out here, J.D.?"

"Things are gettin' a little touchy in town, Mr. Drummond," J.D. started, not sure of himself or how he should say what he wanted. "What I mean is—a lot of the folks are pushin' me pretty hard to do somethin' about the trouble out here between you and the McCraes."

"It's none of their damn business what goes on between me and the McCraes," Drummond replied. "Sounds to me like you ain't lettin' 'em know who runs things in Whiskey Hill."

"Yessir," J.D. responded respectfully. "I've been tryin' to let 'em know just that, but they're complainin' that the trouble is spillin' over in town—especially with that new feller you hired. He walked right in Dewey Jenkins' house and shot his son."

"Those people were hidin' that murderin' Colt McCrae," Drummond said. "Bone said he had to shoot in self-defense." When he saw J.D. wincing, trying to think of a better way to state his request, Drummond was quick to cut him off. "I thought we had an understandin' on what I'm tryin' to do here, and that you would handle things in town, and I'd take care of troublemakers like Colt McCrae. Now, if you ain't up to the job, maybe it's time we had a talk about that."

"Oh, no, sir," J.D. was quick to reply, "it ain't about that. I was just makin' sure you knew what that man is up to. I mean, I thought you'd wanna know. I can handle my job all right."

"Good," Drummond said, "I thought for a minute you'd lost your nerve."

"No, sir."

"All right, then," Drummond concluded, getting to his feet. "Anything else you need to talk about?" When J.D. shook his head, Drummond left the room, saying, "Go out to the kitchen. Alice will find you somethin' to eat before you go back."

J.D. didn't bother to stop by the kitchen. For once, he didn't have any appetite. Aside from that, he was never comfortable around Drummond's irritable housekeeper. She had never made any attempt to hide her disgust for him. His intention upon riding out to talk to Drummond had been to ask that he put a tighter rein on Bone, and confine his activities to the open range outside of town. In Drummond's presence, he lost the courage to argue his case. As he rode out past the gate of the Rocking-D, his mind was over-taxed with conflicting thoughts and fears. The town council decided who was sheriff of Whiskey Hill, not Frank Drummond. Yet Drummond had held the entire council in his hand for quite a few years. J.D. was afraid that a time of decision had come for him, a moment he had been unwilling to face for some time. During the slow ride back to Whiskey Hill, he thought about his future and the future of the town. When he finally arrived at his office, he was no closer to knowing what to do.

Seeing Stoney's horse tied at the hitching rail, he was surprised to find his deputy still there so late in the afternoon. Stepping inside his office door, he found Stoney there, but not at the desk. Instead, he was laid out on a blanket on the floor, stone dead.

J.D. recoiled, seeing his deputy cold and stiff, his eyes gaping wide as if he had stared into the face of death. Stunned, J.D. just stood there staring at the body until shaken from his stupor by the sound of boot heels on the porch behind him. He turned to face Roy Whitworth, followed closely by Raymond Fletcher, Oscar Anderson, and Barney Samuels. They all crowded around him.

"I see you found your deputy," Roy said. "That's the work of your friend Drummond's hired killer—shot him down in Oscar's place while you were gone somewhere."

"I was out to talk to Drummond," J.D. offered weakly.

The mayor slowly nodded his head as if confirming a suspicion. "J.D., it's time to pull the reins back on

Frank Drummond. This time he's gone too far. If this keeps up, he's going to destroy our town." He looked around him then to receive the nods of support from the other members of the council before continuing. "We've been discussing the problem all afternoon, and we've decided that it's time to rid the town of Drummond and his gang of killers and thieves—maybe time to call up the vigilance committee again. You being the sheriff, it's your job to take charge of that and see that our laws are enforced."

J.D. didn't know what to say. He had not yet recovered from finding Stoney laid out on the floor. He looked at the members of the council, all waiting for his reply, and he thought about his meeting with Drummond just finished. Now was the moment he hoped never to come, when he would have to decide to fight Frank Drummond and his killers. Finally he spoke. "It ain't gonna be so easy, fightin' Drummond. Wasn't but one of you fellers rode with the vigilance committee back in 'sixty-eight." He nodded toward Barney Samuels, the blacksmith. "The rest of the committee was men from Drummond's ranch. He'll most likely hire on more men if we was to come after him."

"Dammit, J.D.," the mayor blurted, "he's strangling the town. We've got no choice but to fight for our homes and businesses. And that means Drummond has to be stopped. No more range wars, no more grabbing free-range land, no more killing of livestock and innocent men. Whiskey Hill could be as big as Cheyenne, but not with Frank Drummond holding a gun over the entire town."

"All right," J.D. conceded, his baleful eyes looking

into the determined faces around him. "I reckon if you've all made up your minds to take on this fight, then I reckon that's the way it's gonna be."

"Good, then," Roy said, turning to nod to his following. "We'll meet at Fletcher's store after supper to organize our plans."

His decision made, J.D. nodded solemnly and said, "I'll have to ride out to my place now." He waited until they had all left before turning to take another look at Stoney's corpse in the corner. *I reckon I oughta go tell the undertaker to come get Stoney,* he thought, but he took no action upon it. Walking over to the rack on the wall, he took his extra rifle out and pulled his rain slicker from a peg by the door. Then he took one more look around the room before walking out and closing the door behind him.

When he reached the modest cabin he called home, he led his other horse from the small corral and loaded his meager belongings into four packs. When that was done, he looked up at the sky to determine how many hours of daylight remained, and satisfied himself that there were maybe a couple. With a weary sigh of resignation, he climbed back in the saddle and led his packhorse toward the hills to the south. He figured to reach his brother's place southeast of Denver in about a three days' ride.

Back in Whiskey Hill, while the members of the town council were beginning to gather in Raymond Fletcher's dry goods store, Pearl Murray drove her buggy out of the stable, Mary Simmons seated beside her. A lone figure watching from the pine-covered hills above the town waited until they took the south trail, then mounted and followed along behind them.

After spending the last few nights in the home of Jared Simmons, Mary's father, Pearl was ready to return to her little cabin. She figured that the man called Bone would hardly have the gall to hang around Whiskey Hill after he killed the deputy. And, besides, she was not comfortable in the same house with Jared Simmons. Most of what little bit of money Mary brought in was spent by her father to buy whiskey, and when he drank, he was a mean drunk, heaping verbal abuse upon his Cheyenne wife and half-breed daughter. Pearl took it as long as she could before telling him he was a sorry son of a bitch who didn't deserve the two women he abused. Quite understandably she was invited to leave. Mary and her mother tried to intercede on Pearl's behalf, but she had no desire to stay in the same house with the no-account drunk, and tried to persuade Mary to move in with her. But Mary insisted that she did not want to leave her mother alone with him.

After driving about a mile from town, Pearl pulled the buggy off the road beside a weathered board house. Mary got out after attempting to persuade Pearl to stay just one more night. Pearl declined, saying she'd rather risk having Bone show up at her cabin than watch another night of Jared Simmons' abuse.

"You be careful," Mary called after her friend as Pearl drove the buggy back on the road.

"The no-good son of a bitch," Pearl muttered to herself, still thinking of Jared Simmons, as she guided her horse up the narrow trail to her house. Driving the

buggy straight into the barn, she climbed down and
unhitched the horse. After watering and feeding it, she
turned it out in the corral and stood watching it for a
few minutes as it kicked its heels, showing apprecia-
tion for being free of the traces. Pearl glanced up at the
sky and the growing darkness. "I'd best see if the rats
moved in while I was gone," she said, and walked
across the yard to the house.

Inside, the cabin was dark with just barely enough
light from the windows to keep from bumping into
things. Making her way to the kitchen, she lit the lamp
on the table, while shivering with the cold. "I need to
get a fire goin' in here," she said as she turned up the
wick in the lamp. Leaving it on the table, she turned to
the fireplace and the kindling box beside it. Kneeling
before the fireplace, she raked some of the old ashes
away before placing the kindling, pausing when she
suddenly felt a slight breeze across her shoulders as if
the back door was open.

Thinking the latch had come undone, she got up to
close it, but before she could take a step, she staggered
back, stunned, as if an icy hand had suddenly clutched
her throat, sending a surge of ice water racing through
her veins. He stood there, motionless, watching her,
his dark clothes barely distinguishable from the cabin
wall behind him. The flickering lamp reflecting from
the metal frame of his gun butts were the only points
of light. Like the eyes of an evil spirit, they seemed to
be damning her. The stick of stove wood she had just
picked up dropped from her hand and clattered noisily to the floor. She did not hear it, aware only of the
beating of her heart that seemed to have risen in her

throat. For a long moment, she was helpless to move, a fearless woman who was suddenly met with paralyzing fear.

Content to let the startled woman experience her fright to the fullest, Bone remained motionless and silent until Pearl showed signs of recovering her senses. "Where is he?" he rasped, his voice low and menacing. When Pearl failed to answer, he took a step toward her. "You caused me a helluva lot of trouble, old woman. I know you carried him off. He ain't here. Where is he? Is he at that house you stopped at on the way up here?"

Recovering a measure of her spirit, she tried to regain control of her senses so seriously broadsided moments before. Unable to think of any answer to appease this monster, she said, "He's dead."

"What?" Bone blurted, taken aback. "Whaddaya mean, he's dead? Where's his body?"

Thinking as fast as she could, she stammered, "I don't know." Seeing the anger flashing in his evil face, she blurted, "Some of the folks from the church took him up in the hills and buried him! I don't know where. They just took him off in the hills."

Her claims stopped him momentarily. This was not a possibility he had foreseen. His first thought was that he had been cheated. He looked hard into the woman's eyes. Could she be telling the truth? With newfound defiance, she returned his steely gaze, unblinking. Within those few seconds, his mind raced over the trail he had followed to this cabin. McCrae had been wounded seriously, judging by the amount of blood he had found. It could have been a mortal wound. Still, Bone could not be totally satisfied until he saw the body. "You old bitch," he suddenly exclaimed. "You're lyin' to me."

Having recovered most of her grit, Pearl replied matter-of-factly, "Well, he ain't here, is he?"

"If you're lyin' to me . . ." he threatened, then stopped to decide. He was of a mind to put a bullet in the sassy old woman for the trouble she had caused him. She had lied to him from the start, when the man he hunted was right under her feet in the church. She could be lying to him now. "I want that bastard," he blurted, and pulled one of his pistols. "You're lyin', and I don't like liars." He pointed the weapon at her head.

She was helpless to stop him, but she refused to give him the satisfaction of seeing her whimper. "Go ahead, damn you. He'll still be dead."

Although his frustration was growing over a trail that had gone cold, he was still undecided about Pearl's truthfulness. But it appeared he was not going to scare her enough to admit it if she was lying. Maybe he *was* dead, but Bone couldn't be satisfied until he saw the body. "I expect I'll have a look in that other woman's house tomorrow," he said. "If I find out you're lyin', I might be back to visit you again. Next time I might not be in such a good mood."

Pearl was afraid to move until she heard his horse pull away from the house, but then she ran to the door, closed it, and inserted the crossbar to lock it. Only then did she dare to take a gentle breath and sigh, "Lordy mercy, I thought I was done for." Then she went to the cupboard to find the bottle she had used when treating Colt's wound.

"Damn, I need a drink bad," Jared Simmons mumbled to himself as he squinted painfully at the plate of food before him. His belly felt as empty as a dry well, but he couldn't eat. Whiskey had made the thought of food sickening to him. "Blue!" he yelled. Blue was the name he called his wife, shortened from her Cheyenne name meaning Blue Sky In Morning. "Go into town and fetch me a bottle. I'm hurtin'."

"There is no money," his wife replied. "Mr. Coolidge told me not to come back for whiskey unless I had money to pay for it."

"That son of a bitch," Jared groaned. "Tell him to put it on credit, and Mary will pay for it on her next payday."

"I did that last week, but he said no," she lied. Mary's meager pay barely covered the cost of food for the three of them. There was no money left over for his whiskey.

He shoved the plate away from him and laid his aching head on the table. "I swear, woman, I'm sick. I need my medicine." Blue gazed at him for a few moments before shaking her head slowly, thinking of the man she had left her father's tipi to marry—so many years ago. Her mother had been right about the white man and the white man's firewater. But the union had produced her daughter, Mary. That was the thought that gave her joy and sustained her. Leaving him there to suffer, she picked up her basket and left to search the cottonwoods by the creek for firewood.

Only vaguely aware that his wife had left the house, Jared remained with his head on the table, bemoaning his need for strong spirits, and alternately cursing Turk Coolidge for refusing to sell him whiskey on credit. During past years, when he still had a job with a freighter in Cheyenne, he had spent plenty of his pay in Turk's saloon. "The greedy son of a bitch," he mumbled. Lost in his sorrows, he failed to hear the front door open.

Walking quietly until he had a chance to determine what manner of welcome he might receive, Bone eased into the front room of the shabby plank house. Looking straight through the doorway to the kitchen, he could see the man seated at the table, his head down and mumbling to himself. Seeing a door to his left, he stepped over to it and peered inside the bedroom. It was empty. On the opposite wall of the bedroom, another door led to a second room next to the kitchen. Like the bedroom, it, too, was empty. Retracing his steps, he then walked into the kitchen and stopped behind the man at the table. "Looks like there ain't nobody home but you," he announced loudly.

Too miserable to be startled, and too sick to be scared, Jared didn't bother to lift his head. "Whatever you want, we ain't got any. Now get the hell outta my house unless you brought a bottle with you."

Bone was mildly astonished at the man's reaction to an intruder in his house. He guessed then the cause of Jared's malaise. Whiskey could do that to a man, if the man was weak enough. He stepped around in front of the table. "I'm lookin' for a man—name of Colt McCrae. Maybe you might know where he is."

"I don't know nothin' about no Colt McCrae," Jared slurred. "If I did, I wouldn't tell you."

"Is that a fact?" Bone replied. His anger never far below the surface, he bristled. Drawing his pistol, he grabbed Jared by the hair of his head and jerked his head up from the table. With the barrel of the pistol almost touching his nose, Jared's eyes opened wide in instant enlightenment. "Suppose I tell you I'm gonna blow a hole in your head if I don't get an answer outta you?"

"Hold on, now," Jared begged. "Just hold on a minute!" A few minutes earlier, he might have welcomed a shot in the head to alleviate his misery. Now with the opportunity at hand, he was of a different mind-set. Until this moment, he had not taken a good look at the intruder. After looking wide-eyed at the sinister face of his visitor, he had no doubt that the man would do exactly as he promised. The problem for Jared was that he did not know where Colt McCrae was. His wife and daughter were careful not to mention it when he was around, feeling him unreliable to keep it secret. "Oh, Lordy, mister, I swear I don't know where he is."

Disgusted, Bone cocked the hammer back, but then another possibility crossed his mind. "What if I was to buy you a bottle? Would that help your memory?"

Despair turned to salvation for an incurable drunk. He still had no notion where Colt McCrae was, but he could not pass on the possibility of a bottle of whiskey. He had to think of something, and the only thing that came to mind was to send this conveyor of doom off someplace far away from here. "Red Moon's camp!" he blurted just as Bone looked about ready to pull the trigger. Bone paused. "Red Moon's camp," Jared repeated, encouraged by Bone's hesitation. "It's a Cheyenne camp my wife came from. If they took him someplace, it was most likely there."

"How do I get there?" Bone asked, lowering the pistol.

"Where's my money?"

"Not till you tell me where that Cheyenne camp is."

"Let me see the money. How do I know you ain't gonna cheat me outta it?"

Bone was losing what little patience he possessed, but he continued to dicker with Jared. Holstering his pistol, he took a roll of paper money from his pocket and counted out ten dollars. "That'll buy you enough whiskey to kill you," he said. "I'll lay it right here on the table so you can look at it."

Jared's eyes opened even wider. "Mind you, it's been a spell since I've been back to Red Moon's village, and he don't stay in one place too long. He moves when the grass is grazed up." When Bone cocked a suspicious eye, Jared was quick to continue. "But he'll always stay somewhere along the same line of hills that rim Bear Basin. That's his huntin' ground. He's been movin' up and down that trough for as long as I can remember. You'll find him if you scout up and down that basin."

"I better," Bone warned, "or I'll be back to pay you a little visit."

Jared went on to give Bone directions from the north road out of town to the little stream called Bitter Branch. "Follow that branch northwest for a mile or so, you'll see a table-sized flat rock at the foot of a notch between the hills. That notch will lead you up into the hills to Bear Basin."

"Good enough," Bone proclaimed, and turned to leave while Jared eagerly grabbed the money from the table. He took two steps past Jared before drawing a pistol again and, striking a hard blow against the back of Jared's skull, knocked the unsuspecting drunkard to the floor, unconscious. Bone reached down and took the money from Jared's hand, then unhurriedly took his leave.

Chapter 13

Colt led the buckskin gelding down to the creek to drink, wincing occasionally when his foot landed unevenly on the ruts close by the water and jolting his sore ribs. He was not fully recovered from the loss of blood, but he could feel himself getting stronger each day, thanks to the meat stew that Walking Woman forced upon him two or three times a day. The bullet wound in his side was healing nicely, although there was still a small amount of blood on the bandage whenever the old woman changed it.

Two Cheyenne women greeted him cordially as they passed him on their way back to the lodges with water skins. He smiled and nodded in return. During his short stay in the camp he had picked up a few words of Cheyenne, but not enough to really communicate. He was thankful that Walking Woman knew more English words than he had learned in her language. The two words that he heard most often from her were "too soon." Knowing that he could not afford to linger long in the care of the old woman, he pushed himself to get back on his feet. She would wrinkle her brow in a deep frown, and scold, "Too soon, too soon." Picturing her now, as he stood watching his horse drink, he couldn't help but smile. He owed the old woman a lot, and he was sorry that he had nothing to give her in return. There were others he was indebted to: Red Moon, Pearl, and Mary, as well as the people of Red Moon's village, many of whom had brought food to Walking Woman's lodge for him.

Reaching for the saddle sling, he drew the rifle his uncle had sent with his horse. It was a Winchester '73, just like the one he had lost. Still, it would not ease the disappointment he felt over losing his own rifle, because that rifle had belonged to his father, and his father had specifically willed it to him.

He had not had a chance to test his new weapon, so he pulled it up to his shoulder now to get the feel of it. *Maybe*, he thought, *I can take the time to go hunting to repay Red Moon's people for their kindness.* He felt the obligation, but he could not escape the urgency to help his family. It had been a week since he had dropped off the face of the earth, and he was anxious to get back. Concerned over what his uncle and brother might be encountering with Drummond's men, he harbored a feeling of guilt for having been shot. Mary came to visit him a couple of times during the week, but she could not tell him what was happening between his family and Drummond, and as each day passed, he became more and more worried. "It's time to go," he announced to Buck. His decision to go was delayed, however, when Red Moon strode down to the creek to meet him.

The old chief was calling something out to him, re-

peating it over and over. Colt had no clue as to what
Red Moon was saying. It sounded like "wa'tis, wa'tis."
When Colt gestured that he didn't understand, Red
Moon tried to act out his meaning with gestures and
signs until Colt began to guess. "Buffalo?" Red Moon
shook his head and continued his pantomime until
Colt guessed, "Deer?"

Red Moon nodded excitedly. It sounded like the
white man's word he had been trying to remember.
Then he pointed to Colt's rifle and pretended to be
shooting an imaginary deer. "You want me to shoot a
deer?" Colt asked. Red Moon nodded again, even
though he did not understand Colt's words. Satisfied
that the white man understood, he beckoned Colt to
follow him. Not without a small measure of pain, Colt
climbed up in the saddle and followed the chief back
to the lodges, where he found several of the men preparing to ride. They were armed with bows and a couple of old single-shot rifles. When Red Moon told them
that the big white man, with the *spirit gun* that shoots
many times, was going to hunt with them, they raised
their weapons in a spontaneous cheer.

The hunt was on. Some of the young boys had
spotted a herd of deer moving through the hills beyond the village on their way to a shallow basin a mile
or so away. Colt and four of the older men rode out of
the camp, guided by the boys who had found the
deer. From the excitement among the group, Colt
guessed that game had been scarce recently, so his ea-
gerness for a chance to repay his hosts for their kindness and generosity with what food they had

overshadowed the slight discomfort caused by the jostling of the saddle.

The deer were sighted at the upper end of the basin, feeding beside a pool formed by the narrow stream that wound its way along the base of the hills. Considering the weapons they carried, the Cheyenne hunters were inclined to make a sudden strike into the herd, hoping to get in close enough to be effective. Through signs and gestures, Colt persuaded them to wait until he crossed over the range of hills and came up on the herd from the other side. He figured he could kill a couple of the deer from the hillside before they suspected they were under attack. The Winchester was not a true long-range rifle, but it was of considerably longer range than the old single-shot weapons he saw the hunters carrying. If he was lucky, and got in the right position, he might drive the rest of the herd toward the waiting Cheyenne. When finally he was sure of Colt's meaning, Red Moon nodded his agreement. Leaving their ponies with one of the boys to watch them, the hunters crept down the slope to take positions near the bottom, while Colt circled back to cross over to the other side of the basin.

The fact that he still had some healing to do was the thought in Colt's mind as he grunted with each breath when he left his horse on the ridge and worked his way down to a rocky crag about one hundred yards beyond the grazing deer. Bracing his weapon against the trunk of a stunted tree, he prepared to begin the slaughter. Drawing a bead on a large doe closest to him, he squeezed off his first shot. The rifle fired true. As the animal collapsed, Colt ejected the shell and

shifted his aim to down a second doe. The rest of the
herd, too startled to run when they heard the shots, realized the danger then, and bolted into flight, but not
before Colt dropped one more of their number. Luck
was with him, for the frightened deer bolted toward
the hunters waiting in ambush. Before the confused
animals could scatter into the hills, three more fell victim to the bullets and arrows of the hunters.

The hunting party returned to the village to a joy-
ous welcome. It had been some time since they had
seen a good supply of fresh meat. Watching the skinning and butchering, Colt was glad that he had delayed his departure long enough to lend a hand with
the hunt. The hunt had also satisfied him that he was
well enough to end his convalescence. Riding pro-
vided some discomfort, but it was tolerable. Firing the
Winchester offered a little stab of pain, but nothing he
couldn't deal with.

He lingered long enough to enjoy some of the feast
that was under way, then sought out Red Moon and
Walking Woman to thank them for their kindness.
Walking Woman seemed genuinely sad to see him
leave. She embraced him with an awkward hug, taking care not to squeeze his ribs, and scolding him with
the words he heard from her most often, "Too soon,
too soon. Dark soon, wait till morning."

"It's best for me to ride at night," Colt replied.

The chief had seen fit to give Colt a new name, a
Cheyenne name. "Nanose'hame," he said, "come back
to stay with us again."

Since it was all said in Cheyenne, Colt could only
respond with a smile and nod. "Nanose'hame?" he

repeated as well as he could, then looked at Walking Woman for help.

"New name," she explained, then thought hard, but could not come up with the English translation of his name. Finally, she shook her head and said, "Good, good."

He nodded again and repeated his new name a couple of times, hoping to remember it. Then he said good-bye to the people gathered around him, and stepped up in the saddle, preparing to leave. He hesitated when someone at the edge of the creek called out that a rider was approaching. Colt dismounted and drew his rifle.

Mary prodded her father's reluctant sorrel for more speed as she saw the smoke from the campfires wafting up into the fading light. The fires were larger and more numerous than usual as if the people were celebrating some occasion. It worried her, knowing that Bone was searching for Red Moon's village. If he was anywhere in the valley, he could hardly miss the glow from the fires. Afraid she would arrive too late to warn Colt, she had pressed the horse mercilessly all the way from town. It was with great relief, and somewhat of a surprise, to ride into the camp to discover Colt standing there by his horse.

"Colt!" she cried out upon seeing him. "You've got to get out of here!" Nodding and trying to smile at the people who crowded around to greet her, she pushed her way through to him. In the firelight, he could see the concern etched in her face, and came forward to meet her. "Thank God you're still alive," she exclaimed upon reaching him. "We've got to go at once. That monster is on his way here."

"He knows about this place?" Colt asked, surprised.

She hurriedly told him of Bone's visit to her father's house, and that her father had inadvertently told Bone that Colt was in Red Moon's village. "The foolish drunk," she complained, "he had no idea where you were. He just said you were here so he could get money for whiskey. He got his skull cracked for his trouble. Bone's not going to stop until he finds you. Pearl came to work this morning and said he followed her home last night. She thought he was going to kill her if she didn't tell him where you were. She told him you were dead, but he showed up at my house, and my father told him you were here."

Colt showed no emotion as she frantically told her tale. His first thought was to wait for the determined killer right there in the Cheyenne village. He was as eager to settle with Bone as the determined assassin was to kill him.

Seeing him hesitate, obviously weighing a decision in his mind, Mary pleaded urgently. "You've got to get out of here. He's coming to kill you." Still Colt hesitated. "If you don't care about yourself," Mary implored, "think about my grandmother's people." Gesturing at the people gathered around them, she went on. "These old men and women are not warriors. If the shooting starts here, innocent people will be killed."

Realizing that he had not given that possibility serious thought, he wavered. She was right. It would not be fair to bring Bone's wrath down on these innocent Cheyenne. It occurred to him then that to wait for Bone here would also place Mary in harm's way.

"If you are not here, he may search the village, but when he does not find you, he will go on his way— maybe think you really are dead," Mary argued.

Colt considered the possibility that Bone might do harm to someone, even if he didn't find him. Thinking it over, however, he decided that Bone probably wouldn't chance an arrow in his back if he was surrounded by Indians. "All right," Colt said, "climb on your horse, and I'll take you home."

Taking only a moment, Mary hugged her grandmother, then climbed up in the saddle. Red Moon said farewell to Colt once more, calling him by his Cheyenne name, as they wheeled their horses and splashed through the shallow creek and disappeared into the darkness. Since she was more familiar with the trail back to Whiskey Hill, Mary led the way as they galloped through the trough that served as the passage from Bear Basin. Once clear of the gulch, they stopped to rest the horses at Bitter Branch since Mary's horse had already been ridden pretty hard.

Watching the horses drink from the shallow stream, with the soft night enveloping them, they felt the sense of urgency fading considerably. "We'll let the horses rest for a little while longer," Colt said as he sat down on the bank beside Mary. "We drove 'em pretty hard through that gulch." He had something on his mind that he felt needed saying, but he wasn't very good at expressing his thoughts, so he hesitated a few moments before getting it out. "Mary," he started before pausing again, then continued. "I've been thinkin' about how much I owe you—and Pearl, too—for stickin' your neck out to help me. I just can't figure out why you're takin' the chances you have to help an ex-convict that everybody else is either tryin' to kill or run out of town." If he had not concentrated his gaze on the bank between his feet, he might have seen the warm smile on her face. "Anyway, I want you to know how much I appreciate what you've done for me."

"Colt McCrae," she replied, "if I thought you really did shoot that bank guard, or had anything to do with it, I wouldn't be lifting a finger to help you."

"I thank you for that," he said.

Amused by his shyness, she commented, "Evidently, old Red Moon took a liking to you. I heard him call you Mountain Lion."

"Mountain Lion?" Colt asked, surprised. "I thought it meant *good*. At least, that's what Walking Woman said."

Mary smiled. "No, he called you Mountain Lion." She was thinking it was a good name for him. There was something in his manner that suggested the savage strength of the mountain lion. "You should be honored," she said. "Red Moon doesn't think much of white men in general."

He thought about what she said for a few moments. Then, finding no words to express his feelings on the matter, he said, "I reckon the horses are rested enough." He reached down to help her up, taking her arm when she extended it. Light as a feather, she came up a little too fast, and fell against him, remaining there for a few seconds before regaining her balance.

He quickly released her arm, but the sensation of her body pressed against his, if only for that moment, reminded him how long it had been since he had felt the touch of a woman. He immediately hoped she had not taken offense.

He acted like I burned him, she thought. She prepared to climb up in the saddle, thinking that it might have been nice to remain pressed against his body for a little while longer. *Pearl would scold me for thinking such a thing,* she thought, smiling. Leaving Bitter Branch, they set out across the prairie toward Whiskey Hill.

It was just past midnight when Colt and Mary reined up before Mary's house. A lamp lit up in the window when they walked their horses up to the front porch. Moments later, Mary's mother came out on the porch to greet them. Worried for her daughter, Blue Sky In Morning rushed to embrace her.

"I'll put your horse in the barn for you," Colt said, and reached down to take the reins.

"What are you planning to do?" Mary asked.

"I guess I'll go on out to my uncle's place. Oughta get there by sunup."

"Colt, you must be hungry," Mary said. "You come on in the house after you put my horse up, and I'll find you something to eat."

"There's no need for that," Colt said. "I won't put you to the trouble."

"No trouble," Blue Sky In Morning insisted. "You come in."

"You need to build your strength," Mary reminded him. "Mind my mother. Mothers know best."

He laughed. "All right, if you're sure you don't mind," he said.

Colt turned Jared Simmons' horse out in the corral and returned to the house to find Mary preparing to fry some bacon while her mother freshened the fire in the stove before placing a cake of corn bread on the edge to warm. Colt hadn't realized he was hungry until the sharp aroma of the frying pork filled his nostrils. There was still coffee left in the pot from supper as well, so Colt graciously sat down at the table. When the food was ready, Mary sat down across from him to watch him eat.

"What's he doin' here?" Jared Simmons demanded as soon as he saw the stranger sitting at the kitchen table. Asleep until moments before when the aroma of bacon awakened him, he stumbled out of the bedroom, a rag bandage wrapped around his head, the gash it covered the result of Bone's parting blow.

"He brought me home," Mary quickly replied. "I just fixed him a little something to eat before he leaves." She exchanged a worried glance with her mother.

"Well, food's cheap enough," Jared snarled sarcastically. "Might as well feed every saddle tramp that knocks on the door."

Colt held his tongue, not wishing to cause any trouble for Mary or her mother. He continued to eat while the belligerent drunk glared at him. After a moment, Jared blurted, "You're that son of a bitch everybody's lookin' for, ain'tcha? And you're settin' at my table eatin' my food? Mister, you can get your sorry ass outta here right now!"

Mary jumped to her feet in alarm. "You set down!" Jared roared, jabbing a finger in the air.

"Jared!" Blue Sky In Morning cried out. "I asked him to eat. Mary paid for the food. She can give it to who she wants."

Jared lashed out with a backhand to his wife's face, knocking her back in her chair. "Don't you ever tell me who eats food in my house," he threatened. He drew his hand back to strike her again.

Like the mountain lion for which he had recently been named, Colt sprang from his chair, knocking it across the kitchen floor. Before Jared's hand could strike again, Colt caught it in an iron grip, and with one violent move, slammed Jared against the wall, bouncing his head on the planking. "Yes, damn you, I'm the son of a bitch everybody's lookin' for. And I'm the son of a bitch who's gonna string your guts on the clothesline if I ever hear you hit one of these women again." He grabbed a handful of the stunned man's hair and rapped his head sharply against the wall again. "Do we have an understandin' on that? 'Cause I don't like cowards who beat women, and I'd just as soon shoot your cowardly ass as look at you." He released him then, and Jared slid down the wall to sit dazed on the floor.

"Come," Blue Sky In Morning said to her husband, "I will help you back to bed. You'll be all right in the morning." She pulled his arms, but could not budge the stunned man. Colt reached down and, grabbing him by the back of his collar, pulled him up on his feet. Jared stared straight ahead in bewildered silence.

"Come," Blue Sky In Morning repeated, and he allowed her to lead him back to the bedroom.

Colt, his rage still simmering, watched the belligerent man with eyes flashing lightning until he was out of the room. Only then able to calm himself, he turned to Mary. "You'll be all right?"

She nodded. "I think so." Then, seeing the red stain on his shirt, she exclaimed, "Your wound's bleeding again!"

He looked down at the deerskin shirt Walking Woman had given him to replace the one ruined by his gunshot. Blood had begun to seep through from the bandage. "I guess I pulled it apart," he said. "It'll stop soon." Walking over to pick up the chair he had knocked over, he pushed it up to the table. "I'll be goin' now." He looked at Blue Sky In Morning. "I'm obliged for the food, ma'am."

Mary followed him outside and stood by his stirrup while he mounted. "Where will you go?" she asked.

"I'll go to the Broken-M tonight," he replied. "I expect they're wonderin' where I am."

"Colt, be careful." She stepped back. He nodded and wheeled Buck around. She watched him until he faded into the night. *I wonder if my feelings for him are getting too strong,* she thought. That could be a bad mistake with a man like that. Pearl would certainly tell her that quick enough.

Brownie Brooks sat close to the fire while he strained his eyes to examine the wound in his leg. "Bad business," he mumbled as he picked at a little pocket of pus that had formed on one end of the wound. "It mighta had a chance to heal up proper if Mr. Drummond coulda let me rest it like the doctor said." Unhappy with the job he had been given to keep an eye on the Broken-M ranch house, he crowded even closer to his small campfire. "What in hell could a man see out here in the dark, anyway? Hell, I couldn't see a dozen riders from this ridge at night." The ridge, some five or six hundred yards from Burt McCrae's ranch house, was as close as Brownie dared to get. Even that was too close to suit him. A man who was half good with a rifle could pick him off at that distance. For that reason, he intended to move back a couple hundred yards before sunup.

Finished with picking at his wound, he made himself as comfortable as he could, and pulled his blanket over him. "Ain't nobody comin' or goin' this time of night," he said as he pulled his hat down tight and tucked his whiskers inside his blanket. In less than a quarter of an hour, he was sleeping. An hour before sunrise, his snores still resonated off the chill night breeze as he slept the peaceful sleep of the simpleminded—unaware of the man quietly walking into his camp.

Pausing to look at the sleeping form for a brief moment, Colt recognized him as the man he had shot in the leg. He reached down and picked up the rifle resting across the saddle. Brownie snorted, but did not awaken. Colt stepped around him and walked over to Brownie's horse. Removing the hobbles from the horse's fetlocks, he led the obedient animal away.

•　　　•　　　•

Tom Mosley came out of the bunkhouse to spot a rider approaching, leading a horse. He squinted against the sunlight for a moment until the rider reached the creek and he identified the visitor. "Colt," he exhaled softly, then sang out for those in the house to hear. "Colt!" he yelled. "It's Colt!" He was soon joined by Bill Wilkes, followed in a few seconds by Burt coming from the house. They stood waiting to greet his nephew as he walked the horses up to the porch.

"Where'd you get the extra horse, Colt?" Tom asked as Colt dismounted.

"From a feller back there on the ridge," Colt replied. "He wasn't usin' him."

Tom threw his head back with a hearty chuckle, well aware of the constant surveillance. "It's a long walk back to Drummond's ranch totin' a saddle."

"Especially with a bad leg," Colt said.

"Lord knows, you're a sight for sore eyes," Burt McCrae said. "How's the wound comin' along?"

Colt replied that the wound was healing fine, that Walking Woman had given him the best of care. His ribs were the cause of most of his discomfort. "Sorry I had to leave you shorthanded," he said.

"Well, come on in the house," Burt said. "Rena will fix you some breakfast."

Inside, they were joined by Vance and Susan. Colt was disappointed to see how slowly his brother was recovering from his wound, but he had not been counting on Vance's gun in the business to be concluded with Frank Drummond. "Have there been any more raids since I've been gone?"

"No," Burt answered. "They've been satisfied with just settin' on that ridge up there and watching us. I think Drummond ain't got enough men left to do any real fightin'. They plundered Vance's place, but at least they didn't burn it down. We're just too thin to cover both houses."

"What about the sheriff?" Colt asked. "Has he done anything about it, one way or the other?"

"Hell," Burt snorted. "There ain't no sheriff. That gunman Drummond hired shot Stoney Yates, and J.D. just cut out and headed for who knows where."

Colt let that register in his mind before responding. "Well, I reckon that wasn't much of a loss for the town."

Burt watched his nephew eat for a few minutes before asking, "What are you aimin' to do now?"

"I'm thinkin' I'd best get back to that Cheyenne camp. Mary's pa told that gunman of Drummond's that I was there. He's been lookin' all over creation for me, and I think it's time he found me. Then I reckon we've got to settle this fight with Drummond."

When the early rays of the sun lit upon his face, Brownie Brooks stirred briefly before shifting his body, looking for a more comfortable position. Still half asleep, he reached down to pull his blanket up closer around his shoulders, only then remembering that he'd planned to move his camp back from the ridge before full daylight descended. Reluctantly, he sat up and poked around in his campfire in an effort to rekindle a flame. "Damn, it's cold," he commented. It occurred to him then that there was no sound from his horse. Knowing the horse wouldn't be far away, he looked all around him. "Well, where the hell . . ." he started to question, but his eye caught sight of his hobbles lying on the ground some twenty feet away. At once alarmed, he reached for his rifle. It wasn't there. Near panic then, he jumped up and looked all around him on the ridge. There was no one in sight. He strained to see down the ridge toward the ranch house he had been watching. He could see no activity as yet on the frosty morning.

Knowing he'd better not linger on this spot, lest Burt McCrae and one of his hands decide to ride out again to challenge him, he hurriedly picked up his belongings, not waiting to make breakfast. It didn't make sense, he thought, as he hefted his saddle up on his shoulder and started walking as fast as he could manage under his burden. *Injuns?* he wondered. *That don't hardly figure, since I still got my scalp.* No, he told himself, somebody from the Broken-M had to have a hand in this. The more he thought about it, the more foolish he felt. How in hell was he going to explain this to Mr. Drummond?

The sun was just beginning to climb above the hills as Brownie trudged along. The load of his saddle was already bearing down, rubbing a sore spot on his shoulder, and he was forced to limp to favor his wounded leg. He was reluctant to leave his saddle behind, so he had no choice but to continue on, placing one already weary foot before the other. His simple mind was a mass of confusing thoughts as he berated himself for being fleeced while he slept, and tried to picture the storm he could expect to see in Frank Drummond's face.

So much occupied with these thoughts, and thinking about the distance he had to walk, he failed to notice the slow plodding of the horses following along some thirty yards behind him. Finally realizing he was not alone when one of the horses snorted, he jerked his head around to look behind him. A new panic arose when he discovered the stern countenance of the man astride the big buckskin, casually content to follow along behind him. *Colt McCrae!* The name screamed out in his brain, and he dropped the saddle on the ground. Then he stumbled over it as he reached for the pistol on his side. Once it was free of the holster, he hesitated to raise it when he considered the Winchester aimed at him. He knew he was a dead man if he raised the weapon. Easing it back in the holster, he decided it better odds to beg for his life. He sat down on the saddle and waited.

"I reckon you got the drop on me," he said as the somber-faced man rode unhurriedly up to pull his horse to a stop before him. "You got no call to shoot me. I wasn't killin' no cattle or nothin'. I just camped for the night—wasn't doin' no harm to nobody."

"Is that a fact?" Colt replied and continued to fix his gaze on the nervous man. "I figure you've been spying on the Broken-M. This is war, and spies are shot durin' wartime."

"Whoa, now wait a minute, mister," Brownie quickly replied. "I ain't no spy!"

"Then what the hell are you doin' on McCrae range?" He cocked his rifle.

"Wait! Dammit!" Brownie blurted. "I'm just a hired hand. I got no quarrel with you or your uncle."

"Is that so?" Colt replied. It was plain to him that Brownie was becoming a bit unraveled. "I've been lookin' at that rifle I picked up this mornin', and I'm thinkin' it's the rifle that put a bullet in my father's back. Somebody's gotta pay for that."

"Wait! Wait!" Brownie cried as Colt brought the rifle up, the barrel looking at Brownie's face. "Mister, I swear, I ain't ever shot nobody. I weren't anywhere around when your pa got shot."

"That may be, but somebody's got to pay for it, and you're the one that got dealt the losing hand."

Colt brought the Winchester up to his shoulder, preparing to pull the trigger. "But I know who did!" Brownie blurted, his eyes wide with terror.

This was what Colt had hoped to scare out of the frightened man. "All right," he said. "You've got about two minutes to tell me what you know. If it doesn't sound right to me, you're on your way to hell."

"God's honest truth," Brownie pleaded. "Me and Lon Branch rode over to the Bar-M and waited while Mr. Drummond rode in to talk to your pa. When Mr. Drummond came back, he was madder'n a hornet. He grabbed Lon's rifle and went back about two hundred yards or more. When your pa rode out, Mr. Drummond cut down on him. I ain't never seen Mr. Drummond dirty his hands like that before or after."

Though he gave no indication, Colt was stunned. After a moment, he said, "That's the story you wanna take to your Maker?"

"It's the truth, I swear it," Brownie stammered.

"Please don't kill me. Let me go and I'll ride outta Wyoming Territory right now."

With the answer to the one question he wanted answered most, Colt continued to fix his gaze on the defeated man's face. Was Brownie telling the truth? Colt decided that he was. He brought the rifle up to his shoulder again.

The doomed man's eyelids began to flutter uncontrollably as Colt took deliberate aim and squeezed the trigger. Terrified, Brownie braced himself for the shot. His heart skipped a beat when he heard the metallic click of the hammer falling on an empty chamber. "Shit!" he screamed involuntarily as if it had been the sound of a gunshot.

"If I see you around here again, I'll kill you," Colt pronounced. Then he dropped the reins to Brownie's horse and tossed his empty rifle on the ground. Without another word, he nudged the buckskin into a lope, and left the shaken gunman on the prairie.

"You ain't gonna get the chance to kill me," Brownie mumbled to himself when Colt had ridden out of hearing distance. "I've had enough." Feeling it was high time for him to find a healthier climate, he struck out for parts unknown.

Chapter 14

Frank Drummond scowled at the three men left to run his ranch as they stood nervously waiting for his orders. He had not slept well during the night just past. Thoughts of frustration had kept his mind churning with the anguish of seeing his once invincible gang of men reduced to these three sorry specimens standing before him. For a man accustomed to the conqueror's role, it was excruciating to admit defeat so far in this contest with the McCraes.

What troubled him most at this moment was the question of whether Burt's nephew, Colt, was alive or dead. Rafe was halfway convinced that McCrae had been mortally wounded in the ambush on his buckboard. Bone had not returned to collect his money, and Drummond was determined not to pay him a cent without positive proof of Colt's demise. Where in the hell was the notorious killer? Drummond wondered with the dawn of a new day and Bone still not returned.

Drummond was anxious to move on Burt McCrae. Young Vance's ranch had been abandoned, according to his lookouts, and it appeared that both families were holed up on the Broken-M. Had Drummond not lost so many men, he would already have sent in a half dozen guns to claim the Bar-M. But with only three, he could not spare any of them when he moved against Burt McCrae. It had to be a complete victory, with no one left to talk about it—man, woman, or child. Still, he would prefer to know for certain that Colt McCrae was not out there somewhere waiting. He decided to wait one more day for news from Bone.

"Rafe," he ordered, "ride on out to Broken-M and relieve Brownie. He's probably bellyachin' already about bein' out there all night. And, Rafe, take some grub, 'cause you're gonna be there all night. You keep a sharp eye. I wanna know who's comin' and goin', 'cause tomorrow I'm gonna make him an offer he ain't gonna turn down this time."

"Whaddaya want us to do about the stock, Mr. Drummond?" Charlie Ware asked. "We got cattle strayin' all over hell and then some." During the past week, Rocking-D cattle were finding their way onto Bar-M and Broken-M land. It had become more than Drummond's skeleton crew could control.

"We'll worry about that next week," Drummond replied. "It won't matter where they stray then, they'll still be on my land."

His mind was racing to weigh the decision he was about to make, after Brownie Brooks' startling revelation. Colt would never have suspected that Frank Drummond was the man who actually pulled the trigger that killed his father. He figured Drummond to be a man who never dirtied his hands, preferring to hire gun hands to take care of things of that nature. When he first heard, he was ready to forget all other issues. The most important reason he had returned to Whiskey Hill was to settle with the man who had killed his father. He immediately turned his horse toward the Rocking-D.

The farther he rode, however, the more other things crowded into his thoughts. Mary Simmons and her grandmother came to the forefront of his conscience, and the lethal shadow that was bearing down on that peaceful village preyed upon his sense of duty. Red Moon and Walking Woman were not prepared for a poisonous snake like Bone to slither into their quiet camp. He tried to tell himself that the Cheyenne men of that village could easily handle one gunman. They could certainly take responsibility for their own protection. Even as he thought it, he knew it was not the case. Red Moon and his people were no longer warriors. They rode the warpath too many years ago. The young men had left the small band of old people long before this time. No, he, Colt McCrae, must be the warrior to face Bone. Frank Drummond would have to wait. With these thoughts weighing heavily upon his mind, he turned Buck's head toward Bear Basin and the inevitable showdown with Bone.

It was late afternoon when Bone's horse topped the last ridge between the basin and Willow Creek. He pulled the horse to a stop and sat looking down for a while on the tiny Cheyenne village on the opposite side of the creek. There was very little activity other than a few cook fires started before several of the tipis. A few old women trod back and forth to the water. A group of four men sat talking before one of the fires. There was no sign of a white man. There was still the question of how badly McCrae was shot. If his wounds were minor, Bone might have spotted him outside one of the lodges—more serious, he could still be inside one of the lodges. Bone meant to find out which.

With a kick of his heels, he started down the slope, angling across the ridge toward the camp at a fast walk. He had approached to within one hundred yards before one of the men in the circle of four stood up and pointed toward him, alerting the others. Bone continued his steady approach, crossing the creek at a shallow ford, then climbing the bank, his rifle cradled in his arms. The entire village was alert to his arrival by this time, and began to slowly converge on the four men by the fire.

When within a distance of forty yards, Bone held up one arm and spoke in the Cheyenne tongue. "I come as a friend of the Cheyenne," he announced.

Red Moon raised his right arm and answered, "Come, then. If you come in peace, you are welcome." Red Moon and his friends watched the white man dismount. A curious man, he carried the look of a dark spirit, and Red Moon wondered if this was the man Little Star had fled the village to avoid. "What brings you to our humble village?" he asked.

"I come to find a man," Bone replied, "a bad white man. I heard that he was in your village. He is wounded, and I have come to get him." Holding his rifle with his right hand on the trigger guard and the barrel resting across his left forearm, Bone stood ready in case his peaceful ploy failed.

Red Moon noticed the two pistols, their holsters reversed so that he could see the butts facing forward, and he remembered Mary's description of the evil man she feared. "There is no white man in our village," he replied truthfully.

"Is that a fact?" Bone responded skeptically in English. Then in Cheyenne, he said, "This is a bad man, and the soldiers sent me to find him. He will do bad things to your people. I fear he is hiding in one of your tipis, and is threatening your people. I'll look in your tipis to make sure he is not here." He watched Red Moon's face closely to see if the chief was buying his story, but there was no change in the old man's expression. There was, however, a general restless stirring among the people gathered around them that immediately put Bone on guard.

Red Moon held up his hand to quiet his people. This man was not sent by the soldiers, of that he was sure, but some of his people would surely be killed if they determined to deny him. "I say to you, there is no white man in our camp, but you may look for yourself if it pleases you."

Bone stood looking into the chief's eyes for a few moments. Then he shifted his gaze to scan the passive faces of the people gathered around Red Moon. *He ain't here*, he thought, disappointed. There was no need to search the tipis. "All right," he said. "I believe what you say. But he *was* here. Where is he now?"

Red Moon saw no need to put his niece, Little Star,

in danger, so he lied when he said, "He left here, but did not say where he was going."

"He was wounded," Bone insisted. "How bad was his wound?"

Red Moon shrugged as if unconcerned. "Wounded bad, maybe he went off to die."

Bone studied Red Moon's face intently. He could not be sure if the old chief was sincere, or just an accomplished liar. He looked around him at the other old men standing by, their faces as devoid of expression as their chief's. He knew he was wasting his time. "Which way did he go?" he asked. Red Moon pointed toward the way from which Bone had just come. Making no attempt to hide his disgust, Bone stepped up in the saddle and took his leave. It was useless to think about scouting around the camp to try to pick up McCrae's trail. There were too many tracks coming and going, and he wasn't familiar with the horse's tracks he wanted to follow, anyway. Added to that was the scarcity of daylight. It was already late in the day, and he was not familiar enough with the trail to find his way in the dark. He decided to head back toward Whiskey Hill and ride until darkness caught up with him. If McCrae was still alive, he would pick up his trail somewhere. It was just a matter of time before he tracked him down. Bone was confident in the knowledge that he was the best. He was a born tracker and he had never failed to bring his prey to ground.

A heavy layer of low-lying clouds crept steadily over the foothills, borne on a northwest wind as Bone departed the Indian camp, and darkness descended upon him at the southern end of Bear Basin. If his memory served him, he estimated the notch that led him to Bitter Branch was probably no more than half an hour's ride. Figuring another half an hour to pass through the notch, that worked out to about an hour to a campsite with water. Bone could do without water, but his horse couldn't, so he pushed on into the night. After a little more than the hour he had figured, he made camp on the bank of Bitter Branch. With fingers stiff with the cold, he fashioned a bed of tinder to receive the spark from his flint and steel. In five minutes' time, he had a small flame fighting for its life. He carefully fed it twigs and small limbs to sustain it until it breathed full life. With nothing to eat but a handful of dried jerky, and needing nothing more, the hunter of men settled in to wait for daylight.

Separated by a distance of less than a quarter mile, on the opposite side of the ridge, another camper replicated many of the same motions as those just made by Bone. On his way to Red Moon's village, Colt McCrae made his camp upstream on Bitter Branch. A cold wind freshened as he built his fire in a shallow dry wash, after hobbling Buck. Looking up at the clouds, he guessed it likely that he might wake up to a blanket of snow.

The night passed peacefully. It was still a while before sunup when Colt was awakened by a soft dusting of snow. He took some of the limbs he had gathered the night before and rebuilt his fire. It was still not light enough to get started, but he figured by the time he made some coffee and cooked a little bacon over the fire, it would be. He was satisfied to see that the snow had not amounted to much. The wind was still up, so it was probably responsible for moving the snow clouds along. Unbeknownst to him, the wind took on the responsibility for another task, one more threatening than the movement of snow clouds.

On the opposite side of the ridge, Bone's eyes flickered open, and he lay there listening. Like a hungry timber wolf, he sensed something, but there was no sound other than the patient labor of the stream. He rose on one elbow and sniffed the morning air, realizing at once what had alerted his senses. He smelled smoke. He got to his feet at once, sniffing like a predator on the prowl. His curiosity aroused, he looked to the tops of the pines to determine the wind direction. He could see no smoke, but the wind was coming from the west, causing a downdraft after it crossed the ridge, and there was no doubt in his mind that the scent of a campfire was being carried on that wind.

Could be Indians, he thought, *or a hunting party maybe. I'd best take a look on the other side of that ridge.* Taking only enough time to saddle his horse, he picked his way carefully up the dark slope to within a few dozen yards of the top before dismounting and leaving the horse; then he crawled the rest of the way. Settling on his stomach, he looked down the slope. Unable to spot the source of the smoke, he scanned the shadowy banks of the stream on both sides, straining to see in the predawn light. Convinced that there was someone below him, he determined to wait out the sunrise to see who it was.

The light of a new day gradually began to empty the gullies and switches of their dark shadows, although it would still be a while before the sun climbed high enough to illuminate the cloudy sky. Colt reached for the coffeepot now boiling busily on the fire. It suddenly jumped as if alive a split second before his hand touched the handle, and clattered nosily against the side of the dry wash, a bullet hole drilled neatly through its middle. Colt dived away from the fire, rolling over against the edge of the gully as the sound of the rifle rang out over his head. Two more shots followed in quick succession, digging chunks of clay and rock out of the bank.

While cursing himself for being careless, he crawled over to retrieve the rifle he had left beside his saddle. Two more shots closer to the fire told him that his assailant could probably not see him, but was just hoping for a lucky shot. He quickly moved farther down the dry wash to take a position behind a brace of young pines. Then with eyes straining to search the slope above him, he watched for some movement in the shadows or a muzzle flash. With no clue as to where the shots had come from, there was nothing he could do but wait.

Dammit! Bone berated himself for missing with his first shot. *The son of a bitch moved. I had him dead in my sights.* Unsure of the identity of the man camped below him, he had hesitated, watching as Colt tended his fire. As the predawn light brightened, he caught a glimpse of the horse a few yards away. It was a buckskin. He had been told that Colt McCrae rode a buckskin. That was confirmation enough for him, and he quickly leveled his rifle and fired, but his man had moved by that time. Furious with himself for not firing when he had a better shot, he was now frustrated by the fact that he could no longer see his prey, and he wasn't sure if one of his shots had found the target or not. Wasting no time speculating, he scrambled over the top of the ridge and made his way from one spot of cover to the next, descending the slope as fast as he possibly could. His main concern at this point was to prevent his prey's attempt to escape. He reached a point halfway down the hill in time to get a glimpse of the buckskin horse disappearing under the bank of the stream. *He's running!* he thought, and made a dash for a rock formation overhanging the water.

Forty yards downstream from the spot where Bone had taken cover, Colt dropped down behind a grassy hummock on the bank. With his horse safely under the cover of the stream bank, he scouted the slope above him. He saw nothing for a few seconds. Then there was a sudden movement in the corner of his eye, and he jerked his head around in time to see his assailant a step or two away from an outcropping of rock near the bank. He raised his rifle and fired, but there was no time to take dead aim.

Breathing hard from his flight down the hill, Bone ducked low behind the rocks when a slug ricocheted overhead. Realizing then that the man he hunted was not in frightened retreat, he reconsidered his first impulse to charge after him. He then remembered Drummond's warning that Colt McCrae was a different breed. The thought drew a thin smile across Bone's face. *He might be a different breed of cat*, he thought, *but I've skinned every breed there is.* He drew confidence in the knowledge that no man had ever bested him when the stakes were life and death.

There was no doubt in Colt's mind that the gunman stalking him was the man called Bone. He showed no sign of retreating after his first attempt to bushwhack him failed, unlike the typical riffraff Drummond hired. Consequently, Colt decided he had better show the notorious killer some respect. He looked around him at the spot in which he had landed. It would not have been his first choice for a defensive position. The stream widened out at that point before converging again to take a sharp turn around a stand of willow trees some thirty yards behind him. If Bone decided to work back up the slope a ways, he might very easily pin Colt down against the bank.

He had no sooner given birth to the thought than it apparently occurred to Bone as well. Suddenly, there he was, but only for a second as he dashed from the rocks and dived into a clump of pines a few yards up the slope. Colt got off a shot, but it kicked up dirt harmlessly behind Bone's boot heel. Trying to guess what his adversary was up to, he followed the belt of thick pines with his eyes. There was a narrow ledge about three-quarters of the way up the slope just beyond the pines. *I can't stay here*, he thought. *If he gets up on that ledge above me, I won't be able to hide or run.* He considered his options as he hastily saddled Buck. If he made a run for it downstream, he would present his back as a broad target for thirty or forty yards before reaching the cover of the willows where the stream made a turn. The only option left was to ride hell-for-leather back upstream to the rock formation Bone had just vacated, and gamble on the notion that Bone was still moving along toward the ledge. It was impossible to know for sure because of the solid screen of pine trees that led up to the ledge. One thing for certain, the closer Bone got to that ledge, the more the angle improved to give him a clear shot at anything in the streambed.

Working furiously, he finished saddling his horse and jumped on his back. The buckskin bounded into a full gallop. With Colt lying low on the horse's neck, they raced away up the shallow stream toward the rock formation. The quick retreat must have taken Bone by surprise, for no shots rang out after them. *So far, so good*, Colt thought. Then another thought crossed his mind. *Bone's horse has to be on the other side of this ridge.* If he could beat him back to his horse, he would have his adversary on foot.

Calling for everything the faithful gelding had in reserve, Colt gained the cover of the rocks just as bullets started flying around him—Bone having realized Colt's sudden flight. Once he found cover, Colt pulled his horse to a stop while he studied the slope before him. In the morning sunlight now, he could see Bone's tracks where he had descended the hill. He nudged Buck, and the big horse responded.

Back in the pine thicket, Bone was caught in the middle of reloading when Colt broke from the rocks. At first he thought that his man was running again; then he thought of his horse left near the top of the slope. "I'll be damned," he uttered defiantly, realizing what Colt had in mind. He started back up the hill as fast as he could manage. Since he was farther up the slope to begin with, he was just able to win the race with the man on the horse. He whistled twice and his horse obediently trotted to him. With his horse safely out of harm's way, he dropped to one knee and prepared to fire as soon as Colt appeared over the crest of the hill.

Damn, I hadn't counted on that, Colt thought as he reached the top in time to see the blue roan trotting away across the brow of the ridge. He didn't wait. Throwing caution to the wind, he went after the roan at a gallop, hoping to get a shot at Bone. He charged over the top of the ridge to discover he had ridden headlong into an ambush.

It happened in an instant, Colt saw Bone kneeling, waiting, his rifle aimed at him, and he knew he had but one option. He didn't take time to think about it. Rolling off his horse as the startled buckskin skidded to a stop, he heard Bone's rifle shot snap over his head while he was in midair.

Landing hard on his side, he grunted with pain as his still tender ribs protested the rough landing on the hillside. Struggling to get to his hands and knees, he found he could not breathe. The fall had knocked the wind out of his lungs, but in spite of the pain, he forced himself to scramble back below the rim of the ridge. The impact with the ground had also almost caused him to lose his rifle, but he had somehow managed to hold on to it, knowing it determined whether he lived or died. The pain in his chest was excruciating, but he didn't know what he could do to restore his breathing. Once when he was a boy, he had come off a horse and landed on his back. The same thing had happened then. But that time his uncle Burt had moved his legs up and down until his lungs relaxed and he could breathe again. Remembering that, he tried to work his legs, but there was no relief. The one thing he knew he must do at the moment was to find cover. Feeling as though he might black out at any moment, he collapsed behind a low evergreen shrub. It offered no real protection other than a visual screen, but he had no time for anything better. Gradually, after a few more seconds, he felt his chest relax, and his lungs began to take in air again, and he crawled over to the edge of the shrubs. Bone was bound to come over the top of the ridge after him, so he trained his rifle on the spot he figured him to show.

When his target came off the horse, Bone wasn't sure if his bullet had hit him or not. If Colt was shot, Bone was anxious to finish him off before he had a chance to drag himself off somewhere to hide. Far too smart to charge recklessly over the top of the hill, however, Bone proceeded to work his way along the ridge to his right, taking care not to expose his body above the brow. The anticipation of a kill swelled in his mind, and his senses told him it would be soon now.

Colt crowded even closer to the edge of the pine shrubs in an effort to broaden his field of fire, his gaze still focusing upon the spot where he thought Bone would show. When there was no sign of the hired killer for a few minutes, Colt decided that Bone might be trying to flank him. A few seconds after that thought, movement off to his left caused him to shift suddenly, set to pull the trigger, only to discover he was about to shoot his horse. In less than an instant, he shifted back again when Bone rose to shoot. Both rifles fired at the same time. Bone's bullet passed so close to Colt's ear that the snapping sound made Colt's ear ring, but otherwise caused no damage. Colt reacted in time to see his bullet strike Bone in the arm, spinning the surprised gunman around.

Stunned, Bone retreated a few yards down the slope. He dropped to one knee to examine the wound in his arm. Just below the shoulder, it was beginning to bleed. He could feel the blood spreading on his shirtsleeve although he could not see it beneath the long black coat he wore. Almost staggered by the fact that he had been shot, he was caught in an emotional whirlwind between astonishment and anger. There was no time to shuck the coat and determine the seriousness of the wound before McCrae might appear on top of the hill. He tested the movement in his arm, and while there was now pain involved, the limb seemed to be functioning. With some relief then, he cursed. "I'll cut you up in little pieces for that, you son of a bitch!" Realizing he was not in a good spot to defend, he ran back to retrieve his horse.

Colt cautiously inched his way up the slope, expecting to be met at any second with a bullet. He knew he had hit Bone with one of his shots, but he was reasonably certain it had not been a fatal wound. He dropped to the ground before exposing himself above the brow of the ridge, and crawled the rest of the way on hands and knees. Peering carefully over the top, he was surprised to see Bone on horseback, galloping away. Springing up on one knee, he attempted to get off a shot, but there were too many trees in between. He wasted a cartridge anyway. He knew very little about the man who hunted him, but his instincts told him that Bone had not quit the fight, so Colt hurried to catch his horse and give pursuit. The hunted was now the hunter.

His features twisted in a furious scowl, Bone bent low over his horse's neck as he sped recklessly down the slope toward Bitter Branch, glancing over his shoulder frequently to see the buckskin hard on his trail. The blood dripping from his fingertips told him that he needed to tend to the wound before he lost too much of it. Finding cover to give him a chance to stop the bleeding, and maybe set up an ambush, was his main concern at the moment. When he reached the bottom of the slope, he pressed the blue roan harder, splashing across the stream, and heading for the hills beyond. With each stride the roan took, Bone's anger burned hotter and hotter. This was not a role he was accustomed to, being chased, and his very soul screamed for vengeance.

Colt bent low in the saddle as Buck gave chase. There was no need to press the horse for speed. The buckskin understood the game, and Colt knew he would force himself to falter before he willingly gave up the race. Bone was obviously looking for a place to hide, probably intent upon reversing the roles to become once again the stalker. One thing Bone did not know, however, was that Colt had spent much of his boyhood roaming these foothills of the Laramie Mountains.

Both horses began to tire as Bone galloped down a grassy draw toward a line of low hills to the west. *In a short time*, Colt thought, feeling Buck strain to lengthen his stride, *this race will be at a slow walk.* At the base of the first in the line of hills, there was a narrow gulch that divided it from the second hill. Colt knew the place. When he was a boy, he had followed a deer into the gulch. He figured Bone would seek cover there. It appeared to be a perfect bastion to hold off an attack, but Colt knew there was a back door to that gulch, for he had lost the deer many years ago. With horses now tiring to the point of faltering, Bone did just as Colt figured.

Veering sharply to the west, Bone drove into the gulch, coming out of the saddle before his horse had pulled to a full stop. Crouching beside the entrance, he laid down a series of rifle shots, causing Colt to veer off to the north and press Buck for one more burst of speed. It was just about all the weary horse had left, and Colt dismounted as soon as he reached the cover of the trees at the base of the hill.

Both men were on foot now, for the horses were spent for the time being. Wasting no time, Colt grabbed some extra cartridges from his saddlebags and started up the hill on the run. The gulch that Bone had taken refuge in looked for all the world to be a box canyon, but Colt knew there was a narrow passage between the rocks that required a sharp eye to discover. If he was quick enough, he should be able to get in behind his adversary before Bone knew what he was up to.

Climbing up the side of the slope, in some places so steep that he had to use his hands, Colt made his way through the rocks toward a thick clump of pine trees wedged between two huge boulders. The trees were considerably larger than when he had lost the deer many years before—concealing the opening even more—but he was certain this was the passage. If his memory served him, once through the trees, he would find himself on a short ledge above the gulch.

Pushing up to the trees, he struggled to keep from sliding on the loose gravel before the gap in the boulders. Finally reaching a point where he could grasp one of the trunks with his free hand, he pulled himself up on the ledge and into the trees. Moving quickly between the tightly crowded pines, he emerged onto an open shelf at the top of the gulch to suddenly discover that his adversary had been scouting it from the other side. The two found themselves face-to-face at the top of the gulch. Though it was for only an instant, both men were stunned motionless, before both raised their weapons to fire.

The shots rang out simultaneously, both wide of the mark due to a lack of time to aim. With no immediate cover available, Colt could only fall backward to land on his back between two small pines. He automatically ejected the spent cartridge as soon as he hit the ground, and set himself as best he could to fire again. In less than a second, Bone appeared on the ledge with both pistols drawn, ready to finish what he thought was a wounded man. His evil eyes opened wide in shocked surprise when he felt the solid slam of Colt's bullet against his shoulder. The impact sent him staggering backward to lose his footing on the ledge and tumble back down the inside slope of the gulch, both pistols firing into the air.

Wasting no time, Colt scrambled to his feet and

plunged through the pine thicket to the edge of the ledge. Some thirty feet below him, Bone managed to drag himself behind a sizable rock shelf, causing Colt to hesitate before rushing recklessly down the slope after him. He was certain he had put two slugs in the man who hunted him, and he was anxious to end it, but not to the point of exposing himself carelessly. A wounded bear was a dangerous bear. He stopped to decide what his next move should be.

Below him, Bone lay grimacing in pain behind the rock shelf. With bullet wounds in his left arm and right shoulder, he was taken with fear for the first time in his evil life. Feeling his life's blood seeping out to soak his shirt, he was too stunned to realize that he was experiencing the trauma he had administered to his many victims. His only thought now was to somehow extract himself from this certain death situation. Clutching his two pistols, he looked behind him toward his horse, wondering what chance he had of reaching it. Admitting to the horrible truth that he had at last been beaten, he now cared about only one thing—to save his life. To make a run for it was his only hope. He was afraid that if he stayed where he was, he might bleed to death.

Struggling to pull himself back to the edge of the shelf, he peeked around the end in an effort to spot his antagonist. His efforts were immediately rewarded with a rifle shot that glanced off the rock beside his head. "Damn!" he swore and jerked back. He was effectively pinned down. His chances of running to his horse were nonexistent. *But*, he thought, *the horse can come to me. I ain't licked yet.* Rolling over on his stomach, he whistled for the roan. The weary gelding stood, lathered, with head down, steam still rising from its body. It rolled its eyes in Bone's direction, but did not respond. Bone whistled again, but the horse would not come. "Damn you!" Bone cursed, and the chilling thought occurred to him that his horse would be unable to run, even if he did manage to get to him without being shot. In angry frustration, he reached up over the edge of the shelf and fired his pistols blindly in the direction of the man on the ledge.

Colt lay flat against the ledge, counting the shots until the firing stopped, then listening for the click of empty cylinders. On the ground beside him lay the rifle Bone had left there when he had pulled his pistols in preparation to finish him. He glanced again at the rifle and realized that it was *his* rifle, the Winchester his father had willed him. He quickly picked it up and cocked it. Then he laid his other rifle aside. It was ironic that Bone had been the one to find his rifle, so he felt it fitting that the rifle be used to eliminate Bone.

Seconds passed since the barrage of pistol shots from the rocky shelf near the bottom of the gulch. Although he had not heard the sound of empty cylinders, Colt guessed that Bone had to be reloading both pistols. *What the hell?* he figured, ready to end the standoff, and disregarding the advice he had earlier given himself. With the rifle his father had left him in hand, he leaped off the ledge, landing on the steep shale-covered slope some six or seven feet below, sliding wildly down the loose gravel to the bottom.

Startled midway in the act of painfully reloading both his revolvers, Bone rose when he heard what sounded like a small avalanche. With no time to finish loading the pistols, he snapped the cylinder of one in place and stood ready to fire at the man just then scrambling to his feet. Seeing he had the advantage, since Colt had not had time to aim his rifle, Bone could not help but gloat. With his pistol aimed directly at Colt's head, he warned, "Hold it right there, damn you. You raise that rifle and I'll put a bullet right between your eyes." With his wounded shoulder in pain from the strain of holding his arm pointing at Colt, he took a few steps closer. "You son of a bitch," he cursed, "you put a couple of holes in me. Ain't no man ever done that before. You made me earn my money. I'll give you that."

Colt stood motionless during what was evidently supposed to be his eulogy, thinking all the while that it may have been the dumbest move he had ever made—jumping off that ledge. *Might as well turn over my last card,* he thought. Looking the sneering Bone in the eye, he said, "You never finished loadin' that pistol. I ain't sure you ain't settin' on an empty chamber." When he detected a question in Bone's eye, he added, "I know my rifle's ready to fire."

Uncertain now, Bone involuntarily glanced at the revolver in his hand. It was all the time Colt needed. He dropped to one knee, raising his rifle at the same time, firing before his knee hit the ground. Hit in the center of his chest, Bone staggered backward, his finger squeezing the trigger. The firing pin struck on a loaded chamber, but his shot went high over Colt's head. He was dead before he had time to get off a second shot.

Feeling as if he had been granted a double helping of luck, Colt rose and walked up to stand over the body. It was the first opportunity he had to study the man who had come to kill him. A tall man, his face was drawn into an angry scowl in death. His eyes, deep-set and dark, peered up at Colt as if staring at him from hell itself. This, then, was Frank Drummond's hired demon. Now Drummond would have to stand alone to answer for his sins, without help from the devil. Colt drew his skinning knife, and kneeling beside the sinister corpse, he cut off Bone's long greasy ponytail with the single eagle feather interwoven in it. After taking the late hired killer's weapons, he took his boot and rolled the body over, leaving it to the buzzards.

Chapter 15

Frank Drummond had reached the end of his patience, a quality he had precious little of to begin with. Where the hell was Bone? He was supposed to be a deadly tracker and killer, and yet Drummond had no clue as to the whereabouts of him or Colt McCrae. And what happened to Brownie? His hired hand, Rafe Wilson, thought it a strong possibility that McCrae was dead, but Drummond couldn't count on that. *The son of a bitch has a habit of showing up to kill a couple of my men*, he thought.

Unaware that J. D. Townsend had fled the territory, he decided that it was time to ride into Whiskey Hill and order the sheriff to form a posse to hunt down Colt McCrae. Charlie Ware, one of Drummond's three remaining men, was Drummond's choice to accompany him. One of the last men Drummond had hired, Charlie came highly recommended as an obedient brain with a fast trigger on an indiscriminate gun. Drummond selected him to accompany him on this day primarily because Charlie was the only hand he had left who had not as yet failed him.

Upon arriving in town, Drummond was puzzled to find the sheriff's office door padlocked. His anger flaring immediately, he figured the most likely place to find the bungling sheriff was in the local diner, so he headed for the Whiskey Hill Kitchen.

"Uh-oh," Pearl Murray murmured as she stood drinking a cup of coffee while gazing out the window. "Here comes trouble."

"What is it?" Mary asked, moving to the window beside her friend. Seeing then the cause of Pearl's comment, she said, "Frank Drummond—better tell the meeting in the back room." In the years that Mary had worked at the diner, Drummond had not crossed the threshold on more than two or three occasions. Seeing him headed this way now brought a feeling of deep foreboding.

Always one to enjoy seeing someone else's behind in the fire, Pearl said, "Let's not. Let's let 'em find out for themselves." She found it ironic that the mayor and the council members were at that moment in a meeting to discuss available action to break Frank Drummond's choke hold on the town. "They oughta be tickled to have him come to the meeting," she said with a chuckle.

Drummond strode forcefully through the door, followed by Charlie Ware, barely noticing the two women standing at the end of the counter. "Well, howdy there, Mr. Drummond," Pearl sang out as the determined owner of the Rocking-D breezed past her. Ignoring her greeting, he headed straight for the room in back of the dining area. Pearl grinned and winked at Mary. The two women moved closer to the door of the back room.

Roy Whitworth abruptly stopped in midsentence when the imposing figure of Frank Drummond suddenly appeared in the doorway. In reaction, all attendees of the meeting turned to see what had interrupted the mayor. The room went silent as Drummond stood searching the faces of the men seated around the table. A group of the usual council members save one, J. D. Townsend, sat gaping back at him, wondering how he could have discovered the purpose of their meeting. "Where's J.D.?" Drummond demanded.

There was a heavy silence for a moment before Roy answered, "J.D.'s not here anymore."

"I can see that. What do you mean he ain't here *anymore*?" Drummond shot back. "Where is he?"

The mayor glanced at the others seated around the table, seeking support and receiving only blank stares. "Well, we don't rightly know," he said. "He just decided to leave—it's anybody's guess where he went."

Drummond hesitated a few seconds while he considered what he had just been told. It was surprising news and it was obvious that it didn't please him.

"That's a fact," Barney Samuels spoke up, since everyone else seemed to have been struck tongue-tied. "J.D.'s lit out, and he ain't likely to come back, so we're left without no sheriff—since your man shot Stoney Yates." Drummond frowned at the mention of Bone, causing Barney to stop short of revealing the main purpose of the meeting, which was to stand up to Drummond.

"But we're discussing the business of naming a new

sheriff in this meeting," Roy Whitworth was quick to interject.

Drummond's gaze shifted back and forth around the table as if he was judging every face in attendance. "Hell," he finally stated, "I can end your meetin' right quick." He turned and gestured toward Charlie Ware, who had been standing bored and sullen during the exchange. "Charlie, here, is your new sheriff. He's highly qualified and I give him my endorsement."

The announcement was met with a shocked silence that settled over the table like a sodden blanket. Drummond stood there, feet widespread, arms crossed before his chest, fully expectant that there would be no question and no debate. Charlie Ware's sullen expression turned into a moronic grin. The idea seemed novel to him. It was a side of the law on which he had never trod.

Roy Whitworth knew that this was his time to stand up for the best interests of Whiskey Hill. The purpose of the called meeting was to form a solid front to counter Frank Drummond's bullying, enlisting all council members to stand together. With Drummond's premature visit, there had been no time for a roll call of pledges. Roy glanced at Oscar Anderson for a sign of support, but Oscar hurriedly looked away. He received the same reaction from Raymond Fletcher. Only one, Barney Samuels, the blacksmith, met his gaze, and gave him a solemn nod.

After an exaggerated period of silence with no spoken reaction, Drummond considered the matter settled. "First thing Sheriff Ware is gonna do," he said, "is get up a posse and run Colt McCrae to ground."

Knowing he had no choice, Roy spoke up, trying to step as softly as possible. "Well, Mr. Drummond, we appreciate the suggestion, and I assure you we'll certainly consider your candidate for sheriff. There'll be some other candidates to consider, I'm sure, and we'll try to do what's best for the town."

Drummond's eyes narrowed as his heavy eyebrows lowered into a deep frown. He could scarcely believe his ears. With his eyes locked on the mayor, he spoke slowly and distinctly, his voice low and threatening. "I don't make suggestions," he rasped. "What I said was, Charlie, here, is your new sheriff. Now, who don't understand that?" He glared directly at Oscar Anderson.

Wilting under the intensity of Drummond's stare, Oscar's face was drained of color. "I don't reckon there's any objection to that," he stammered. "Mr. Ware's probably a good man." He glanced apologetically at Roy Whitworth, then looked quickly away.

"All right, then," Drummond blustered, "we're just wastin' time here. The sooner we hunt McCrae down, the faster things are gonna get back to normal here."

Showing an obvious look of despair, the mayor started to speak, but the words would not come forth. With the town apparently falling back into its former position as the personal pawn of Frank Drummond, Barney Samuels looked to Roy to voice some opposition to the self-elected tyrant. When the mayor failed to speak, Barney accepted the challenge. "Now, wait a minute, here, folks. Things can't be decided just like that. The town council has to discuss the problem of replacin' J.D. with a new sheriff, and we have to vote on it. Then the council has to offer the job to whoever we decide is best qualified."

The silence that followed Barney's blatant statement was deafening. Outside the door, the two women who had inched up close to eavesdrop on the meeting backed away as if expecting the room to explode. Inside, it was as if time had stopped. No one dared move as all eyes at the table shifted toward Frank Drummond.

Drummond directed his icy stare at Barney, his dark eyes challenging. When he spoke, his voice was deadly calm, his tone low and hoarse. "Samuels, ain't it? I wanna make sure I remember your name." He let that sink in for a moment before continuing. "Anybody else hard of hearin'? I said the matter of sheriff is settled. The next order of business is to raise a posse."

Barney's face drained of color, his courage fading away as he realized he had been marked as a result of his comment. He swallowed nervously when a grinning Charlie Ware stepped over close to the table to smirk at him. Roy Whitworth attempted to support Barney's statement, hoping it would generate a united front with the others joining in. "Barney meant no offense, Mr. Drummond. We're just trying to do things accordin' to the rules, you understand, so they'll be legal."

Drummond had reached his limit of patience with the irritating town council. "I'm done talkin'," he said. "I want the key to that padlock on the jailhouse door. Who's got it?" The cowered eyes that instantly turned to Roy Whitworth told him that the mayor was in possession of the key. Drummond turned back to glare down at Whitworth, his hand extended, waiting for the key.

"This ain't accordin' to Parliamentary Procedure," the mayor meekly protested as he reached into his vest pocket and produced the key.

Drummond took the key and handed it to Charlie Ware. "Here, Sheriff, go on over to the jail and get yourself a badge. Then go down to the saloon and round up a posse. Tell 'em there'll be a cash reward for the man who shoots Colt McCrae."

With his malignant grin spread wide across his face, Charlie took the key, and with a condemning wink at Barney Samuels, turned to leave the room. Outside the door, Mary and Pearl scurried out of his way as the intimidating gunman tromped toward the front door.

Inside the back room, Drummond returned his attention to the men seated at the table. "I don't like what I saw here today," he said, his tone threatening. "Let me make myself clear, I'll burn this damn town to the ground if you people get in my way. I don't wanna hear about any more of these town meetings. I'm rememberin' ever' one of you men settin' around this table. You think about that." He stood glaring down at them for a few moments more, then turned and left the room.

The meeting a shambles, the participants slowly scraped their chairs back and got to their feet, feeling like schoolboys caught in a naughty scheme. Roy looked balefully at Barney Samuels, who shook his head in defeat. They both then turned to stare at Oscar Anderson and Raymond Fletcher, who had failed to support their show of unity.

"We didn't really have a helluva lotta choice," Oscar said in defense of his lack of backbone. "We need a sheriff, and we didn't really have a man for the job."

"That ain't the point, Oscar," the mayor said. "We need to get Frank Drummond's bloody fingers off of our necks. If we don't do somethin' to stop him, he's gonna soon make Whiskey Hill his own little town."

"Hell," Barney interjected, "it's damn near been that way already for the past two or three years."

"Barney's right," Roy said. "It was bad enough when J.D. was sheriff. At least he was one of us. Now look at what we've got—Charlie whatever-his-name-was, nothin' but a hired gun hand. It's time we stood up together to take our town back. It's time to revive the vigilance committee, only this time without Frank Drummond's gunmen."

"That's easy enough to say," Raymond Fletcher replied. "But we're talking about going up against Drummond's professional killers, and I, for one, think we're outmatched in that department."

"Dammit, Fletcher," Barney spoke out, "we've all got to stick together on this." His concern was possibly greater than the others' since he had been singled out by Drummond. "We need to talk to Turk Coolidge and Judge Blake to make sure we have their support." He stopped to think about what he had just said, then added, "You know, the judge might be the one to tell Drummond that he's the one supposed to appoint a new sheriff."

Oscar quickly jumped on the comment. "I think you're right. Judge Blake oughta be the one settin' Drummond straight on that. It ain't up to us."

"Hell, Oscar, the judge is gettin' too damn old to tell anybody what to do. Drummond don't understand talk, anyway. We need to fight fire with fire." The mayor shifted his gaze around to fall on each man there. It was not a reassuring sight. The reality of their situation struck him forcefully then. Drummond was too strong for these peaceful men.

"What about Colt McCrae?" a voice from the doorway asked. They turned to see Pearl Murray standing there.

"What *about* Colt McCrae?" Roy Whitworth countered.

"Pearl, you and Mary get on back to the kitchen," Oscar quickly chimed in. "This ain't no concern for womenfolk."

Ignoring Oscar's chiding, Pearl replied, "He's the only one I've seen around here man enough to stand up to Frank Drummond. If you stay outta his way long enough, he might take care of your problem for you. Hell, you outta make him sheriff."

No one seemed to take her suggestion seriously until Barney spoke up. "You know, that ain't a bad idea. Hell, him and Drummond are already at war with each other, and from the way Drummond's been losin' men, Colt looks to be gettin' the best of him."

"Maybe that's the way things *were* goin'," Roy said, "till Drummond hired that man, Bone, to take care of McCrae. Besides, we can't have an ex-convict for a sheriff."

"Well, we got a damn outlaw for one now," Barney replied. "At least Colt's done his time and paid for his crimes." From the expressions on the faces of the others, he could see that his idea was still met with a great deal of skepticism.

"I still think we're going to have to form a vigilance committee to confront Drummond," Roy said. "I'll talk to Turk Coolidge and see where he stands."

The owner of the Plainsman Saloon seemed properly astonished to hear of the mayor's proposal to reform the vigilantes. "Why in hell would I wanna do that?" he exclaimed. "Frank Drummond accounts for over half of my business—him and his cowhands. Just what are you figurin' on doin' to him, anyway? Take my advice and just let things go their natural way, and everything will be all right."

"Have you met the new sheriff?" Roy asked.

"Yeah, he was in here lookin' for men to ride in a posse to go after Colt McCrae. He's a rough-lookin' son of a bitch, I'll say that for him—gonna be a helluva change from ol' J.D."

"Did he get up a posse?"

"Yeah. Well, five men signed up. They were all drunk with no money to buy any more whiskey. Maybe they'll be sober enough to see straight in the mornin' when they're supposed to strike out for the Broken-M, but I doubt there's a steady hand among 'em."

Roy left the saloon burdened with further disappointment. He had counted on Turk's support. There was nothing to do but try again to persuade Oscar Anderson and Raymond Fletcher to have the courage to take their town back from Frank Drummond.

• • •

It was late that night when Frank Drummond returned to the Rocking-D. Stepping down from the Appaloosa gelding he rode, he handed the reins to Rafe Wilson. "Evenin', Mr. Drummond," Rafe said. "What happened to Charlie?"

"He got himself a new job," Drummond replied. "He'll be stayin' in town." That was all the explanation he offered as he climbed up the steps to the porch. About to enter the house, he stopped short when he saw what appeared to be a small critter of some kind on the door. "What the hell?" he exclaimed, and waited a moment to see if whatever it was would flee. When it remained there, he pulled out a match and struck it on his boot. Holding the match up to the door, he was baffled at first until he recognized what he was looking at—a long greasy length of hair with an eagle feather intertwined. He felt a stifling rage building inside him as he realized the message—*Bone was dead.*

He turned back to Rafe, who was already leading his horse to the barn. "Damn you!" he bellowed. "How does somebody ride right up to my front door and nobody sees him?"

"Who?" Rafe asked.

"Colt McCrae, dammit, that's who!" Drummond roared, then threw the offending ponytail at Rafe. The anger inside him was threatening to explode as he formed a picture in his mind of Colt McCrae blatantly riding onto his property—walking right up to his front door, stealing around the house, looking in his windows, searching for him. This was the second time McCrae had ridden into his stronghold like a ghost nobody sees. The first time was when he left the bodies of Jack Teach and Lou George, their horses tied to his front porch. "That son of a bitch," he growled. "Rafe, as soon as you put my horse away, saddle yours. I want you to ride into Whiskey Hill and tell Charlie to meet me at the south end of Pronghorn Canyon at sunup in the mornin'."

Staring stupidly at the dark object his boss had thrown at his feet, Rafe looked up then. It was lucky for him that it was too dark for Drummond to see the scowl on his face. A long ride into town at this hour of the night meant he would be going without sleep. "Yessir," he replied dutifully. "Where do I go to find Charlie?"

"In the sheriff's office," Drummond answered. "Tell him to bring that posse with him. We're gonna clean out a hornets' nest once and for all."

"Ah, yes, sir," Rafe replied respectfully, "I'll tell 'im." He was not quite clear why Charlie would be in the sheriff's office, or exactly what Drummond had in mind, but he knew better than to question him.

What Drummond had in mind was the annihilation of the McCrae clan and all who worked for them. He was weary of waiting for his hired guns to handle the problem. He would lead the slaughter himself to make sure the job was done right.

Chapter 16

It had been a good two hours past dark when Colt had slow-walked Buck past the tall gateposts of the Rocking-D. There had been no one about the corrals or barnyard, and no sound other than the soft padding of the buckskin's hooves on the bare ground. There had been a lantern lit in the bunkhouse, and Colt held his Winchester ready to answer any challenge from that quarter. There was none, however, and he had silently continued on his way to the house of the man who murdered his father.

His intent on this night had been to extract payment for the sin against his father, a simple elimination of a deadly predator. There were no thoughts of a duel, merely the execution of a mad dog. Consequently, he had no intention of giving Drummond any opportunity to defend himself.

Walking as softly as he could manage, he had cautiously climbed the steps to the porch. Very slowly, he had tried the door handle and found it unlocked. Pushing the door open, he had peered inside the dark hallway. There was no sound and no light. He continued past the great room, carefully placing one foot after the other until he reached an open door to a bedroom that was obviously that of the master. There was no one there. He continued walking to the end of the hall to the kitchen where he had stopped upon hearing a noise—snoring—and it had come from behind a closed door at the back of the kitchen. Moving silently to the door, he eased it open and stood ready with his rifle, only to find Drummond's housekeeper, Alice Flynn, snoring away peacefully. He backed carefully out of the room.

His plans had been thwarted. Drummond was not there, but Colt knew that the meeting would come in time. He would find Drummond, or Drummond would find him. Either way, it made no difference to Colt as long as his father's death was avenged. He left the house as he had come in, taking less care to avoid noise. After closing the front door, he took his knife and cut a splinter in the door, and hung Bone's ponytail on it as a notice to Drummond that he could get to him anywhere. As he rode past the bunkhouse again, the thought had occurred to him that he would have set fire to the house if the old woman had not been sleeping in the back room.

Vance McCrae painfully made his way to the kitchen table and sank heavily into a chair held for him by his wife. "Look who's strong enough to eat at the table this morning," Susan said to Rena. The Cheyenne woman smiled and nodded. It was the first time Vance had been able to stand without help since he had been shot.

"He oughta be about ready to go back to work in a day or two," Burt said, joking, as he walked in from outside.

"I feel like I oughta do somethin' around here to help out," Vance said.

"We're doin' all right," Burt quickly reassured him. "We've got cattle—yours and mine—scattered all over hell's half acre, but it don't matter a helluva lot. Drummond's short of help, and the men he's got are spending most of their time watchin' us instead of worryin' about stealin' cattle." He paused. "Although Tom says there ain't nobody up on the ridge this mornin'."

"I need to get back to take care of my place," Vance said.

"You'd best stay here," Burt assured him. "We're a lot better off together, and Drummond knows it. I figure it's the only thing that's kept him from makin' his move. With you and me, and your two men, we can match him in numbers. If we split up, he's got the advantage."

"I reckon you're right," Vance said, "but I still ain't much use to us."

Burt smiled. "Well, we still got Rena." He looked at the Cheyenne woman and winked. She nodded emphatically, returning his smile, causing Burt to chuckle when he recalled the somber Indian woman's confrontation with Drummond's foreman, Tyler.

While Burt and Vance had breakfast, two groups of riders met in a grassy coulee near the south end of Pronghorn Canyon. Rafe Wilson and Charlie Ware had ridden in from town with five men who had volunteered to join the posse. Waiting for them, Frank Drummond sat impatiently on his Appaloosa gelding, his remaining gunman, Fred Singleton, beside him. Drummond urged his horse forward and rode out to meet the posse.

Feeling it important to make sure every man knew the purpose of their mission, Drummond prepared to address the group. Judging from the appearance of the five men Charlie signed up, they were a sorry-looking lot, all obviously hungover from the prior night's drinking. They had guns, however, and he figured they would better his odds.

"All right," Drummond started as they pulled up around him. "Sheriff Ware has probably told you we're goin' after Colt McCrae, and that's the main thing. But to get to him, we're gonna have to go through the rest of the McCraes. And that's what you're gettin' two dollars a day for. We're gonna wipe out the whole lot of those murderin' coyotes and burn their damn nest to the ground." He paused to judge the reaction from the five volunteers.

One of the volunteers, Ronnie Skinner, spoke up. "The sheriff said there's extra bonus money for the shot that takes Colt McCrae, but he didn't say how much."

"That's a fact," Drummond replied, pleased that none of the volunteers showed a reluctance to continue. "Fifty dollars to the man who gets him." His response brought a smile to Ronnie's face. "Colt is the most important one to kill," Drummond went on to emphasize, "but for the good of the town, the whole bunch of low-down murderers have to be wiped out, men, women, children. It ain't no different than wipin' out a nest of scorpions." Again, he waited. When there were still no negative protests, he prodded the Appaloosa and led out to the south. "Come on, then, we've got work to do."

Burt McCrae looked up to see Bill Wilkes flailing his horse's flanks as he charged down the east ridge at breakneck speed. Laying aside the bridle he had been in the process of mending, he stepped out of the barn and went to meet him. In the corral, Tom Mosley climbed over the top rail and ran to join Burt.

"They're comin'!" Bill yelled before he had passed the well at the edge of the yard. "Drummond!" he blurted as he pulled his horse to a sliding stop before them. Breathless with excitement, he gasped, "Drummond and a gang of riders are headin' this way, and they look like they mean business!"

"The ol' son of a bitch himself," Burt muttered. "How many?"

"I counted nine of 'em," Bill said.

Burt considered that, but just for a second. "Nine, huh? Drummond musta hired some extra guns." There wasn't time to wonder where he managed to get them on such short notice. "How far?"

"On the other side of the ridge, following the creek."

"Well, that don't give us much time, does it?" Burt replied calmly. The fact that Drummond was leading the bunch told Burt that this was a serious strike against his family. Drummond was usually careful not to be part of the raids he had instigated before. "All right, let's get back to the house," Burt said. "Bill, turn your horse in the corral and we'll stand 'em off from the house." With nine to defend against, Burt feared the siege might last for a long time. "Tom," he said, "grab a couple of buckets from the barn and fill 'em with water. We may need it if this is what it looks like."

"I don't reckon they're comin' to apologize," Tom said facetiously. "We might need more'n two buckets."

Inside the house, Burt hurriedly organized the defense of his home. The house had not been built to defend against Indian attacks like some older houses in the territory, but there were not many windows, and all but two of these were on two sides of the structure. Consequently, it was easy to decide where to place each rifle. Burt chose the one window in front near the door for himself. He stationed Tom on one side, with Susan to help load for him. Bill and Vance manned the other side, Vance insisting that he was strong enough to handle a rifle. Rena, with her rifle ready, took a station by the kitchen door. There was no shortage of weapons or ammunition, courtesy of the unsuccessful prior raids on Burt's ranch. With everyone in position, Burt took a final check to make sure everyone was ready. Then he took his derby off a peg by the door and situated it carefully on his head. As they quietly waited for the siege to begin, Burt cracked the front door ajar, and stood by to receive his visitors, expecting Drummond to first demand that he turn Colt over to him.

Contrary to Burt's thinking, Drummond planned to waste no time talking. He had come to destroy the last obstacle in his quest to own all the land between Lodgepole Creek and Whiskey Hill. When his force of nine men crested the ridge east of the Broken-M, he signaled a halt while he surveyed the house and outbuildings below. No one was seen moving about. He guessed that they had been spotted, so he turned his gaze to focus on the house. "They're holed up in there," he said to no one in particular, "waitin' for us."

Moving forward again, he led his men halfway down the ridge to within two hundred yards before halting again. "Charlie, since you're the sheriff, I'll let you show 'em we mean business." Charlie moved up beside him. "See that door opened a crack? Let's see if you can put a bullet through that crack." Charlie grinned obligingly and raised his rifle and took aim.

"Hadn't we oughta tell 'em why we're here, and give Colt a chance to surrender?" This question came from one of the posse volunteers who had sobered up enough to question the legality of their actions.

Drummond jerked his head around to seek out the source of the question. Focusing his scowling gaze upon the man, he demanded, "Didn't you hear me back there when I said they're all murderers and thieves? We didn't come here to talk. We came here to kill scavengers." Turning to the sheriff, he said, "Shoot, Charlie."

Charlie was not accurate enough to put a bullet through the small opening in the door, but it splintered the frame beside it, causing Burt to jump back, startled by the shot. Susan released an involuntary squeal when she heard the report of the rifle. "Damn!" Tom

Mosley exclaimed. "They ain't wastin' no time on talkin'."

"Damn you, Drummond!" Burt yelled. "There's women and a child in here. If you've come for Colt, he ain't here."

"Send everybody outside," Drummond called back. "I've got the new sheriff here, and we'll search the house and see for ourselves. Everybody outside."

There was a silent pause inside for a few seconds. "Hell," Burt said after a moment's consideration, "he's come on a killin' spree." Inching back close to the crack in the door, he yelled out, "You go to hell!"

The response was what Drummond had hoped for, providing what he considered justification for what he had come to do. "All right, boys," he announced, "you heard him. I gave him a chance to come out and he wants a fight. Well, we'll give it to him. We'll shoot that place to pieces." Sizing up his target, he decided it best to concentrate his fire on the sides of the house where the windows were located. Looking to his own men to lead the assault, he gave his orders. "Charlie, you take three men with you and find you some cover on yonder side of the house—maybe in the barn— wherever you can get a clear shot. Rafe, take the other three and find you a spot on the other side. And, boys, don't spare the ammunition." He held back while his men rode off down the slope to take up their positions. As soon as the shooting started, he turned his horse and rode along the ridge until he came to a narrow break with a clump of pines. This, he decided, was a good place to watch the assault while safe from direct fire.

Once the shooting started, there was no letup. Drummond's crew of outlaws and drunks were soon caught up in the conscienceless sport of target practice with little risk to themselves. Empty cartridges gathered on the ground like hailstones and rifle barrels grew hot from rapid firing as round after round smashed windows and tore chunks from the siding.

Inside, Burt and the others did their best to answer while trying to stay behind what protection they could find. Caught in a storm of flying glass and deadly lead hornets, they hugged the floor amid the constant hammering of bullets against the sides of the house. Risking random shots from the windows at uncertain targets, they were forced to shoot quickly before diving back to the floor for protection. Crawling from one side of the house to the other, Burt tried to help out where he could, offering encouragement while knowing they were caught in a hopeless situation. But he also knew to surrender was certain death. There were no choices.

The siege had carried on for more than an hour with no way of telling what damage they had inflicted. Charlie Ware was sure that there was a decrease in the return fire from the house, but he could not be sure anyone had been hit. He started to tell the man next to him, one of the volunteers, to move around more to the front of the house, when the man suddenly reared up and cried out in pain. Charlie was astonished to see the man clutching his chest as he fell back on the ground. "I've been shot!" were Ronnie Skinner's last words.

Bad luck, Charlie thought, *lucky shot*. He reciprocated by throwing three shots in rapid succession through the front window from where he guessed the shot had come. He turned to warn Fred Singleton to keep behind cover. His words had not formed in his mouth when Fred dropped his rifle and fell face-first on the ground. "Gawdamn!" Charlie exclaimed. "We're in a bad place." He looked over to one of the volunteers, who had taken cover behind a wagon. "Let's get to better cover!" Not waiting for his response, Charlie retreated to the barn behind him. Once safely inside, he looked back to see the volunteer crumple to the ground as soon as he stepped out from behind the wagon.

Far from being an intelligent man, Charlie nevertheless had the brains to conclude that the killing shots were coming from someplace other than the house. Struck motionless in a moment of indecision, he wasn't sure what he should do. Finally, he deemed it in his best interest to go out the back of the barn and try to circle around the rear of the house. Moving cautiously, he went past the empty stalls to the back door. Outside, he was surprised to see a buckskin horse standing saddled among the cottonwoods by the creek. While waiting for his sluggish mind to digest the significance of this, he heard a soft voice behind him. "Hey." He whirled around to confront the solemn countenance of Colt McCrae. It was not close enough to be considered a gunfight. Charlie was cut down before he raised his rifle past his leg.

Inside the embattled house, Tom Mosley called out, "Hey, they've quit shootin' on this side."

With bullets still flying from the other side, Burt

crawled over to Tom's side. He paused a few seconds before agreeing. "Damn, you're right." He waited a few moments more, then eased up to the windowsill to hazard a peek. "There's a dead man layin' by the wagon," he said. "I can't see nobody else. You musta hit him."

"I don't see how," Tom replied. "I don't have time to aim at anything."

"Well, he's sure as hell dead. Keep your eyes peeled. Maybe they're up to somethin'." He crawled back to the other windows to help out where he could.

Moving at a trot, Colt returned to the trees by the creek to retrieve his horse. In the saddle again, he guided the buckskin through the cottonwoods, across the creek, and taking cover behind a long rise, rode toward the west ridge on the other side of the house. When he reached a line of gullies that led back to the creek, he dismounted and left Buck while he continued on foot.

Rafe Wilson paused when he suddenly realized that the firing from the other side had stopped. He was not sure what it meant. He glanced down the line of volunteers that were still firing away blissfully from the cover of a hogback between the house and the ridge. If there was some cause for the end of the shots from Charlie Ware's side, they, too, were unaware. He crawled up out of the gully to see if he could get a better look. The bullet that struck him in the shoulder spun him around, staggering him. Trying to return fire, he pulled the trigger before he could recover his balance, the shot glancing off the brow of the hogback where the three volunteers had taken cover. Startled, the man closest to him turned to discover Rafe stumbling drunkenly with blood spreading on his coat. Rafe tried to call out a warning, but Colt's second bullet smashed into his breastbone, dropping him to the ground.

The bloody sight of Rafe's demise was enough to dishearten the man who was almost hit by Rafe's errant shot. He stopped shooting at the house, and paused to look around him, trying desperately to see where the fatal shot had come from. As he knelt there, another bullet zipped past his head and embedded in the side of the hogback. Fearful for his life, he crawled over the top and scrambled away through the brush. Seeing their partner fleeing for his life, the other two volunteers didn't wait to find out why, and all three were in full flight back to their horses. By the time Colt emerged from the gullies, they were effectively out of range and galloping away.

Stunned, Frank Drummond could not at first believe what he was seeing. Perplexed by the sudden cessation of rifle fire from Charlie Ware's men, he strained to see what had caused it. Unable to tell from his position in the pine trees, he could only wait to see what developed. It seemed like little more than moments later when he saw Rafe go down, followed by the rout of the posse members. To his horror, he then saw Burt, Tom, and Bill filing out of the house and running to the barn. He realized at that moment that he alone remained. Reasonably sure that they couldn't see him, he considered making a hasty retreat, but as he was about to do so, he saw Colt McCrae step up on the hogback that had shielded Rafe and the three members of the posse. The sight infuriated him. He raised his rifle and fired at the man he hated with such passion. The shot missed, kicking up dirt near Colt's feet.

Not sure where the shot had come from, Colt turned unhurriedly, almost as if he were invulnerable to bullets. The deliberate manner in which he stood, searching the ridge, fearlessly scanning the cuts and hogbacks, struck a sudden fear in Frank Drummond's soul. In a panic then, he recklessly fired at Colt again, missing by a foot or more, but Colt saw the muzzle flash in the pine thicket. He dropped to one knee and fired at the spot. Colt's shot clipped a pine branch barely inches from Drummond's face. Wanting no part of a duel with the prison-hardened young rifleman, Drummond almost stumbled over his own feet in his haste to escape. Stepping up in the saddle, he whipped the Appaloosa mercilessly as he galloped out the other side of the thicket. Colt ran back to his horse, and was soon in the saddle after him.

Fear, cold choking fear, gripped Frank Drummond's throat as he thrashed his horse for more speed. Caught in a position he had never experienced before— alone with no one to do his evil bidding—he was unable to decide what to do. He rejected his first instinct—to flee to his ranch—because of the thought of having to face alone the relentless killing machine that had decimated his band of outlaws in such work- manlike fashion. Daring to look behind him, he glimpsed the buckskin climbing up out of the series of gullies. It was enough to make him decide to head for town. There was enough of the bully's confidence left in him to believe he could find safety among the men of the town council.

Hard on his adversary's trail, Colt let Buck dictate the pace. The buckskin sensed the race to be a serious one and needed no encouragement, but found the Appaloosa to be a worthy match. Consequently, Colt could gain no advantage, but neither could the Appaloosa increase the interval between the two horses. Racing down the length of Pronghorn Canyon, stride for stride, past the spot where Colt had been ambushed, Drummond held the horse to the demanding pace. Buck stayed doggedly on the Appaloosa's tail until both horses, tiring rapidly, threatened to founder. With no other choice, Drummond took advantage of an out-cropping of rocks within a couple of miles of the town.

Pulling the weary horse to a stop, he jumped down from the saddle and led the Appaloosa up behind the largest of a group of boulders. With his rifle in hand, he scrambled up near the top of the boulder and waited for Colt. Colt, however, saw him disappear behind the rocks and guessed he had an ambush in mind. He picked a spot some two hundred yards from the boulder at the base of a low hill where Buck could rest safely. He had no sooner dismounted than shots from Drummond kicked up dirt on the top of the hill.

Working his way around the brush that covered most of the hill, Colt found a dry wash that afforded a good firing position. Lying on his belly, he inched up close to the top and watched for Drummond's rifle barrel to appear on the boulder. When it did, he fired two shots in rapid succession, chipping rock on either side of the rifle. Drummond immediately scampered down to find a new position. Drummond was not through running—Colt was sure of that. Knowing how tired Buck was, Colt figured Drummond had no choice but to stop. His only thought now was to keep him at bay, but Colt had other ideas. Spotting a stand of pines off to his right, he made a dash for them as soon as Drummond's rifle had disappeared from the top of the boulder.

Reaching the safety of the pines, Colt found that he had a better angle. He could almost see the whole pocket formed behind the boulder, leaving Drummond exposed if he ventured too close to the outer edge. Drummond, unaware that Colt was no longer behind the hill, edged over closer to the side. He was met with a bullet so close to his head that the resulting chips of rock stung his face, leaving a series of tiny cuts. In a panic, he jumped back, crowding his huge body into the corner of the rocky angle. Colt could no longer see him, but he guessed that he could make it extremely hot for the big man in that tight pocket. Taking aim at the near wall, he methodically cranked shot after shot at the boulder.

Pressing as tightly as he could into the corner where the two stone walls joined, Drummond was terrified as the bullets ricocheted from one side of his rocky tomb to the other, chipping off chunks of the walls while whining their deadly song—searching. Drummond feared that it was only a matter of time before one of the deadly hornets found him. Eyes wide with panic, he finally bolted from the boulders and scrambled back in the saddle. The Appaloosa was reluctant to run, but Drummond whipped the exhausted animal until it finally broke into a halfhearted gallop.

Colt ran back to his horse, determined not to let Drummond escape. When he reached the weary buckskin, his better judgment overcame his desire for instant revenge. One look at Buck told him that his horse was spent. He turned to watch Drummond riding away, knowing that Buck would respond to his commands, even if it broke his wind—and Colt had no doubt that one more gallop would indeed cause the horse to founder. Taking the reins, he said, "Come on, boy," and started toward town leading the horse.

At the edge of town, after a walk of about thirty minutes, he came upon the Appaloosa standing riderless by the blacksmith's forge. Head down, the horse was done for, heaving as if trying to take double breaths, its wind broken.

When his horse had refused to take another step, Drummond was forced to run from the edge of town. It was not something a man of his size was accustomed to, so it was a stark, red-faced man that burst into the Whiskey Hill Kitchen, searching the room with desperate eyes. "Where are they?" he panted, out of breath. "They're always here. Where are they?"

"Who?" Pearl asked. One look at the frantic owner of the Rocking-D Ranch was enough to discourage employment of her usual barbed remarks.

"The goddamn town council!" Drummond roared impatiently as he stormed straight for the meeting room in back.

"In the back room," Pearl answered, "where they

are every afternoon." Never far away, her flippant tone returned as she figured surely everybody knew that.

Having already heard him coming, all five members of the town council gaped at the door, surprised by the second unannounced visit by the dominating owner of the Rocking-D. This time, there was an obvious stressful condition displayed as Drummond burst into the room, rifle in hand. Struck silent by the frenzied look on the huge man's face, no one said a word.

"Get your guns ready!" Drummond commanded. "That murderer is on his way here. You're all members of the sheriff's posse now. When he comes in that door, we're gonna shoot him down!"

With everyone at the table properly stunned, only Roy Whitworth attempted to make a sound. "What . . . ?" was all he could manage at first. Never having seen the formidable Drummond in such a flustered state, Roy realized suddenly that it was fear he was seeing in the belligerent bully's face. He didn't know what to make of it. "Where's the new sheriff and his posse?" he asked.

"Dead!" Drummond exclaimed. "Dammit, that's what I've been tellin' you! He killed 'em all, and now we've got to stop him!" He waved his arms frantically toward the still-seated council members. "Get up, dammit, get a gun in your hand. We'll meet him in the street."

"I don't have a gun with me," Raymond Fletcher offered weakly.

"Me neither," Oscar Anderson said.

Backed against the wall, still holding the coffeepot in her hand, Mary Simmons watched horrified. She had just been in the process of filling the cups when

Drummond charged in. Witnessing the rage building in his eyes at the lack of response from the men at the table, she feared, not only for them, but for Colt as well. She wanted to run from the room to warn him, but Drummond stood in the doorway.

Always the one person less fearful than the others to speak up in Drummond's presence, Barney Samuels said, "We ain't members of no posse. I don't know what's goin' on, but it ain't up to the council to do anythin' about it."

Anger, like lightning, flashed in Drummond's eyes. He leveled his rifle at Barney. "You're wearin' a gun, and you'll stand with me, or by God, I'll shoot you down right here and now." He motioned toward Turk Coolidge. "You're wearin' a sidearm, too, Coolidge. Get on your feet." Using the barrel of his rifle to gesture, he motioned for them all to rise. Afraid not to, they all did as they were bade. Seeing their reluctance, he attempted to change his tone and appeal to their sense of community. "We'll all stand together against this murderer before he destroys our homes and families." He took a step back from the doorway. "Now let's all go out in the street to face this convict and protect our town."

Like sheep, they all did as they were told, filing out of the room and walking to the front door. It was apparent to each one of them that they were seeing a vulnerability unseen in this tyrant before, but with his rifle leveled at them, no one wanted to be the one to object. To Barney Samuels, the prospect of being caught between Frank Drummond and Colt McCrae was a desperate place to be, a sentiment shared by the other four members of the council.

"I know you've got guns in here, Anderson," Drummond said, and stopped his reluctant squad at the door.

Before Oscar could respond, Mary spoke up. "He's got a shotgun and a pistol in the kitchen. I'll get them." She disappeared through the kitchen door. As quickly as she could, she ran past an astonished Pearl Murray and went to Oscar's desk where he kept the weapons. Breaking the breech on his double-barrel shotgun, she pulled the shells out and closed it. Then she emptied the cartridges out of his revolver and hurried back to the front door where she handed a weapon to Oscar and Fletcher, receiving an incredulous look from Oscar. She stepped quickly back out of the way, bravely meeting the approving gaze of Frank Drummond. He, in turn, drew his revolver from the holster and gave it to Roy Whitworth, the only remaining member without a weapon.

"Now we'll show this bastard who owns this town," he said and opened the door. "Just remember, I'm standin' behind you with my rifle in case anybody gets rabbit's feet," he warned.

Rounding the corner of the blacksmith's shop, Colt stopped at the end of the street to discover a line of six armed men awaiting him in the street. In the middle, and slightly behind, Frank Drummond stood. He had evidently managed to organize another posse, this one with faces recognizable to Colt. *The crowd that sent me to prison*, was the thought that ran through his mind. It was a fitting ending to this drama that had cost him his father and ten years of his life. Once again, the odds were stacked against him. *Well, so be it*, he thought. *I'll damn sure get Drummond before I go down.*

Though fifty yards away, the line facing him looked less than committed. He immediately dismissed Fletcher and Anderson, as well as Roy Whitworth. When the shooting started, he counted on wild shots from all three of them, or none at all. At least, that's what he hoped for. That left three to command most of his attention.

His rifle in a ready position and cocked, he started walking toward the waiting firing squad, but stopped when he heard horses coming up behind him. Ready to defend himself from that quarter, he turned to see three riders coming toward him, the leader wearing a derby cocked to one side and held in place by a red bandanna tied under his chin.

Suddenly experiencing a sick feeling deep in his stomach, Drummond realized the odds were no longer in his favor when Burt galloped into view, followed by Tom Mosley and Bill Wilkes. In a fit of panic, he shoved Roy Whitworth aside and took a wild shot at the man he had come to hate above all others. Reduced to total alarm, his reluctant posse bolted, all members running for their lives as Colt spun back, dropped to one knee, and returned fire.

Drummond grunted with the impact of Colt's rifle slug slamming deep into his chest, the force knocking him back a few steps. Looking down at the hole in his coat, his eyes wide with fear and disbelief, he lurched backward, looking around him for the support that had already deserted him. Overcome with fear when he saw Colt running toward him, he turned and staggered for safety inside the Whiskey Hill Kitchen.

With vision already blurring and feeling his life draining from his body, he determined to take Colt McCrae with him. Stumbling drunkenly, he willed himself to remain on his feet long enough to hold on to the counter for support. Once behind the counter, he supported his rifle on it and aimed it at the door. Fighting to hold on to life long enough to complete this last evil deed, he waited for Colt to come through the door. As his shirt filled with blood, his sight became hazy, but he forced himself to focus on the door. He heard Colt's footsteps on the boards of the porch, but in the next instant, everything went black and he crumpled to the floor. Behind him, Mary's fingers vibrated from the impact of the heavy iron skillet against his skull.

Frank Drummond never awakened from the blow that helped send him on his way to hell. Colt charged through the door seconds later to find a trembling young woman staring down at Drummond, terrified that he might get up again. Near the end of the counter, Pearl stood, a butcher knife in hand, eyes as wide as saucers. Colt quickly checked the body to make sure Drummond was dead, then turned to face the two women. "Are you all right?" he asked, looking at Mary. Still shaken, she nodded.

"Yeah, we're all right," Pearl said, assuming he was concerned for them both. "Remind me to wash that damn skillet before we cook breakfast in the mornin'."

"He was going to shoot you when you came in the

door," Mary said, still trembling, her eyes wide in shock.

"I expect so," he said gently. "That's a fact, sure enough."

She stood gazing at him for a long moment before seeming to recover her composure. It was then that she noticed the blood soaking through the buckskin shirt he wore. Her eyes grew wide once more, and she scolded him. "Colt McCrae, you're bleeding again!"

"Yeah, I caught one in the shoulder," he replied. Drummond's wild shot had not been far off target.

She handed the frying pan to Pearl and came immediately to him and made him sit down in a chair while she looked after the wound. "You're going to the doctor with this one," she admonished. "And then you're going to let it get well before you make it worse again."

He smiled at her. "I might need someone to look after me to make sure."

She looked up to meet his gaze and held it for a moment. Watching from the end of the counter, Pearl shook her head, then commented, "Yeah, if anybody ever needed lookin' after, it's him." They were still gazing into each other's eyes when Burt and the others burst through the door.

Chapter 17

Frank Drummond was gone, and with him, the murderous gang of bushwhackers that rode for him. There were issues to be taken care of, and there was some discussion about who should be responsible for overseeing the equitable disposal of Drummond's vast cattle empire. It fell upon Burt McCrae to handle that chore, so along with Tom and Bill, he rode over to the Rocking-D to see what had to be done. They rode up to the ranch house to find Alice Flynn sitting in a rocking chair on the front porch.

"I was wondering when somebody was gonna show up," the acid-tongued woman said as a greeting. It had been two days since Frank Drummond had been killed, with no word to her.

"Yes, ma'am, Miz Flynn," Burt said. "Somebody shoulda been out here sooner—you out here all alone like this. I'm sorry about that."

"Drummond dead?"

"Ah, yes, ma'am," Burt replied, taken aback by her indifferent attitude. "He died of a gunshot wound in the Whiskey Hill Kitchen."

"That figures," she said. "He ran with a rank crowd of riffraff. Had to happen sooner or later."

Burt really had no notion as to the best way to settle Drummond's holdings when he arrived at the Rocking-D. It had generally been assumed that since the McCraes won the war, they would automatically claim the spoils. But upon meeting the ramrod-straight old woman, a better solution occurred to him. "I expect you must be wantin' to get away from this lonely stretch of prairie, maybe move into Whiskey Hill where there's other folks around," he said, testing the seemingly indifferent woman's state of mind.

"Hell no," she replied at once. "Why would I wanna move into the middle of that tomfoolery? I've been living alone for more'n fifteen years—same as, living with Frank Drummond. No, thank you, sir. I'll get by fine living in one of the line shacks or the smokehouse. I don't need nobody around me."

Tom and Bill exchanged glances of astonishment at the salty old gal's declaration. Burt grinned. He had never met the lady before, but he had heard she was hard as nails. He made his decision. "Well, now, it seems to me that with Drummond gone, you're the only rightful heir to his estate. So I reckon this house, this ranch, belongs to you now." The only indication of emotion he detected after that statement was a slight flicker of one eyelid. He continued. "Now, you're gonna need some help runnin' this place. It's bigger'n the Broken-M and the Bar-M put together, and until you can hire on some hands, I figure me and my nephew can help out. We'll be shorthanded, for sure, but we'll manage through the winter. I expect we'll lose a few head to wolves and coyotes, but we'll do all right. Does that sound all right to you?"

Although the facial expression was not obvious, Tom Mosley would brag afterward that he was one of only three souls on the face of the earth to have ever seen Alice Flynn smile.

"We can help each other out," Burt went on when there was no reply at once. "Whaddaya think? I know it seems like a helluva lot for a woman to take on."

She got up from the rocking chair and walked over to the edge of the porch. Without a word, she spat in the palm of her hand and extended it toward him. Understanding, Burt spat in his hand, and they shook on it. "I'll get Judge Blake to handle the legal part of it," Burt said. She nodded.

Tom and Bill were left to look after the ranch while Burt and Vance, along with Susan, rode into Whiskey Hill for a meeting Roy Whitworth called to discuss the future of the town. Little Sammy begged to stay with "Uncle Tom" and "Uncle Bill," which was fine with Vance since it would be far past Sammy's bedtime by the time they returned.

"I'm glad you folks decided to come to the meeting," Roy said when the McCraes arrived at the Whiskey Hill Kitchen. "We've been talking about a lot of things that need taking care of if we're gonna build this town into a respectable place to live and work. Now that Frank Drummond is gone, you folks, along with Miss Alice Flynn, of course, are the major landowners outside of town."

"We were wonderin' if Colt was plannin' on stayin'

around, now that the trouble with Drummond's done," Barney Samuels spoke up. "We ain't seen him since the shoot-out."

"Can't say for sure," Burt replied. "You ain't seen him 'cause he's gone back to that Cheyenne camp. Mary Simmons went with him—said she was stayin' with him this time till he healed up proper." He shook his head and smiled at that. "Colt wouldn't have come to the meetin' anyway."

"He's left me shorthanded," Oscar Anderson complained. "Pearl's had to do all the work with Mary gone."

"The way I heard it," Burt replied, "she didn't give Colt much choice in the matter."

"We sent word through Pearl for Colt to come to the meeting," Roy said. "The town ain't been too friendly to him since he got out of prison. I don't reckon I blame him for not coming."

"In fact," Barney said, "some of us think we could do a lot worse than Colt to take J.D.'s job."

"Colt as sheriff? I don't know about that." Burt shook his head slowly.

"We only talked about it," the mayor said. "I don't know if we could have a sheriff that's been to prison."

"Hell," Barney insisted, "he didn't shoot that bank guard, he was just involved in the robbery."

"Well, he was part of the bank robbery. That's pretty serious," Oscar commented.

"He wasn't even there when it happened." Startled by the comment, all three turned their heads at once, surprised that it had come from Susan McCrae.

Her husband was more surprised than the others. "Why do you think that?" he asked.

"I don't think—I know," she replied. "He was twelve miles away at that little creek between my daddy's land and your father's place."

Confused, Vance asked, "How could you know that?"

"I was there," she stated softly. Her confession left the room silent, waiting for details. Vance, completely bewildered at that point, was struck speechless.

"That's right," a voice from the doorway sang out. "She saw me, all right." So enthralled by Susan's statement, the gathering had failed to notice the appearance of the broad-shouldered mountain lion in the buckskin shirt. "Caught me butcherin' one of her daddy's calves just for somethin' to eat."

A common thought ran through everybody's mind at that point. Vance was the first to express it. "If that's true, why in the world didn't you come forward?" he asked his wife.

Again, before Susan could answer, Colt said, "I told her if she told on me for killin' that calf, I'd slip into her room one night and slit her throat. She was awful young then. I guess she believed me."

"Ten years in prison for killin' a calf," Burt uttered, then swore softly, "Damn!"

Vance, finding it hard to believe his wife could be so vindictive, looked at Susan in disbelief. "Susan, how could you let Colt sit in that prison and not tell somebody?"

Again, Colt stepped in. " 'Cause I scared the hell out of her. She thought I would cut her throat. Hell, Vance, don't blame Susan. It was my fault, and I'd just as soon drop it." He glanced at his sister-in-law to discover her gaze locked upon his face. A tear slowly formed in the corner of her eye and she lowered her chin slightly, a nod of gratitude that only he could see.

Impatient to get on to more important business, Barney Samuels interrupted. "Well, there you go! He wasn't even guilty, just like he said. Ain't no reason he can't take the sheriff's job now. Right, Roy?"

"Well, I reckon that's true," Roy said. "How 'bout it, Colt?"

Colt couldn't help but smile at the irony of the offer. He still harbored ill feelings toward the fickle little town that shunned him. He looked over at Vance and his uncle Burt. They were both grinning like dogs eating briars. Lawman would be a helluva stretch for him. It had certainly never occurred to him. Finally, he said, "I'll think about it, but right now I'm gonna lie around Red Moon's camp till my shoulder heals up. I'll think on it, though." He left them with this final word. "If you find somebody before I get back, go ahead and give it to him."

Two weeks had passed since the town meeting, and Colt's wound was healing nicely under the care of Mary and her grandmother. It was a peaceful time for Colt, a welcome respite from the trouble that preceded it. His only concern was that he had been captured again, this time by a pretty young half-Cheyenne maiden. And he had to admit that he had no thoughts of escape.

Returning from hunting one frosty morning, he was

surprised to find a buggy tied up beside Walking Woman's tipi. As he stepped down from the saddle, Mary came out of the lodge to meet him. She was accompanied by a thin, ramrod-straight woman dressed in a long woolen coat, wearing a bonnet that concealed most of a silver-gray bun. "Colt," Mary said, "this is Alice Flynn. She wants to talk to you."

"Oh?" Colt responded. "What about?" He was well aware of who Alice Flynn was, even though this was the first time he had ever actually laid eyes on the lady, other than one brief glance while she lay sleeping.

As was her nature, Alice cut right to the point "About you doing something besides lying around this Injun camp," she blurted. "I've got the biggest spread in this valley, and I need somebody to run it. I want you to be my partner. Whaddaya say? It beats sheriffing."

Astonished, Colt didn't know what to say. He looked at Mary, who was beaming happily, waiting for his response. Looking back at Alice, he said, "I'll think on it."

"Burt said you'd say that," Alice huffed. "Yes or no?"

Colt looked at Mary again, flustered. "I reckon," he finally said.